What readers are saying about Linda's books

"Ms. Hughes weaves a riveting mystery that keeps you on the edge of your seat from the very first page. The history and fiction were meticulously woven together to create a perfectly believable story—one you will not put down until you finish."

"Amazing story!"

"Linda creates vivid settings and characters, which makes this an excellent read…I loved her characters—complex, funny, loving, and very real."

"A good, fast read."

"This book reads like a cross between a generational saga and a finely-tuned mystery…The author does an amazing job of providing just enough information to cause a reader to begin to see the truth… and will be shocked at the denouement."

"I highly recommend this book and I will read more of this author's work."

"The story leaves you guessing till the end! I cannot wait to read the continuation of this series."

"The book is rich in descriptive and historical detail. Even more importantly, it is an intriguing read that leaves the reader wanting more. Fortunately for us, the story will continue."

"Must read!"

"This was a very good and well-written book, and I enjoyed it. It was so well done that I was not aware it was part of a series, and it was completely able to stand on its own as a novel."

"I so enjoyed the characters, the mysteries, and the camaraderie of the friends and family searching for clues in *Secrets of the Island* that I didn't want this book to end. On a recent trip to Mackinac Island, I reread *Secrets* while scouting out the places in it. It was just as good on the second read as on the first. *Secrets of the Island* is as incredible as the island itself."

"The author interweaves history with the characters' very interesting stories that keep us turning the pages. The reader wonders how many hidden secrets are in their own past!"

Novels by Linda Hughes
Becoming Jessie Belle (Indie Book of the Day)
Secrets of the Asylum (eLit Bronze and Silver Falchion finalist)
Secrets of the Island (Baltic Writing Award finalist)

Non-Fiction by Linda Hughes
The Spark that Survived (with Myra Lewis Williams)
What We Talk about When We're Over 60 (with Sherri Dailey; eLit Gold)
Atlanta's Real Women (with Christine Martinello)

SECRETS OF THE SUMMER

SECRETS OF THE SUMMER

a novel

LINDA HUGHES

Dear Claudia,
Enjoy!
Love,
Linda
7-26-19

Deeds Publishing | Athens

Published by Deeds Publishing in Athens, GA
www.deedspublishing.com

Printed in The United States of America

Cover design by Mark Babcock. Text layout by Matt King.

ISBN 978-1-947309-75-3

Books are available in quantity for promotional or premium use. For information, email info@deedspublishing.com.

First Edition, 2019

10 9 8 7 6 5 4 3 2 1

For people in small towns everywhere.

1

Summer Rose Krause opened her eyes and moaned upon recognizing where she was... again.

"Oh, cra-a-a-p..."

Instinctively rolling over to avoid what seemed like a strobe light overhead pulsating directly into her burning line of sight, she tumbled off the rock-hard cot and hit the cement floor.

"Ow-w-w."

"Well. Look-ee here. Lady Godiva has awoken."

The strange voice sounded amused.

Doing her best to ignore the hammer pounding inside her skull, Summer shielded her eyes with her hand and dared look up. Yup. A stranger with big eyes and big hair stared down at her. A second cot sat nearby. Bars made up the front and side walls of the space, which connected on either side to more jail cells with more glaring eyes.

The big-haired woman reached down. "Here, let me help you up."

Afraid to decline, Summer took the strong hand and sat up. But that was the best she could do. She let go and waved off the assistance.

"I... I can't go any further." Now a bulldozer dug into the muck that made up her brains. She dropped her face into her hands and tried to get a grip on some semblance of sanity. But, she couldn't grasp it. She knew where she was but had no idea why.

"Hey," somebody with a breathy voice said from one of the other cells. "Is she okay? Maybe she needs a doctor." That one sounded like a nice enough person, given where they were, but maybe not too bright, the way that Summer thought of Marilyn Monroe.

"Looks like somebody slipped her some really bad junk." A cynic guffawed.

Big Hair squatted down to inspect her. "Lady Godiva, do you need a doctor?"

Summer looked up to realize that the woman was pretty, with amber skin and thick black hair.

"No. No. I could use a drink of water, though. And I have to use the ladies' room."

The surly one in the other cell went into hysterics over that. "The 'ladies' room.' Ha. Good luck with that, 'Lady.'"

Ignoring their neighbor, Big Hair took hold of Summer's arm and stood up, hauling Summer up with her.

"The toilet is over there." She pointed to a stinky-looking thing in the corner of the cell. "Here, I'll hold up a blanket if it makes you feel better." She pulled the thin gray blanket off Summer's cot.

"Aw, look at that. Lady Godiva is shy all of a sudden." The cantankerous woman wouldn't relent.

"Oh, shut up," the Marilyn-like woman insisted. "Let the girl pee in peace."

Summer did her business as quickly as possible while her cell-mate held up the blanket as a shield. When finished, she turned to the tiny sink to wash her hands but took one look at the filthy porcelain and opted for rubbing her hands up and down the sides of her prison attire, an anything-but-attractive pea green jumpsuit.

"Why are you calling me Lady Godiva?" she asked as she took her blanket from her cellmate's hands, folded it, and laid it back down on her cot.

"You really don't remember, do you? Come sit here and let me tell you all about it." Big Hair sat on her own cot and patted the thin mattress beside her.

Terrified of this place, even though her cellmate seemed nice enough, Summer felt she had no option. After all, the woman must be some kind of criminal or she wouldn't be in jail. Summer sat down as instructed.

"You see," her iffy new companion began, "you were brought in last night, wrapped in a beach towel, wearing nothing but your birthday suit underneath. At least on top. You had that pair of panties on." She pointed to a pair of pink lace bikini panties hung over a horizontal bar. "But they were wet from your dance in a fountain, so I took them off you."

Summer clutched at the front of her jumpsuit, embarrassed that this woman had undressed and dressed her.

"From what we could weasel out of the deputy who checks on us all the time, you were stoned out of your mind at some party downtown, and you decided it would be a good idea to prance through the streets, strip off your clothes like some kind of Gypsy Rose Lee, and dance in the fountain by the bank." She stood and swayed around as she talked, mimicking a striptease act. Flinging her last imaginary bit of clothing away, she sat down again to finish her tale. "Apparently, you were like a naked Pied Piper, gathering quite a crowd as you went. I mean, of course you would. Look at you: so tall and thin and blond and pretty. Your striptease wouldn't have been so bad, but police found drugs at the house where the party started. So, you got busted for drugs, as well as indecent exposure." The woman shrugged, as if it happened all the time.

"What? What are you talking about?" Summer ruffled her hand through her tangled hair, trying to understand. "Never in a million years would I have done something like that. That's crazy. That's not me. They made a mistake. It must have been someone else."

Her cellmate squinted at her. "Well, believe that fairytale if you like, honey buns, but it was you who they put in this cell wrapped in a beach towel and me who dressed your limp, nude body in the lovely prison attire you have on at the moment." She swished her hand around to indicate their jumpsuits.

"You have a very nice body, by the way."

"Yeah, very nice." Cynic snorted after what must have been a rare compliment.

Summer looked at the female prisoners around her. They'd all seen her naked. No one ever saw her naked. She was shy. Not only them, but if this wacky story was true, lots of people had seen her almost naked. She could never go out in public again for the rest of her life. Never.

But that was nothing compared to what would happen when her family found out.

"Hey, the deputy said your grandpa is the governor. Is that true?" Cynic asked.

Summer glared at her, then burst into tears.

"Now look at what you've done," Marilyn scolded. "Give her some toilet paper to dry her eyes," she recommended to Big Hair.

4

The woman did as suggested, and Summer wiped her face. "I'm so a-ashamed," she hiccupped. "My grandpa worked so hard to become governor and my grandma is so-o-o conservative and my parents are the best parents in the w-world. They're all good Catholics. And I have a great-grandpa, my Popo, who's a hundred and three years old. In all those years, he's never been in jail. What's wrong with me? I'm such a screw-up." With that she wailed like a condemned woman headed for the hangman's noose. "I swear to God I never break the law but this is the second time I've been in jail. I don't drink. I don't do drugs..."

"Ah ha," Big Hair mumbled, looking over Summer's head and rolling her eyes in disbelief at the others.

"It's true. I've never even had sex." Summer Rose Krause had never admitted that to any other living soul, but in this traumatic situation her confession escaped as she struggled to make her case for innocence, even though that admission was embarrassing as all get out. From what Summer could tell, she was the only twenty-one-year old virgin left on the planet in 1965, this era of "free love."

"You've never had sex?" Cynic sounded incredulous.

"It's possible," Marilyn insisted optimistically.

Big Hair looked Summer up and down suspiciously, then her features softened as she seemed to accept the possibility. "Oh, my god. I don't think I've ever met a grown-up virgin. You should be in *Ripley's Believe It or Not*."

"Ladies," a booming voice interrupted. They all looked up as a muscular man in a deputy sheriff's uniform came into the hallway in front of their cells. "Ginger Snapper, Naughty Nellie, and Betty Boobs, you are free to go, thanks to your loving friend and pimp, Randy Finkbinder, better known as Randy the Rake, who has once again ever-so-kindly paid your bail." The deputy opened cell doors as he made his sarcastic announcement. Big Hair, Marilyn, and another woman joyfully bounded out of confinement.

"Yay," Big Hair clapped as she hopped out of the cell.

"Thanks so much, Deputy," Marilyn thought to say.

The other woman did a merry jig with her arms pumping in the air.

The deputy relocked the cell doors as the freed prisoners vaulted down the hallway.

When the officer opened the heavy metal door that led out, Marilyn turned to wave. Then they all disappeared through that door.

Summer stood alone in her cell staring after them, stunned.

"It's okay," Cynic said. "I can't hurt you through these bars."

Slowly, Summer drew her gaze away from the door through which her only excuse in the world for friends had vanished. She stared at Cynic.

"They're strippers," the tough broad explained. "That's not illegal, but they all got busted for selling a little nookie on the side. All three of them, all at the same time, with the same man."

Summer opened her mouth to ask a question but couldn't get one to formulate in her muddled mind. She couldn't put it together: three women and one man, doing what? The question finally came to her.

"What's nookie?" she asked.

2

"Summer, I have your record right here. I have to be honest, it's not good. I want to help you out here, but there's only so much I can do."

Summer sat in Sheriff Smith's office, thankfully sipping on a frosty bottle of Coca-Cola he'd brought her. Shortly after the three women prisoners had been released, the deputy returned to bring her here. She'd be eternally grateful, seeing that Cynic's run-down of "the seedier side" had started to make her feel ill. She took a big chug of her pop to ease the queasiness in her tummy. She definitely now knew the definition of "nookie."

"You know I'm a friend of your dad's. I'm grateful to him for the benefit he holds every year at his winery for local law enforcement officers and firemen. And I've always supported your grandfather in politics." The sheriff was a roly-poly guy who shifted his heft in his chair as he spoke. "I've managed to keep this hush-hush, so it won't hit the papers. But I have to follow the law here, and that means I can't dismiss this charge. It has to go through the proper legal channels. In the meantime, why don't you tell me what happened from your point of view?"

Tears sprung to her eyes again. Bravely, she swiped them away.

"Well, I met this girl at the beach when I went for a swim this morning. Carol something. She seemed nice. We talked for a while and she invited me to a party. I almost didn't go, but then I decided I was bored. So, I went. I swear to you, I don't drink hardly at all. Only a small glass of my dad's wine every now and then. My dad never even let me have any of that until I turned twenty-one. I didn't have anything to drink at that party. Not even pop." She lifted her Coke bottle to emphasize her point.

She didn't add that she'd gone to that stupid party, which was totally out of character for her, because she was starved for friends her own age. Two of her best high school friends were married now and had moved away, and her other lifetime friend was her Aunt Charlotte. Only two years older than Summer, she'd always been more of a chum than an aunt. But Charlotte was ga-ga in love and getting married in a couple of months, so it seemed like all she cared about anymore was planning her wedding. Aside from the rest of her extended family, which was admittedly ginormous, Summer felt lonely.

"What about drugs?"

"No. Never. I would never do that."

Sheriff Smith rubbed his chubby chin, as if stirring up a question in his mouth. "Did you eat anything while you were there?"

Summer thought that over. "Yeah, I had a couple of brownies. They were really good. I admit I'm a chocolate addict. In fact, I think I went back and got a third brownie, but that's when things start getting fuzzy. I can't believe what they say I did. I would never do that." Her voice rose to a shrill and she took a deep breath to calm herself. "I am never going to a party like that again. I may never leave home again."

The lawman folded his hands on top of his barrel of a belly and let out a long sigh. "It's possible the brownies were laced with something. Maybe marijuana; maybe something stronger.

But there was also a garbage can full of drugs in the house. Are you sure you didn't take any of those?"

"Yes, I'm sure. I didn't even see a garbage can."

He nodded. "They call them 'garbage can' parties. Guests bring whatever drugs they have on hand and dump them into the can. Then the 'cool' thing to do is dip in and take a chance on what you'll get. A person can die that way, but these idiots think it's cool to take the chance." He shook his head in disbelief. "We arrested the owner of the house for illegal possession and distribution of drugs. He'll be in jail for some time. But you'll be able to get out as soon as somebody comes to pay your bail. I know your mom and dad are celebrating their anniversary in Hawaii, so I had no choice but to call your grandfather."

"Grandpa? Oh no. He'll think I'm an idiot."

The sheriff studied her for a few moments. "No, Summer, he won't think you're an idiot. I'm a granddad myself. I know what he'll think: he'll want everything possible to be done to help his granddaughter, who he loves. Everything within the law, that is. And he'll hope you learn a lesson from this."

Summer chewed on her lower lip, then relaxed. "Maybe it won't be so bad. He'll probably send my Aunt Charlotte. That's what my parents did last time." In her nervousness, she unnecessarily added, "Even though she's my aunt she's only a couple of years older, so we're friends. I'm going to be Maid of Honor in her wedding on the island at the end of the summer." She knew she didn't need to explain "the island." Everyone around here knew that meant Mackinac Island in Lake Huron. This town, Summer's hometown and the site of her incarceration, Traverse City, sat nestled into a bay on Lake Michigan. But traveling by water once out of the bay, with a wide right turn, Lake Huron and Mackinac Island lingered nearby.

Sheriff Smith frowned and looked at the papers in front of him. He picked up one sheet. "As for the indecent exposure charge, all I have to say is keep your clothes on from now on, young lady. I don't ever want to have to call the governor of our fair state again to tell him his beloved granddaughter streaked through town for a moment."

Struck by a glimmer of hope at his words, Summer said, "'Streaked?' You mean it didn't last very long?"

"Streaking" had become a popular pastime with college kids who wanted to test the limits of the law and the ability of lawmen to catch them. Miscreants would run through campus naked and usually disappear back into a dorm before campus police could get their hands on them to throw their bare butts in jail.

"From what I understand, no one really saw much of anything," the sheriff said. "Your sundress came off on your way to the fountain. Witnesses disagree as to whether you took it off or it fell off while you were dancing around like a maniac. Apparently you didn't have anything under it... on top." He cleared his throat, uncomfortable with this topic. "Anyway, some woman threw you a beach towel. You wrapped that around yourself and wore it in the fountain. So, you were only, um, exposed for an instant."

Summer silently cursed herself for hating those clingy brassieres. She didn't always wear one but figured no one would ever know, seeing that her breasts were so small. She made a silent vow to wear the cloying paraphernalia every day for the rest of her life from now on.

"As for that other time you were arrested...." He picked up another sheet of paper and read off it. "Traverse City, Michigan, 1964." He looked up. "Last summer right here in town, while I was away on vacation, although I heard a bit about it when I got back." He looked at the paper again and continued to read. "Vandalism: destruction of public property: tulips. Tulips? What in he... What on earth was that all about?"

"Well, it was my best friend's bachelorette party and she loves tulips and so we picked the first ones we drove by. Unfortunately, they happened to be in the yard of the college president and we didn't know that was 'public' property because it's a state college. We got caught and were arrested and they put us in one of those horrible cells." She pointed in the direction of the women's section of the jail. "Then..."

"Okay," he interrupted. "I've got it. Your grandfather should be calling soon to make arrangements for your release. Once bail is paid, you can go but will still have to appear in court tomorrow morning. The judge will most likely set a fine with no more jail time. This is a misdemeanor, like before, so you won't have a record. Stay here and finish your Coke while I go out and get some other work done."

He hoisted himself out of his chair and started to leave but his phone rang, so he turned back to his desk to answer it.

He picked up the chunky black receiver. "Sheriff Smith here."

He listened for no more than half a minute.

"Yes, sir. Thank you, Governor. We'll take care of it."

He hung up the phone with a clunk and looked pitifully at Summer.

"What?" she wanted to know. When he didn't answer, panic clawed its way from her belly up into her throat. "What?" she croaked.

3

Cynic, whose name was Carla, as it turned out, droned on and on.

"And so then I knew I was too damned old to turn tricks anymore, so I decided to start a cleaning business so I could get into hoity-toity houses and steal them blind. Some of those fat cats have so much junk I figured they wouldn't miss a diamond necklace or two..."

Summer didn't bother mentioning that her own family was one of the wealthiest in the state, maybe in the country, and that there were plenty of diamond necklaces in her parents' and grandparents' homes. She also didn't point out that Carla's plan was totally lame-brained, as proven by the dame's presence in a jail cell.

Summer tossed and turned on her cot, which was too short for her five-foot-ten-inch frame. It was impossible to get comfortable on the thing. She longed for her cushy bed and fluffy pillows and thick comforter at home. She'd never take that for granted again.

Last year she'd been in a cell for only an hour before Charlotte came to bail out her and her friend. Never in her life had she expected to spend a night in jail.

She pulled up her poor excuse for a blanket and wrapped the wan pillow around her head to cover her ears. It didn't help:

she could still hear Carla's blathering. Although the deputy had turned out the lights an hour ago and ordered Carla to "zip it up for the night," the woman was like a wind-up toy that wouldn't stop. It was as if every flighty thought that inexplicably alit in her otherwise empty head boiled over into her mouth and spewed out.

Thankfully, the two women in the cell on the other side of Summer never uttered a word. If they'd been yappers, too, she might have understood why some inmates hung themselves with their sheets.

The sheriff had been uncomfortable informing her that her grandfather was letting her spend the night in jail, and that no one would be there for her until court time in the morning. So, here she was, back in her cell. No more strippers or prostitutes, "pantie peelers" and "flatbackers" as Carla called them, had been brought in. At least Summer had the cell to herself.

Finally, blessedly, Carla shut up. Unfortunately, snoring quickly replaced her jabbering.

Summer begged herself to fall to sleep, although she was certain it would never happen....

"Rise and shine." The deputy flicked on the lights to groans from all around. "Come on, ladies. Get cleaned up. Breakfast in ten minutes. Court starts in forty-five. Get ready for a new day."

Summer sat up, stunned that she'd finally been able to fall asleep in this place. She pulled at the front of her jumpsuit, disgusted that she'd had to sleep in her day clothes, such that they were. The deputy came over and shoved a paper bag through the bars. "Here you go, Miss Krause. Somebody sent you some of your own clothes."

"Thank you." Summer jumped up and took the sack. Yanking

out a pair of jeans, a pink tee shirt, pink tennis shoes, a toothbrush, toothpaste, and, yes, a bra and panties, she silently vowed to herself to be more grateful to Charlotte for everything she did. In fact, she probably needed to be more appreciative of everyone in her family for everything they did for her.

Forty minutes later the deputy escorted her out of her cell and into the lobby. Surprised to see who awaited her, she yelped, "Uncle Harry, I thought Charlotte would be here."

Her Uncle Harry and Aunt Charlotte O'Neill were brother and sister, but nineteen years apart, so they hadn't even been raised together. Uncle Harry, being Summer's mother's twin, was old enough to be his younger sister's dad. Therefore, Summer had preferred the much younger, much more lenient relative to come fetch her, the one who was more buddy than aunt.

Uncle Harry merely nodded and took her elbow, ushering her out the door. "We meet the judge in her chambers in ten minutes. We can walk over." He pointed at the courthouse across the street from the jail.

Summer glanced at her uncle several times as they walked, trying to read his thoughts. She didn't know why he was here. He didn't even live here; he and his wife Ellie lived on the island. With Summer's mother, Harriet, and her Uncle Harry being twins, they were female-male images of each other. They shared the same sandy-colored hair, hazel eyes, and slim builds. They were extremely close. Summer knew her mother would learn all about this as soon as she got back from Hawaii.

Uncle Harry had never been much of a talker, which was a relief after her night with the blabbermouth-snorer, but Summer ached to know what he was thinking. Afraid to ask, she simply let him lead her into the courthouse, down a hallway, through a courtroom, and to a door with a sign that read "Judge Ames." The door stood ajar, but he knocked anyway, causing it to swing all the way open.

Before them sat a formidable woman behind a big, fancy, wooden desk. She appeared to be about the same age as Summer's mother and Uncle Harry. With her glasses perched on the end of her nose she looked up and pointed to the two chairs on their side of her desk. Fuzzy-wuzzy she was not. Summer and her uncle sat down.

Without preamble and without looking up from the documents in front of her, the judge said, "Miss Krause, I have informed your grandfather and your uncle here that I am requiring one hundred and fifty hours of community service and a fine of five hundred dollars in order to make this 'incident' go away without jail time. It's that or a month in jail." She looked up and squinted at Summer. "Do you understand?"

"Um, yes." It was the first Summer had heard any of this, but it was okay by her, certainly better than going back to prison with yappy Carla. She felt sure her parents would let her help out at one of their charitable causes to work off the community service, so that wouldn't be too bad.

"Mr. O'Neill, have you informed your niece about our agreement as to the nature of her community service?"

"No, your honor, not yet."

The judge looked at Summer and jabbed a finger her way. "You will spend the summer working, free of charge, in the state and federally funded Head Start program. Your uncle has already made arrangements as to where. Do you understand?" she repeated, this time emphasizing the last word, making it sound like two words, *under* and *stand*.

"Yes. I understand. But I've never heard of Head Start." Her voice was weak, but Summer was proud of herself for speaking at all.

"It's a new government summer program for children ages four to seven."

"Oh, gee, I don't really like children all that much. I mean, they're cute and everything, but I guess I have so many little cousins I'm tired of being around them." Summer shocked herself at her bravery. "I'd rather work with one of my parents' charities."

For a moment she thought the judge might leap across the desk and slap her but, inexplicably, the woman started to laugh. The judge looked at Harry. "She really doesn't know yet, does she?"

"No, your honor. I haven't had time to explain."

The judge slapped her desk and let out a final snort. "Well, you'll have to explain it to her somewhere else. I have to get ready for court. Pay your fine to the clerk on your way out." She gestured for them to shoo and they skedaddled out of there.

It took a few wrong turns in the courthouse before they found the clerk, but they finally got there, and Harry wrote a check. As they headed for his truck parked at the curb, Summer said, "Could you explain this whole Head Smart thing to me later? I'm exhausted and want to go home and go to bed."

He stopped and faced her. "It's Head Start. You'd better get that right because it's going to be a big part of your life this summer. And there is no going 'home.' Charlotte packed your bags and found your purse. They're in the truck. You're coming with me."

"Oh… but… I'm so grateful to you for everything you've done, but you don't have to take care of me anymore. I'll be fine."

He shook his head and smirked, and started walking again.

"Oh, don't worry. There won't be any taking care of you. You'll be taking care of everyone else."

"What? What do you mean?" Summer shuffled up to the truck, wondering if she should run like hell.

"Get in," he ordered, swinging open the driver's door and hopping into his beloved twenty-year-old 1945 Ford pickup. When she hesitated, he insisted through clenched teeth, "Get in."

Summer couldn't deny him any more than she would his twin, her mother. She sighed and reluctantly climbed in. She didn't know where they were headed, but it didn't sound good.

4

"West Branch is a great little town. That's where you'll be
staying and working for the next two months." Harry
O'Neill knew this was a shock to his niece. He knew she'd almost leapt out of his truck when he'd passed Peninsula Drive in
Traverse City, the road up Mission Peninsula which led to her
parents' winery and mansion, where she still lived. But he'd kept
driving east, out of town, and she was still with him, at least in
the flesh. Her mind seemed miles away. Struggling to engage her,
Harry said, "You might remember going through West Branch
on your way to Detroit a few times for a Tigers game or to visit
Greenfield Village and the Henry Ford Museum."

"No. I don't remember," she said, her voice dripping with contempt.

Harry had turned on his favorite country music station,
WXKZ out of Windsor, Canada, as soon as they headed out. At
the moment, Roger Miller sang, "Trailers for sale or rent, rooms to
let fifty cents…" Fortuitous, considering he was driving Summer
away from her opulent home. He knew she preferred Motown,
rock-and-roll, and show tunes. But he wasn't in a conciliatory
mood, so kept his favorite music playing, although he turned it
down low so he could be heard.

"Head Start is a program for disadvantaged children, poor
kids," he said, grappling to grab her attention. "It's new but I

18

hope it stays around for years to come. It's a worthy cause. One of the main goals is to make sure the kids get two good meals a day, because many of them don't get supper at home. You'll be an assistant teacher. You'll give lessons, take them on field trips, and do anything else the lead teacher wants. Got that?"

"I guess," Summer groused.

"That'll be from eight in the morning until one in the afternoon. That's your community service. To pay for your room and board you'll be the waitress and chambermaid at the new B&B we have there, right in the middle of town. The W.B. B&B. It's a neat little place. I've really enjoyed getting this one up and running."

Harry and his wife Ellie owned thirteen B&Bs around Michigan, including four on Mackinac Island where they lived, and another half dozen in the Carolinas. They owned a number of restaurants, too, seeing that Ellie was a fabulous cook. Harry loved finding old, run-down spaces and turning them into inviting places where people could relax and unwind. He called it his heart's work; therefore, it never felt like work. He knew he was fortunate to have been born into a filthy rich family, so he'd never had to worry about money. There had been plenty to start with, but now with his twin sister, Summer's mother Harriet, running the family conglomerate, there was even more. No, he'd never had to worry about money, so he'd always been able to do the work he loved. He'd had other crosses to bear, though, that no amount of money could fix.

"Wait a minute, Uncle Harry. Do you mean waitress, like I have to hand food to people on plates?"

"You've got it."

"But, I've never done that. That won't work out."

"Sure it will. Betty, the innkeeper, she'll show you what to do."

"But... but, what's a 'chambermaid?'"

"Oh, that's a quaint old word for maid. You'll clean guest rooms, change bedding, scrub toilets—things like that."

"I don't clean toilets." She scrunched up her face in disgust.

"You do now. You'll also help Betty with breakfast each morning starting at six...."

"Six in the morning? I don't like getting up early."

"Most people don't. But they have to, to make a living. So, as I was saying, you'll do that before school, then when you get home in the afternoon you can perform your chambermaid duties. You should be done by four each day, unless something unusual comes up, like some especially messy guests."

"That's a ten-hour day of work." She thrust her arms across her chest a tight as a straitjacket, a signal she felt shackled by all of this.

"Yes. But, hopefully, you'll enjoy at least some of it so it won't all feel like work."

"Why can't I just write a check to pay for my room and board?"

"Well, first of all, I won't let you. Second of all, there won't be any more weekly deposits to your checking account from your trust fund. Your grandpa has cut them off for the time being."

He glanced over as anger seared into her face.

"Cheer up," he said. "It won't be so bad. For once in your life you're going to see how most people live."

"What do you mean?" She turned toward him with a genuine look of bewilderment.

Harry turned off the radio and Patsy Cline's *Faded Love* faded away. He glanced at his recalcitrant passenger and the denim blue of her dazzling eyes stared at him in a quandary.

His eyes back on the road, he said, "Honey, you know your Aunt Ellie and I love you like our own child, especially because, unfortunately, we can't have kids of our own. But you're not our child, which makes us see you a little differently than your parents do. We see you more objectively. You're spoiled, Summer Rose." He looked her way again in time to catch seeing her jaw drop in shock. "Not 'spoiled rotten,' because, in spite of a couple of stints in jail, you're a great kid. A great young woman," he said, correcting himself. "And it's time for you to grow up."

She glared at him in disbelief.

"In fact, I'm glad your parents are far away in Hawaii and that Dad called me to take care of this. He and your grandma are busy right now, with the governors' conference on the island."

"Oh, crap. I forgot about that." Summer slapped her forehead like an imbecile. "All those governors and their wives from around the country visiting the Governor's Cottage on the island and he gets a call that his bum of a granddaughter is in the clink. I'm so embarrassed."

"Well, I admit, maybe you should be. But he wasn't mad. He and Mom were concerned that you were okay. That's why they sent me, which I think is perfect timing, time for you to have an opportunity to experience a different way of life and time for me to give you that opportunity."

"But, Uncle Harry, I'm no good at anything. Not anything except helping out at the winery."

"You are good at that. But you have to confess, your dad doesn't exactly brow-beat you to work hard. You get to do whatever you want."

"There's nothing else I know how to do. Next to everybody else in this family I'm such a dork. By the time she was my age,

Grandma had lived the high-life in Chicago and then married Grandpa, and was pregnant with you and Mom. By this age my mom had saved lives in a war, and was married and pregnant with me. I haven't done diddly-squat compared to them. And look at you: you fought in a war by my age."

"Honey, these are different times. You can't compare yourself to all that. You've got a whole lifetime ahead of you to discover your own path."

He paused, struggling to bolster her confidence. "Don't forget you're marvelous at painting pictures. You have amazing talent. Ellie and I love the horses you painted that we have on our living room wall. We're such horse lovers, and we love you, so you couldn't have given us any better anniversary gift. And the mural you did at the winery is magnificent. Give yourself credit for your talent as an artist."

"Yeah, but painting pictures isn't a job or anything. Let's face it. I'm a total screw-up." Now her arms flailed in frustration. "Besides that, I'm a giant." With a dramatic flair that would have done any actress proud, she squished down in her seat to emphasize her point, her knees jamming up under the glovebox.

Harry hesitated before responding. This conversation had meandered into girl-talk territory that was totally foreign to him. He may as well have been navigating the orbit of a spaceship around the earth and taking a walk into space like that Russian cosmonaut had recently done. Harry knew as much about that as he knew about girl-talk. He wished to God Ellie was here. She'd know what to do.

"Summer Rose, you're gorgeous." He figured that's how Ellie would put it. He wasn't placating his niece; it was true. "You take a person's breath away when you enter a room. No, you don't look like lots of other women. You're unique; you're beautiful. Your aunt and I, and your parents, and your grandparents, and even your great-grandpa who's getting blind as a bat, we've all told you that all your life."

"Of course you have. That's your job. You're my family."

"You really don't understand how unique you are, do you? Well, I hope this summer helps you figure out that it's okay to be different. It's better than okay; it's wonderful."

"And you think cleaning toilets will help me realize that?"

He peered over to see one corner of her mouth curl into a baby grin. Ah ha, he'd struck a chord somewhere in there deep inside, where she was happy he'd told her she was gorgeous, in spite of the toilets.

Harry's heart melted. He loved this young woman and would protect her until the day he died. Yeah, she needed a good kick in the butt to make her face reality and grow up, but there was one reality she would never have to face, one that no one should ever have to face. Never-ever would she know the truth about her appearance, about the possibilities of her heritage, because the few people on earth who knew; her mother, her step-father, her great-grandpa, her elder Aunt Abby, his wife Ellie, and himself; had all pledged a vow to keep it a secret. So heinous was the reality that no one, not even her grandparents because her grandmother Meg was so tender-hearted it would rip her apart, no one more would ever know. Especially not Summer herself. Her real father might be her mother's first husband who died in World War II after only one day of marriage to Summer's mother Harriet, the man Summer believed to be her father; or her real father might be the German field soldier who ravaged Harriet while she served as a Red Cross nurse in Tunisia. Summer knew a watered-down version of the story of how her mother had killed the German soldier who tried to kill them. But she didn't know the whole story. And she never would.

Were her features those of her mother's husband or the German rapist? There was no way anyone could ever know for sure. As luck would have it, her step-father Richard, a British spy during the war who'd helped save Harriet and Harry himself, was tall, stately, good-looking, blue-eyed, and blond. Just like her. It saved explanations when people noticed how different Summer looked from other women in the family. They took one look at Summer next to Richard and assumed she was his biological child. Certainly, no man could be a better dad. He adored his adopted step-daughter. In every way that mattered, he was her real father.

But all that trauma surrounding the conception and birth of Summer had resulted, Harry believed, in Harriet and Richard coddling their children, Summer and their sixteen-year-old son Shane. Harriet and Richard even agreed. They all knew something needed to be done.

The time had come when that something could be done for Summer Rose.

5

Summer had been vacillating wildly between love and hate for her Uncle Harry. Right now, the barometer weighed heavily on the hate side, like a deep weather depression compressing the air, making an effort of each breath she took.

They stopped in Roscommon for lunch, during which neither of them spoke other than to order their meal. Then they drove on until a sign said: "West Branch, 3 Miles." Although she'd dozed on and off since they quit talking, she'd seen plenty of farm houses and barns. And farm fields. There were lots of those, with rows and rows of sprouts popping their heads up out of the ground, like a million miniature green babies being born. She had no idea what they were. There were patches of forest, too, with blinking views of scattered lakes between the white birch and pine trees. Now they were only a few miles from the town that was to become her home for the next two months, and the scenery hadn't changed. How could they be this close with no neighborhoods or stores or restaurants? Traverse City wasn't a big city, with about twelve thousand people, but at least it had some semblance of civilization.

They drove another couple of miles before coming upon a big hill with a huge, ready-to-tumble-down barn to the side. The road gave them a panoramic view of a valley and town below. A tall, gray, barreled water tower down there said "West Branch" in neat black letters. So, this was it, what there was of it, her home away from home.

"That's Pointer Hill," Uncle Harry said, pointing to the side at the quaint park next to the giant barn. Then he pointed ahead at the valley. "Pretty view, isn't it?"

"Um, how many people live in this place?"

"Almost two thousand. Betty is from here, born and raised and stayed, except for a stint in the military. I'm sure she'll tell you all about it."

"That shouldn't take long," Summer said under her breath as she looked out the window at yet another farm.

"What?"

"Nothing."

After another quarter of a mile they came upon a man riding a horse on a path alongside the road. Harry pulled over, an easy task seeing that no other traffic impeded their way. There, standing right next to her open window, was the enormous left flank of a golden-brown horse. That and a man's long leg in jeans and a boot-ed foot in the stirrup took up her entire field of vision. The boot slid out of the stirrup and the leg disappeared as it swung over to the other side of the beast, leaving her with a view of an intricately tooled black saddle. She inhaled the smell of horse and leather, a pleasing scent, her being an avid rider and horse lover herself.

"Move over, Ranger," the man said. The horse shuffled side-ways and suddenly a head popped into view right at Summer's window.

"Oh." She slapped her hand to her chest. "You startled me."

The man chuckled. "Sorry." Summer thought he didn't sound sorry at all, but rather amused. About thirty years old, with a square jaw and earthy brown eyes, she reluctantly had to admit he was attractive. A fringe of black hair rimmed his face underneath a black cowboy hat.

"Hi, Bogey," Harry said. "Good-looking horse you've got there."

The man rested his arms on the windowsill and leaned in. Summer scrunched back. "Thanks, Harry. Good to see you again. So, this must be her." He jabbed a thumb in Summer's direction.

She flinched and pulled back even further. Did this moron know about her?

"Yeah, this is my niece, Summer Rose Krause. Summer, this is Bogey Bush. He's one of the deputy sheriffs in town."

"Nice to meet you, Summer." He backed away a bit to have enough room to thrust his hand inside and she had no choice but to shake it.

"Nice to meet you, too," she lied.

"Well, take her on in, Harry, and I'll see you later." He clapped the roof of the car twice with the palm of his hand and stepped back, as if he'd been talking about carting a horse to the slaughter house.

Harry waved, and they were off.

"Why does he know about me?" Summer fumed.

"Because the judge wants a weekly report from the sheriff's office about your compliance with community service. The principal of the school will report to this sheriff and they'll send it on to Judge Ames in Traverse City."

"Like babysitters? It's like I have babysitters?"

"Well, yeah. That's what happens when you break the law, whether you meant to or not."

Now her Uncle Harry weighed totally on the hate side of her mood barometer, which was about to break from the steam building up inside her head. Not trusting herself to say another word, she folded her arms, clamped her mouth shut, and glared out the window.

Then a terrifying thought struck. "Hey, when will somebody bring me my car?" She loved her silver Mercedes-Benz Cabriolet convertible her great-grandfather had given her six months ago for her twenty-first birthday.

The look on her uncle's face said it all. "You won't have your car until this is done. I've informed Carlos to keep it stored in the big garage until you get home in August."

Immediately Summer started calculating how she could convince Carlos, her dad's overseer for the estate, to sneak her car to her. She felt certain she could manage that. Carlos was a pushover, unlike this new uncle she suddenly felt like she hardly knew. Uncle Harry used to be a pushover, too. But, even though he'd tried to convincingly lie to her about being beautiful, he'd morphed into a military drill sergeant. Well, she refused to let him get away with taking her treasured car. She'd have it soon.

So there.

A restaurant came into view, Hutch's, with a drive-in called Tait's across the street. Then there was St. Joseph's Catholic School, St. Joseph's Catholic Church, and an accompanying rectory on the left side of the road. At least she'd have someplace to worship on Sundays, she figured, because she needed to beg God to get her out of here. On the other side of the street a stunning, large, dark brick, Victorian-era building with a turret stood majestically proud of itself. An impressive house of the same period sat next to it.

"That's the courthouse and jail," Harry said, pointing to the buildings. "The sheriff and his wife live in the house, with the jail downstairs. Let's hope you never have to stay there."

His attempt at humor did not humor her. She didn't bother to offer so much as a word of polite response.

"The deputies don't live there, of course. There are two, Bogey, who lives on his family farm out on the edge of town where we saw him, and a man who lives in town. And this is it: town."

He pulled over and stopped, letting her take it in. The street sign said this main road was Houghton Avenue. Some "avenue." She thought of an avenue as leading to someplace exciting. The Ogemaw Hills Hotel on the left side of the street was a broad, rectangular, three-story structure. On the right sat two houses made of the fieldstone that was so common in Michigan. She could also see a Dairy Queen.

"Hallelujah," she said, pointing at the DQ. "Dilly Bars. Maybe I can eat myself into oblivion."

Her uncle didn't respond to her snide remark. She truly did like Dilly Bars, so this town had one little thing to offer after all. Probably the only thing.

Up ahead across a set of railroad tracks she could see a couple of blocks of two-story buildings down each side of the wide street, with a variety of store signs jutting out over doors and painted onto the buildings. There was one traffic light down there in-between the two blocks.

If she wasn't so mad she'd admit it was a well-preserved, charming, Victorian-era town. Right out of a storybook, as if a woman with a bustle under her long skirt and a man with a bowler hat might step out of one of those stores at any moment. The woman would open her sun umbrella and take the man's arm. He would touch the brim of his hat in greeting to anyone who passed by.

Harry pulled the truck back onto the road and drove slowly

through town, not needing to stop at the lone traffic light, as it glowed green. He pointed out things she'd never remember. There were two drugstores, a couple of dress shops, a dime store, a movie theater, some restaurants, blah, blah, blah. She didn't care. She was being forced to stay here, with babysitters, no less.

They tooled past the main part of town into an area of mature trees; maples, oaks, and elms; bright green with their early summer leaves, lining the street, with lovely houses interspersed with other places here and there. There were churches, a funeral home, a hospital, a gas station, a Masonic temple, a state police post, and a cemetery. Harry turned around at a cut-off at the end of the road where a Y veered into different directions leading out of town, and went back down Houghton Avenue in the opposite direction as before.

"This is it," he said, pointing to a sign over the door on a brown brick corner building right by the traffic light. Summer couldn't believe she'd missed it on the first pass through town, but the sign hanging over the door said "W.B. B&B." Closer inspection revealed the same thing on one of the front showcase windows. The signs were in sweeping script lettering, cherry red laced in gold. Very Victorian.

"We own what at one time would have been three stores, including the upstairs. We have the B&B, the café next door, and the bakery down there, too." He pointed toward the middle of the block at the W. B. Bakery that sat on the far side of the café. "I rent the bakery downstairs back to the present bakers. The upstairs of all three sections are part of the B&B, but that's not all remodeled yet. The café in the middle down here is where you'll help serve breakfast to our guests in the morning before you go to your job at the school." Now he pointed at the W.B. Café.

Summer didn't mention his lack of imagination in naming his businesses.

"How am I supposed to get to the school with no car?"

"Oh, it's only a ten-minute walk away. In fact, everything you could ever need is only a ten- or fifteen-minute walk away."

Not really, she thought. *I need to go home.*

Harry got out, so she did, too. While he grabbed her bags and took them inside, she stood cemented to the sidewalk, her feet refusing to transport her inside. She looked up at the tall windows on the second floor with their intricate brickwork framing them on the outside and white lace curtains hanging on the inside. She looked down at the cherry red front door with its golden trim and warm "Welcome" sign.

She blinked, and in the blink of an eye, she detested the place.

6

Harry couldn't conceal his pride. "Look at this place. It's moving along wonderfully. Betty, you're doing a great job."

Betty, the "innkeeper," as Harry dubbed her, beamed. "The workers in this town are excellent," she said. "Every electrician, plumber, carpenter, painter, and lookie-loo who's been in here has been a breeze to work with. Kimball's Glass Shop down the street fixed that broken window like it was nothing." She pointed to a side window. "Now no one would ever know it was shattered to smithereens."

Harry and Betty walked around the lobby of the W.B. B&B, with Summer silently plodding along behind them. Harry knew Betty to be in her early forties. She was short with a strong build. Her black shoulder-length hair appeared to be naturally curly, with a few streaks of gray. She smiled easily and had a husky voice. Harry knew she smoked, but she had vowed not to smoke in front of guests. Obviously not much for frill, she wore jeans, a white short-sleeved blouse, and white sneakers. Her red-framed cat-eye glasses emphasized bright eyes with generous crow's feet. Harry knew she'd earned those wrinkles with a lot of merriment and a lot of sorrow.

"You, of course, have been an inspiring boss," Betty said to Harry.

"I love doing this." Harry reverently ran his hand across the heavy wood beam mantle over the Michigan fieldstone fireplace that sat in the center of the outer wall of the lobby. "This fireplace turned out perfectly."

"Yeah, the mason brought those stones from his own farm."

Although he'd left the day-to-day remodeling supervision up to Betty, he'd been spending a day or two a week here to help get things done in time for their opening, only a week away. But he hadn't seen the finished fireplace until now. He wished he'd been there to see how the mason set those heavy, round stones.

Harry loved carpentry and had made the cabinet with bookshelves that covered a section of the inside wall at the back of the room to create a cozy library area. Once a large storage room, now the space was open to the lobby. Drawn into that space, he looked around and marveled at the perfection of the pale green and sky blue and cherry red old-fashioned flowered wallpaper Ellie had picked out for the back wall. She also selected the calming pale green paint covering the lobby walls. The same paint and wallpaper adorned the downstairs guestroom and its bathroom.

He'd made certain that the entire building retained its historic ambiance and that as much original work as possible remained, with any necessary repair. To that end, the oakwood floors had been refinished to a satiny sheen. The wood trim around the windows and deep crown molding surrounding the ceiling had been sanded and varnished to match the floor. The tin tiles on the ceiling had been cleaned, with a minimal amount of need for patchwork.

The only accessory in the room so far was a big, thick Persian carpet in front of the fireplace. Its color scheme matched the rest of the décor. The only furniture was an antique desk and chair on the right-hand side of the entrance, for registering guests. Soon comfortable furniture and interesting décor, appropriate for the original time period of the building, would be brought in to fill the room. For weeks Betty had been collecting antiques from local shops and buying new furniture from the Morse Furniture Store down the block. The store owner had kindly stored all of it for her.

Betty turned to Summer. "Your uncle here is a master crafts-man, you know. He repaired the stairs, all of it, the steps and bannister and handrail and newel post." She pointed to the back of the lobby where a large entrance revealed a hallway, which ran across the back of the building. The stairs resided in that hall and from the center of the lobby the side of the stairway with its rich wood banister could be seen ascending upwards.

"Summer," Harry said, "this is the fun part of the place." He pointed at that back hallway. He knew she hated him right now. That was a shame, but it didn't change anything. His resolution about her fate hadn't waned a bit. Besides, he was so excited about the progress on this place, nothing could dampen his en-thusiasm. He couldn't be more pleased with this B&B. But the pièce de résistance was on the second floor. Excitedly, he shuffled the women toward the hallway with its stairs.

Once there, he turned back to the open entrance they had walked through. "Originally, there was a regular doorway there instead of this big opening. We put this in and made it look au-thentic." He swung his hand up to mimic the arch of the open-ing. "Back in the 1920s and early '30s, during prohibition, that door was kept locked so nobody in the store out front could get back here because this..." he went to the door that led to the side street... "was the entrance to the speakeasy upstairs." He no-ticed that Summer perked up a bit at the mention of a speakeasy.

He unhooked a latch on a lid covering a small window in the door. He opened the lid and looked out. "This door to the outside was locked, too, and folks would knock, a guard would open this little window to see who it was, and then he'd decide if they could come in." He closed the lid and latched it shut. "So, you see, Summer, this place may not be as boring as you expected."

She didn't respond as the three of them went up the stairs. At the top, they turned to walk that hallway to a turn that opened up into a vestibule, a wide hallway in front of more doors. There, on the right, a door led to a guestroom Betty said was ready for occupation. Straight ahead, another door at the front corner of the building was pointed out as another one that was finished, which would be Summer's room. On the left, opulent double doors opened into a cavernous room. They stepped inside, and Summer couldn't suppress a gasp.

"It's beautiful, isn't it?" Harry asked.

"Yeah," she had to admit.

An expanse of newly refinished oakwood floors stretched from the front of the building all the way to the back and from side-to-side to take up an entire store space in the building.

"This was the speakeasy," Betty said dreamily. "I can picture it: A band playing over there." She pointed to a riser at the back end of the room. "A bar with free-flowing moonshine and illegal whiskey over there." She pointed to the far side. "Little round tables with chairs over there by the windows. Women in those fabulous 1920s dresses, although this whole part of the state wasn't wealthy like in the city. But, still, women would have been as fashionable as their budgets allowed. And everybody would have been dancing their hearts out. On warm summer nights the windows would have been open..." she noted, pointing to the long front windows with their lace curtains… "with curtains floating into the room on the evening breeze. It's all so romantic." She sighed.

Harry watched Summer as Betty waxed fantastic. The girl didn't seem to share the woman's sentimental vision. Her brow knitted, Summer studied the ballroom.

"Isn't this town sort of out in the middle of nowhere to have been so popular back then?" she asked.

"Well, yeah," Betty admitted, "except that the Purple Gang liked hanging out around here. They even had a cabin in the woods in Lupton, twenty miles away. So illegal booze was easy to come by around here. Even though it was illegal, it flowed like a river."

"Who's the Purple Gang?"

"Oh dear," Betty said as she looked at Harry. "She has a lot to learn about this town, doesn't she?"

"Uh huh. And I'm leaving it up to you to teach her." He grinned broadly as Betty shook her head.

"Well," he said, "I'll take my leave now. I have to get back to catch a ferry to the island. Betty, thanks for everything. Summer, Betty will show you where the school is. The principal, Miss Campbell, will show you what you need to do. Good luck."

Harry trotted down the stairs and out of the building without one iota of guilt over what he was doing to his niece. It would be the best thing in the world that ever happened to her… he hoped.

7

Summer stood between the lace curtain and one of the front windows of her upstairs bedroom, looking down at the main street, Houghton Avenue. The curtain floated into the room behind her, the balmy summer breeze lifting it to flutter as delicately as a wide-winged butterfly. In fact, she'd thrown open all three windows in her room, two in front and one on the side, which allowed curtains to drift about along both outside walls.

Running her hand down her throat, she shuttered at the pleasure the humid air brought to her clammy bare skin. She could even feel it through her thin cotton nightie. Unusually hot for a Michigan summer night, it smelled like rain, promising to bring one of those downfalls that would barrel away to leave mist steaming up from the surfaces of the ground and creeks and streets. Billowing dark clouds scudded across the sky, giving way only occasionally to unveil a glimmer of stars. The shower would come soon.

She sucked in a long breath, trying to get a grip on her life. She felt so homesick she couldn't sleep, having tossed and turned in that foreign bed behind her for an hour before finally getting up. It hadn't been the bed, which was new and comfy, like her bed at home. She wouldn't be able to feel a pea, or a pear for that matter, underneath this mattress, it was so cushy. No, it wasn't the bed, it was her situation that unsettled her.

She looked up and down the street. Seeing that it was midnight on a Friday, it would seem that more would be going on. From her vantage point on the second floor, she could see all of "downtown" West Branch, one block each way. Old-timey streetlights lined Houghton Avenue, enshrouding the town in its own dim glow that evoked both a spooky and romantic effect at the same time. A street sign told her that N. 3rd. St. ran down her side of the building, so her room sat at the corner of Houghton Avenue and N. 3rd. St.

"Good to remember," she said to herself, "in case I ever get lost in town. Ha ha ha."

The town's only traffic light hung over the intersection at her corner. She'd pulled the shades down to change for bed, but once she donned her shorty nightie and turned out her light, she rolled the shades back up so they wouldn't keep out the breeze. That allowed the traffic light to provide her room with what felt like her own private night light, languidly twinkling through the curtains to leave red, orange, and green patterns on the wall. She supposed that would hypnotize most people right to sleep. That would be normal people who weren't in a crazy quandary over their existence.

Now she watched as the light changed three or four times before a jalopy with two teenagers floundered by, Sonny and Cher's *I Got You Babe* drifting out their window. Appropriate, Summer thought, seeing that the girl practically sat on top of the boy and they smooched as he attempted to drive. The boy had his right arm around the girl's neck and his left hand on the wheel, steering precariously as he tried to manage both his vehicle and his love life.

Summer couldn't imagine being that much in love or carefree or reckless.

"Oh wait, I ran practically naked through a fountain in public."

She'd lain in bed mulling that over and over in her mind. She felt certain the sheriff in Traverse City had been right: somebody had laced the brownies. Her behavior had been totally unlike her. She both envied and scorned people who were free-spirited, but she didn't begrudge them to the point of getting high and naked.

Suddenly there was movement down the block across the street to her right, and she could see a man come out of the Model Restaurant and Bar. He got into one of the four cars in front of the establishment, did a U-turn right in the middle of Houghton Avenue, and drove out of sight.

"Big whoop," she droned. "That must be the big excitement in this place on a Friday night."

Then, down the block on the other side of the street to her left, a tiny flicker of light by the Midstate Theatre marquee caught her attention. Earlier the red sign, with Midstate running up and down in neon, had been by far the brightest light in town. Cars and trucks had been parked along the street, and teenagers had come and gone on foot for the show. But now the streets were empty and the sign was off. The show was over. A large, two-sided sign underneath the neon announced, "Planet of the Vampires, Barry Sullivan and Norma Bengell" in removable black block letters. She'd never heard of the movie or the actress. She wondered if she herself had landed on a planet of vampires.

Still, the little flicker of light continued and it peaked her interest. She craned her neck to see.

"Well, I'll be darned." She couldn't quash a grin.

A lanky, bespectacled teenaged boy sat on the roof by the marquee, obviously having crawled out of the window up there, smoking a cigarette. He must work at the theater and, his work night over, he enjoyed the breeze while having a smoke. His head drifted from side-to-side as he surveyed the deserted street below. Summer wondered if he contemplated his life in this town, calculating his escape after graduation, or if he merely took in the night.

She stepped back so he wouldn't see her staring when he turned his head in her direction, but then his attention and her own were drawn to a sheriff's cruiser that inched its way into town, pulled over in front of Blumenthal's clothing store right across from the B&B, and parked. A tall man in a dark brown uniform got out, his back to Summer. From her vantage point, she could see his deputy cap on the car seat, which laid bare his shaggy, black hair. It looked like he'd slicked his mop back to be nice and neat for work, but the breeze playfully tossed it about. He ran his fingers through it to try to tame it, to little avail. His shirt sleeves were rolled up, too, another concession to the heat. His pistol rested in a holster on his hip.

He waved up at the boy on the roof of the theater, apparently knowing the teen would be there.

"Hey, Tommy. Hot one tonight, isn't it?"

The deep, dulcet voice verified her suspicion that she knew who the man was, even though she could only see his backside.

"Yes, sir, Deputy Bush. It's gonna rain, too." The boy pointed to the cloudy sky with his cigarette and then took another hit on the little stick. "It's a great view from up here. Wanna join me?" An unmistakable tease tinged his delivery.

"Nah, not tonight, thanks."

"You taking Deputy Fitz's night shift 'cuz his wife is having another baby?"

"Yup. She's in the hospital right now."

"Hey, Deputy Bush, when're you gonna get married and have nine kids, like Deputy Fitz?"

Summer liked this young man. He had spunk.

Deputy Bush, "Bogey" as Uncle Harry called him, said, "That, my dear boy, would be never. At least for the nine kids."

Ah, Summer berated herself for being pleased to learn the deputy wasn't married. What difference could that possibly ever make to her?

"Listen Tommy," the deputy said, "it's after midnight, about the time your mom starts worrying about you. Right?"

"Yeah. I know. Time to go."

Summer wondered if everybody in this town knew everybody and knew everybody's business. With her luck, yes. She could only hope, probably beyond hope, that no one except Betty, the sheriff, the deputies, and the principal knew of her plight.

The teen took a last draw on his cigarette and flicked away the stub. He waved. "Good night, Deputy. Stay dry." He crawled through the window to disappear.

Deputy Bogey Bush turned to get into his vehicle and glanced upward, allowing a moment of streetlight to strike his face, emphasizing his strong features. Summer ducked further back behind the curtain in case he looked her way. That man's face was, she had to admit, quite a ruggedly dashing one. She knew he knew why she'd been exiled to West Branch. He must think her a total nincompoop. Oh well, a hick-town deputy-farmer would never be a match for her, anyway. No doubt a guy like him had a girlfriend, probably sporting Annette Funicello boobs and carrying a gun in her purse.

She sighed, having no idea what kind of man might be for her. Maybe nobody. She might end up a withered old maid painting pathetic pictures that no one cared about. One thing was for sure: if she wanted a happy married life she would never find it in this one-horse town out in the boonies. Once her sentence here was over, she'd go back home to Traverse City and do her best to get a life.

The deputy got back into his car and drove off. Summer supposed there wasn't much reason for him to stick around downtown. Sleepy burg though it may be, her own sleep seemed impossible. She went to the small pedestal sink and splashed water on her face, then dried it with a white towel advertising "W.B. B&B" in dark green embroidery.

A small bathroom with a toilet and claw tub was tucked into a room behind the sink. Even though the tiny bathroom floor had checkerboard black and white tiles, and the walls had pretty wallpaper, it felt like a primitive outdoor camping latrine compared to her large, lavish, pink-tiled bathroom at home where her sink sat ensconced in a large counter, a vanity had a lighted mirror, pink marble surrounded her bathtub, a mermaid perpetually smiled down at her from a stained-glass window, and her shower harbored its own skylight. One more reason she couldn't wait for this torturous summer to be over: she could go home and luxuriate in her own bathroom.

Another problem up here in her B&B room was that she was plain lonely and, she had to admit, scared. For the first time in her life, she realized she'd never spent a night away from other people. Betty's small innkeeper's apartment sat downstairs in the back of the building in the second store space that held the café, next to the kitchen. Sure, Betty wasn't far away, a deputy apparently would drive by from time to time, and a teenaged boy might be at hand around midnight on weekends. None of that compared to her house at home where her room sat at the end of a long, wide hallway. On the other end of the hall was her parents' room. On one side of her was her brother's, Shane's, room, and on the other side was what had long been a nanny's suite. Once she and Shane were too old for a nanny, it became a guest suite, occupied by their full-time housekeeper, who usually stayed in her suite in another part of the massive house except on the rare occasions Summer's parents were out of town without taking the kids. Never in her life had Summer been more than a shout away from someone to come to her aid should she need anything.

This felt like being stranded in Hill House from the movie *The Haunting*. She'd seen that bone-chilling show a couple of years earlier and the story of young women being locked into a haunted house still gave her nightmares.

Even during the one month she'd lived in the family townhouse in Chicago for the short time she'd lasted at the Art Academy, her Uncle Harry had found two other wealthy female students to live there, too, and they had a housekeeper and butler. The latter really served more as a bodyguard. So, she knew she'd been safe and she liked everyone there well enough, but had been so homesick she'd taken the train home without telling her parents she was coming, so they wouldn't have time to try to talk her out of it. Later she learned that Uncle Harry had found another well-to-do, rent-paying female student to take her place in the townhouse, so she didn't even feel badly about leaving.

Well, regardless, she reminded herself, she was stuck here in the boonies in West Branch for the next two months. There would be no slipping home this time or she'd land in jail. She had no choice but to try to be brave.

Bravery, however, had never been her strong suit. This was one goal in life she might never be able to meet.

8

Antsy as a caged kitten, she summoned up every ounce of courage she could muster and left her room.

"I can do this. I can do this," she whispered repeatedly to quell her fear.

Her door opened onto the vestibule, an anti-room between the stairs hallway and ballroom. She turned on the vestibule's small antique chandelier. To her delighted surprise, beams of crystalized light shot through the open double doors to splay across the polished ballroom dancefloor, painting the space with a mystical ambiance.

She poked her head in, hesitant because she was alone and was, well, once again almost naked in nothing more than a skimpy nightie. But no one was around, she reminded herself, so she stepped into the ballroom and flicked on a wall switch, illuminating the large chandelier hanging from the center of the ceiling. Her bare feet took her to the center of the room as if operating without a connection to her head. As afraid as she was, she couldn't resist being in that room.

They were there in her mind, the people Betty had reminisced about, the band and boozers and dancers from the 1920s. All her life Summer had heard the story about her grandmother having once been a flapper, the toast of the town in Chicago. Meg Sullivan O'Neill; her conservative, Catholic grandma; the governor's wife. It was hard to picture the wild years of her youth, seeing that the woman had later borne twelve children, giving Summer more aunts and uncles and cousins than she could count. But even in her sixties, Grandma O'Neill was a beautiful woman who craved clothes and style, like her present favorite, the Jackie Kennedy Look.

"Yeah, Grandma, you would have fit right in here, way back when, in your partying days."

She twirled, letting the shards of light wash over her body. She twirled again, feeling bold-hearted and free. Then she did a few rounds of the popular dance from the 1920s, the Charleston, which her grandma had taught her and her female cousins. Remembering with fondness the lyrics to one of the songs her grandma liked to play on her antique Victrola, Summer softly sang while she danced, "Five-foot two, eyes of blue, but oh! What those five foot could do, has anybody seen my gal?" She kicked a foot forward while stepping the other one backward, shook her hands in the air, and repeated the steps a number of times. "Could she love, could she coo! Cootchie-cootchie-cootchie coo! Has anybody seen my gal?" Then, in the quintessential Charleston move, she clapped her knees back and forth with her hands on them, crisscrossing her hands from knee to knee and back again.

Suddenly, shockingly, she realized she was smiling and having fun.

When the wood floor creaked loudly beneath her feet, she stopped, wondering if Betty might be able to hear her from below. Summer loved the sound of the old oakwood, but maybe it wasn't a good idea to get too noisy in the night.

Turning to leave the room, she thought she heard a noise behind her. She held her breath as goosebumps caused the hairs to stand up on the back of her neck. There it was again. This was what she got for letting her chicken self be brave. What was it? A creak in the wood floor? It wasn't her, as she stood frozen in place. Then a muffled thump and thwack came, and came again. She flung around, fists at the ready.

No one was there, yet the muffled thumping and thwacking continued. On tippy-toe, hoping that would render her footsteps silent on the old floor, she gulped. She'd come this far in practicing being courageous on this strange night; she might as well keep going. How could she resist being drawn to that weird noise? She crossed the ballroom all the way to the other side to a locked door that Betty had pointed out earlier. That door led to a large apartment that would later be made into four more guestrooms.

Summer pressed her ear to the locked door and listened. Yup. Someone was in there. Betty said no one had lived there in years. No one should be in there now. Yet someone softly knocked on something. Suddenly, the noise stopped. Did she hear a curse word? She could have sworn somebody swore. Panic struck as she feared whoever it was might come straight for this door. If they had a key, they could barrel through and run right into her. She shuffled backwards.

The sound of the footsteps became a softer clomping. It took a moment for her to realize they went down a flight of stairs. Of course, that apartment would need its own exit stairs to the alley out back.

In the B&B's upstairs hallway that ran along the back of the building, at the top of the stairs, Summer knew there was a window looking down at the alley out back. She dashed through the ballroom and vestibule, and into that hallway, where she flung open the window. She stuck her head out to take a gander.

Totally befuddled, she looked again to make certain she was seeing what she was seeing. A sizzling strike of lightening zig-zagged across the sky to illuminate the scene, making it even more visible. Sure enough, there it was. Summer never swore, but if ever an occasion called for it, this was it.

"What the hell?"

A clap of thunder rumbled above her head as the sky let loose with a smattering of rain. She ducked back inside, slammed the window shut, and raced downstairs.

9

"Betty! Betty!" Summer hollered as she scrambled down the stairs, her bare feet skidding across the varnished wood floors and almost making her fall more than once. She felt like a klutz trying to do ballet. Frantically trying to find light switches, she gave up and found her way by the bits of light trickling in around the sides of the drawn shades. Earlier the innkeeper had shown Summer the door at the back of the stairway hall downstairs, which opened into a short hall that led to her small innkeeper's apartment.

Just as Summer raised a fist and thrust it forward to pound on Betty's door, the innkeeper flung the door open. "Bet..." Summer shouted as she almost toppled over, only keeping her balance with Betty's quick reaction, grabbing Summer's raised arm to steady her.

"Hey, hey, hey. Easy, kid. What's wrong?" Betty looked like she'd been sleeping, with her hair a jumble and no glasses on.

"A man was in the locked apartment upstairs and he left on a bicycle and he's dropping money all the way down the alley. That way." Summer pointed toward the nearby door to the alley outside that sat at a ninety-degree angle to Betty's door.

Betty squinted, jutted out her jaw, and said, "Have you been smoking dope?"

"No. Come, look." Summer grabbed hold of the shoulder of Betty's cotton pajamas and tugged toward the outside door.

The furrow of Betty's brow belied her skepticism, but she stepped out of her apartment and into the hall where she opened a wall cabinet and came up with a flashlight. She unbolted the backdoor and opened it only to be startled by a brilliant jolt of lighting.

"Damn," she yelped, flinching. But, clearly, she'd seen something in that moment of radiant illumination that aroused her interest. Casting her flashlight beam down the alley toward the east, she took one step outside, undeterred by the pouring rain. "Ho-ly shit," she blurted, running out to grab up some of the cash strewn down the alley toward N. 2nd St.

Summer stood in the dry safety of the doorway beseeching Betty to come back in and find an umbrella, but Betty wasn't listening. The older woman got soaked to the bone while thunder rumbled around overhead. Finally, impelled by the terror of a second blaze of lightening, she ran back inside, clutching fistfuls of wet, green bills.

"Holy shit," Betty said again. "These are thousand-dollar bills. Old ones, but big ones all the same. Let's spread them out on the kitchen counter to dry."

Once the bills laid flat on the café's metal kitchen counter, Betty whistled. She'd collected twelve bills. "We have twelve thousand dollars here. What the hell is going on?" She looked up toward the supposedly locked apartment. "You're sure the person who had this money came out of there?"

"I'm absolutely positive."

"And he left on a bicycle."

"Yes."

"Did he drop the money on purpose?"

"No, he had what looked like a burlap bag tucked under his arm. I don't think he realized it was open a little in the back. The money was falling out behind him. It was already raining, so I couldn't see much except that he was short and chubby, bald, and he wore a dark shirt."

"Go look out the front window and see if Bogey is there in his sheriff's car." She ran a kitchen towel through her wet hair as she spoke.

"He's not there. I saw him drive away a little while ago."

Betty considered that for only an instant. "Okay. Let's get dressed. I'm dripping all over the floor. I'll worry about that later. I've got umbrellas; we can collect the rest of the money as fast as possible, then see if we can follow this guy's trail in my car. He can't be traveling too fast or too far on a bike in a storm."

Summer was already on her way to the stairs. Back in her room, she ran from window to window to close them against the rain. Then her frenetic attempt at shedding her nightie proved fruitless, so with one strap off and the other still on, she threw on a tee shirt over it, acutely aware she was already breaking her vow to wear a bra from now on. So much for that pledge. Hopping on one foot, she thrust one leg and then the other into a pair of panties, and then a pair of shorts. "Thank you, Charlotte," she said as she shoved her feet into sandals, "for doing such a great job packing my stuff." She did her best to tuck in her nightie so it wouldn't hang out from under her tee shirt, and flew back downstairs.

Betty; in jeans, a blouse, galoshes, and her red glasses; already stood at the open backdoor, putting up an umbrella. She ran out and grabbed more bills. Summer took an umbrella left by the door and struggled to open it at the same time she pulled the door closed behind her. She, too, picked up bills until the trail ceased at the end of the alley. She calculated that together they picked up about a couple dozen more bills.

"He must have realized he was bleeding cash and stemmed the flow," Betty said as she tromped through mud puddles to the old barn-like structure along the other side of the alley.

Grappling with an umbrella and flashlight in one hand and wet thousand-dollar bills in the other, Betty couldn't open the broad door on the building, so she stuffed the wadded up cash into her jeans' pocket and handed the flashlight over to Summer, who understood this building must house Betty's car. Summer aimed the light at the door handle. One hand now free, Betty released the ancient latch and pulled the rickety door open, having to wade through rivulets of rainwater to push it as far open as possible.

"This used to be the stables in horse-and-buggy days, for store owners," Betty explained as Summer flashed the light inside. "Now we keep our cars here."

There sat a beat-up Volkswagen Beetle convertible. It was white on the upper half of the body and mostly rust on the parts closer to the road, no doubt a result of far too many winters on salted ice-and-snow roads. The ragtop sagged pitifully. The building itself was long, with plenty of empty, dark spaces on either side during the night, but Summer could see how the old stables could handle enough cars for every business owner on the block during regular daylight hours. She could imagine this place once having been filled with horses and drays and broughams and buckboards.

"Hop in," Betty commanded, closing her umbrella and tossing it into the back seat, and jumping into the driver's seat.

Summer followed suit and got in at the passenger's side of the dilapidated vehicle, discovering leather seats so worn they had been covered with colorful, foot-long, plastic stickers shaped like flowers. The same flower stickers decorated the dashboard.

Betty turned the key already in the ignition, spewed mud as she backed into the alley, and took off.

"Geez," Summer said as she crammed bills into her shorts' pocket with one hand while holding onto the dashboard with the other hand, a necessity so she wouldn't get slammed into the window. "You drive like an Indianapolis 500 racecar driver." They jerked around the corner out of the alley and onto N. 2nd St. Once the Beetle straightened up and her life no longer seemed to be in danger, Summer continued. "Think about this: we're chasing a dumpy intruder on a bicycle who drops old thousand-dollar bills like breadcrumbs leaving a trail. And people think I'm weird."

The car's dim headlights barely clawed their way to a few feet ahead in the pouring rain. But, as if a gift from the Norse thunder god Thor, as they veered left onto Houghton Avenue lightening flashed, irradiating the scene ahead. Nature's electricity existed for one mere breath, but that was all they needed to see that five or six blocks up, riding his bike on the sidewalk under the cover of the maple trees, was a short, chubby, bald man in a dark shirt, cradling a bulky bag under his arm.

Thunder rumbled like a freight train careening from one end of the sky to the other, warning them to seek shelter. Summer looked at Betty, the older woman's decision about what to do next plain on her face. Summer agreed. The irresistible allure of mystery spurred them on. They had come this far; they couldn't stop now.

They had to follow this curious quest to the end, no matter where it took them.

10

They lost him.

They stayed a couple of blocks behind the mystery man and turned off the car lights more than once when he looked back, obviously checking to see if anyone followed him. But in the rain, he didn't seem to see their darkened Beetle. Betty couldn't see much, either. So, they lost him.

"Damn," Betty grumbled. "Where did he go?"

They drove past the police station, turned around at the Y in the road, and came back.

"There's his bike." Summer pointed at the Masonic Lodge next to the state police station.

His bicycle stood abandoned, nestled into the soaked bushes by the building.

"Okay, let's be careful from here on out. At least we're close to the police, in case this gets hairy." Betty pulled into the parking area of the lodge with her lights off and turned off the car. "Follow my lead. I want to know about the money, but most of all I want to know why this son-of-a-bitch was in our building. Come on." She twisted toward the backseat to reach for her umbrella, but drew her hand back when the rat-a-tat of rain on the ragtop stopped.

The deluge quit as quickly as if a faucet had been turned off.

"Well, look at that," Betty said. "Thank goodness. Now we can at least see in front of us. Here, take a flashlight." She grabbed one of the flashlights that laid on the seat between them and handed one to Summer. As quietly as possible, they got out of the car.

Summer stood by the car, shining her light nearby. Betty stepped over to check out the bike.

"Hey, look at the footprints. He went that way." Summer motioned toward footprints in the mud that led to the back of the police station.

"Why in blazes would some thief or intruder—or whatever in hell he is—why would he head toward the police station?"

"Beats me." None of this made any sense to Summer.

"Come on. Let's follow. Unless…"

"Unless what?" Summer followed as Betty trudged through wet grass and mud puddles while droplets of rain from giant hardwood trees fell on their heads.

"He might be headed to the cemetery that's behind the police station on the other side."

Betty sped up, hopped over a narrow stream, slipped in muck, righted herself, and scurried on.

"Cemetery? Oh, we don't want to go there, do we?" Summer figured her allotted dose of courage had been spent for the night. Maybe for the year. Or forever.

Betty didn't answer and Summer had no choice but to follow, her feet sinking in mud all the way. When they reached the other side of the back of the police station, Summer could see a sign that said, "Brookside Cemetery." Plenty of spooky headstones loomed ahead in the foggy mist rendered up from the storm.

"I can see a light on in the police station, so they must have a night person on duty. How about we go inside and tell them what happened?" Summer tried to sound encouraging, but it was useless. Again, Betty remained mum. Relentlessly, the woman charged through the gates of the cemetery. Terrified of being left alone among the dead, Summer hurried along close behind.

"Sh-h-h," Betty shushed, holding out an arm in warning. "Turn off your flashlight."

"What?"

"Turn it off, now."

Betty had already turned off her light; Summer did the same. Standing stock still in the darkness, Summer's eyes adjusted to the blackness and tombstones became clearer, even as fog swirled amongst them.

"This way," Betty whispered. Carefully, she moved ahead, following a path that led deeper into the graveyard.

Betty must have seen it at the same instant Summer did, because she grabbed Summer's arm. "Do you see that?" Betty wanted to know, never drawing her eyes away from where a beam of a flashlight bobbed up and down a few tombstone rows up.

"Yeah, I see it," Summer croaked.

"It stopped. Damn, what happened?" Betty kept her voice low and even, but excitement filtered its way into her words. "Come on." She started to forge ahead.

"Come on? How about 'let's go get the police.'"

As if noticing her for the first time, Betty looked at Summer, her face like that of a zombie in the long shadows of the cemetery. "Listen, Summer, that's a good idea. You go back and get a policeman. I'll keep my eyes on this bugger so we don't lose him. Go." She walked away so quickly that in the instant that Summer turned to look at the police station and turn back, Betty was gone.

"Betty?" Summer tried to swallow her panic and keep her voice down. "Betty?" She took a few steps backward....

Without warning, the soggy ground opened up under her feet and she fell for what felt like forever, screaming at the top of her lungs all the way. "Ah-h-h-h-h-h!" Thud. She landed on her backside, sprawled out like a five-point star. "What the hell?" she moaned, shaking her head to fend off her bewilderment. "Where am I?" Her flashlight lost, she looked around and couldn't see a thing, but the unmistakable smell of raw, damp earth surrounded her. "Oh no," she hollered as her senses struggled to put the unbelievable pieces together — falling, blackness, wet dirt... All of that could only mean one horrendous thing.

"Betty! Betty!" she screamed as sheer terror struck. Panic grabbed her heart and lungs and mind, and wrenched them into a worthless blob. "Betty. Betty. I've fallen into a grave," she croaked, her throat having tied itself into a strangled knot as surely as if a killer's massive hands squeezed her neck. "Get me out of here," she sobbed hopelessly.

Forcing herself to remember to breathe, she struggled to stand up but plopped back down. It must have been a large clump of dirt on the bottom that pillowed her fall because she wasn't hurt.

Betty appeared above and shone her flashlight down into the hole. Silently she stared down, her eyes growing wider and wider by the moment. Falling to her knees at the edge of the freshly dug grave and frantically reaching down to try to lend a hand, she bellowed, "Damn. Here, grab my hand. Get out of there." Betty thrust down her hand in a futile attempt to help. Her reach landed about two feet short.

"What...?" Summer, finally managed to get up on her feet in the uneven, muddy ground. She turned to look at where Betty focused her beam of light on the clump that had broken her fall.

"No-o-o!" Summer screamed as horror filled her once again.

"No, no, no. Get me out of here." Hysterically clawing at the wet dirt on the walls of the pit, she'd escape if she had to dig her way out herself. This was far worse than the haunting of Hill House, far worse than anything she'd ever imagined could happen to her in this lifetime. This was a horror story to beat all horror stories.

11

"Okay, let me make sure I've got this right," the sheriff said. His badge said he was the sheriff and that his last name was Kowalczyk, and he'd introduced himself, but Summer had already forgotten how to pronounce that name. She thought it might be like Koe-WALL-zick. This Sheriff Kowalczyk tapped his pencil on his notepad. He'd been asking questions and taking copious notes for the half hour he'd been "interviewing" Betty and Summer. It had been the night shift trooper from the state police post who responded to Summer's screams and pulled her out of the grave, which, as it unfortunately turned out, had not been empty.

But, seeing that these kinds of cases were the responsibility of the sheriff's department and the state police only participated if asked, Ogemaw County Sheriff Kowalczyk had asked. Thus, they sat in the cramped interview room in the state police post, right next to the cemetery where Summer had fallen into a freshly dug grave and landed on top of a dead man. The man, as it so sadistically turned out, she'd seen riding away from their building on a bike. The horror of getting up off what she thought was a pile of dirt to stare into a set of dead eyes wouldn't cease. She felt certain she'd be seeing those eyes in her nightmares for the rest of her life.

She'd been craving excitement, but not like this.

Betty had smoked three of the sheriff's Chesterfield cigarettes so far, and he'd smoked four. Summer sat wrapped in a blanket the trooper had given her. Still, she couldn't stop shaking. She'd never been so filthy dirty. They tried to clean her off, using a hose outside to spray her feet and hands before she came inside. That got off the bulk of the dried mud, but in the end she'd thrown her once-fashionable, expensive sandals away. Why she'd chosen that footwear in such miserable rain, she'd never know. Charlotte had packed her galoshes, which remained clean and dry in her room at the B&B. Now she was barefoot; with arms, legs, and face streaked in dirt; smeared clothes; and broken nails. She'd never had shabby, unclean nails in her life. Her wayward nightie hung out below her tee shirt, and to top it off her hair looked like it had been wrung through a ringer.

Mercifully, the trooper had also brought her a Coke, while everyone else drank coffee. Without the Coke, she thought she might collapse.

"You heard a man in the locked apartment of your building," the sheriff said, pointing his pencil at Summer. She nodded. "Then both of you..." he pointed at Betty and then at Summer with his pencil... "found thousand-dollar bills he'd dropped in the alley. You have a dozen of them at the café and had these twenty in your pockets." Now he pointed at the damp, crumpled up bills lying on the table between them. Both women nodded. "Then, for reasons you can't explain, instead of calling us, law enforcement, you decided to follow the guy on your own, right into the cemetery." Neither woman spoke. "Okay, that's when you," he said to Summer, "fell into a grave where, unfortunately, there was a dead man. The money bag you saw was gone. Have I got that right?"

"Uh huh," Betty said.

"Yes," Summer agreed.

"Then, while she was in the…" He hesitated, mulling over his words. "While Miss Krause wasn't in a position to see, you heard a car race away." He motioned toward Betty.

"Yes, sir," Betty said. "I'm sorry I didn't get a look at it, I was so focused on Summer. The man in the grave must have been killed as soon as he got to the cemetery, because we'd seen him riding close to the police post only about fifteen minutes earlier. He must have planned on meeting someone in the cemetery, and that person killed him right away. The killer must have taken the money bag."

The sheriff was a short, wiry man, with a kindly face. Yet, that face looked totally bewildered at the moment. When called by the trooper in the middle of the night, he hadn't bothered with his uniform. Instead, he'd thrown on jeans and a Michigan State University Spartans tee shirt, arriving at the scene within ten minutes.

He took a sip of coffee, drew on his Chesterfield, and said, "Okay, but we can't make too many assumptions until we do some investigating. You're sure the dead man in the grave is the man you saw in the alley, the one riding a bike down main street toward the cemetery, with a bag under his arm." He addressed Summer.

"It sure looked like the same man," she said. "He was fat and bald and had on a dark shirt."

"That's our guy." Everyone turned toward the door with the intrusion of a new voice into the conversation. Deputy Bush stood there, still in uniform, still sans hat. This time, however, his uniform was covered in mud. He'd obviously been down in that unholy hole.

"How are you ladies doing?" he asked, looking from one to the other.

"Okay, Bogey," Betty said. "We'll be okay after we get over the shock."

The deputy eyed Summer, who still shivered under the blanket. "Um, I'm okay, too, I guess," she said.

He looked at her dubiously, not sure of her answer, then switched to professional mode, looking at his boss. "Fitz came in to help out, Sheriff. He checked in once his wife and new baby were asleep. We got the body to Chuck. That's the coroner," he added by way of explanation to the women. "Of course, he'll do an autopsy, but we can see that the victim was stabbed with a jackknife. None of us have ever seen him before. He's not from around here." He shook his head, and Summer could see a glob of mud stuck in his hair. "We found his bike right where they said it was, and we have it in the trunk of the cruiser. We also found a few more bills in the mud at the bottom of the grave." He held up a lunch-size paper sack. "We'll check them for prints along with the others but everything is so wet and muddy that doesn't look hopeful."

Sheriff Kowalczyk took a final puff of his cigarette before stubbing out the butt in the overflowing ashtray on the table. "Okay, here's what we're gonna do. You ladies have been most cooperative, considering I'm sure you can't wait to get home and get cleaned up and warm. Is that new fireplace working yet?"

"Like a charm," Betty said.

"Go home, sit by the fire while you drink some hot chocolate, then try to get some sleep. I'll follow you and check out that locked apartment. Bogey, go home, clean up, pack an overnight bag, and move into the B&B for the next couple of nights. Betty, you got a room he can use?"

"Yeah. Upstairs, next to Summer's. The apartment is on the other side of the ballroom, so not too far away."

"Good. Everybody needs sleep except me. I was out like a baby when I got the call. Do your best to get some shuteye, then join me in the apartment when you can. Ladies, I'd like you to stop in to be able to verify to Harry the condition it's in. We don't know yet if it's been ransacked or what. Then we'll need you to stay out of the way while we conduct our investigation. Any questions?"

"Uh, I'm not going to jail?" Summer had been dreading the possibility.

"No, Miss Krause. What would make you think I'd arrest you?"

"I don't know. Except sheriffs seem to like to put me in jail." She'd been serious, but couldn't miss the snicker Betty struggled to suppress.

"Well, you haven't done anything here to get you arrested," the sheriff said. "I'm so sorry this happened to you. Let me know if you have any questions or need help in any way. All right?"

"Thank you. Will you have to call my uncle about what I did?"

"No, not about what you did, but about an apparent robbery in a building he owns. I've met your Uncle Harry. He seems like a very reasonable man. I don't suspect he'll blame you for any of this."

"Oh. Okay. I thought you might have to report me to him. And to the judge in Traverse City."

"We'll let them know, but there shouldn't be any ramifications. You're twenty-one; you're an adult; this case doesn't intersect with the reason you're here in town. In fact, you begin Head Start this Monday, right?"

"I guess." She looked at Betty, who nodded.

"We haven't even had time to talk about that yet," the innkeeper said.

"Our other deputy, Jerry Fitzpatrick, Fitz everyone calls him, will have two little boys in your class. He has nine boys now, with the new one born a few hours ago. With that many children, his kids qualify for the program. We all look forward to your service to this community."

Summer didn't know what to say. She'd never thought about what she had to do as anything but punishment, not as actual service to somebody. "Thanks," she mumbled, and she and Betty said their goodbyes. They went back to the B&B, the place the sheriff had called their "home," to try to get back to something like normal living.

12

Harry O'Neill hung up the phone on the nightstand. Ellie sat next to him on the side of their bed, her arm slung over his bare shoulder. All he wore was a pair of boxer shorts while she had on a silky nightgown that had a difficult time containing her ample bosom. He patted her knee.

"Well, you heard both conversations. What do you think we should do?" he asked his wife. When they'd been awakened by the jangle of the phone at two in the morning he'd held the receiver between them so that Ellie could hear, too. Sheriff Kowalczyk had been professional and therefore brief, providing the bare facts. Betty called a few minutes later, lamenting her role in putting Summer in such a horribly traumatizing situation. It all happened so fast, she told them, all she could think about was catching an intruder who had dared to break into their building. Harry reassured her that no one could ever have suspected what eventually transpired.

Ellie nuzzled his neck. After twenty years of marriage, her touch still dazzled him. Harry thought himself the luckiest man alive to have found this woman. She was bold but not brazen, sexy but not trashy, and smart but not snobbishly intellectual. She fussed about having gained weight over the years but he didn't care. To him she'd been appealing as hell as a thin twenty-year-old and now she was appealing as hell as a buxom forty-one-year old. She'd always light his fire, that he knew.

"Well," she said, giving his neck one last nibble, "we know what her parents would do."

"Yeah, they'd be in the car on their way to West Branch right now. Richard would wrap Summer up in a blanket as if she was four years old and take her home, no matter what the judge said."

"Thank goodness they're still in Hawaii. So, you asked what I think. I think we leave her be for now. We wanted her to learn to fend for herself. It's awful what happened, especially on her very first night there, but if we go running to her at this moment it'll be one more time in her life when she didn't have to face reality and somebody came to save her. Call her on the phone in the morning to let her talk it out, if she wants to, but otherwise we know she's in good hands. It might not have been the brightest thing in the world to do, to follow the guy to a cemetery, but I have faith in Betty. She can handle this. She said they saw the guy go in and she followed so they wouldn't lose him, but Summer was on her way to get the police. So, they were thinking clearly enough. Besides, the sheriff said a deputy will be staying there for a few nights. Let's talk to Betty on the phone each day for updates and see how it plays out from there."

"Yeah, the sheriff said he wants to know who owned the building before us, but he can get a copy of the deed of sale from the county. We have nothing else to add; we never met the former owners; it was all done through their lawyer. We don't know that guy from Adam. Remember? It was some brass hat from Detroit.

"How about we consider going to West Branch on Wednesday? We were going to be there on Friday, anyway, for the open house. We'll go a couple of days early to see what's up. How's that? That's four days away, so we won't be running to her immediately, but we'll see her sooner than we originally planned."

She planted a long, deep kiss on his lips. "Perfect," she said upon finally coming up for air.

After a half-hour romp, which left them both naked, breathless, and sated, their conversation drifted back to the B&B.

"What about all that money? It sounds like the dead guy took it out of our apartment. What on earth could that be about?" Ellie laid spread-eagled on top of the satin sheets, basking in the breeze coming in through their bedroom's open sliding doors that led to the balcony overlooking Lake Huron.

"When we saw that apartment there was so much old, dusty stuff it was hard to figure out what was what."

"I thought the place enchanting, sexy even, although it did need a good cleaning after all those years of being closed up."

Harry had come across the building a year earlier while traveling through West Branch. After a search of county records in the basement of the Ogemaw County Courthouse, he learned the owner was a company in Detroit. They owned the entire building, including all three store spaces, downstairs and upstairs. One store space had been empty with a "For Rent" sign so faded it said "Fo Re t." The second space was a record store that wasn't doing well. The owner was about to call it quits and move to Florida. The owner of the popular bakery in the third space told Harry he'd be delighted to have a new landlord, as he'd never laid eyes on the present one nor received a response to enquiries or requests. All he knew was his rental agreement came from a lawyer in Detroit and that was where he sent his monthly rent checks. No one had access to the upstairs portions of the building.

The Detroit lawyer took the three-hour journey from Motor

City to West Branch for the close of the sale, handing over three sets of keys, one for each store space. Excited over their new adventure, Harry and Ellie had gone straight to the building, bought two plump cinnamon twists and hot coffee from the bakery, and proceeded to investigate their purchase. They had never seen the first store space except through the windows. The second one, the record store, had been so cluttered with moving boxes it was hard to tell what it really looked like. The bakery was the only space where they were able to look around before acquiring the keys. They couldn't wait to explore upstairs.

The ballroom had been a complete surprise. They felt like they'd won a jackpot. Later they learned about its speakeasy history from the president of the State Savings Bank, where they opened a business account. They would rent it out, they decided, for events like wedding receptions and reunions, classes like social dance and tap, and club gatherings. Once a month they'd have a band perform and open it up to the public for a modest fee. The possibilities in the ballroom were endless.

But they'd been dismayed to discover they couldn't get into the upstairs of the bakery. That key didn't fit. The rusted old locks, one upstairs on a door in the ballroom, and the other at the downstairs outside alley entrance, had been changed some time long ago. After a locksmith was called and a door finally opened, Harry and Ellie had been agog upon finding an apartment from an era gone by, probably the 1920s. It looked like whoever had once lived there had picked up and walked out without packing a thing. Dust that hadn't been disturbed in decades blanketed a life's worth of belongings.

There was so much to sort through they made the quick decision to remodel and open the other parts of the building first, to give them ample time to assess the value of the stash of belongings in the apartment. It would take weeks, probably even months. They'd planned on starting that process this weekend, after the opening. Summer and Betty were going to be invited to continue sifting through the place after Harry and Ellie left, if they enjoyed that kind of prospecting. There was no telling what they'd run across.

"Too bad we haven't had time yet to go through the apartment," Harry said. "We could've found all that mullah ourselves. According to the sheriff, if the bag of money did indeed come from our property, it's ours. I'm thinking someone must have gone there knowing it was there and might have been in there for some time trying to find it. But how could he possibly have known to meet someone else in the cemetery right at that time? The someone who apparently killed him."

"I have no idea. Do you think there could be others who want into the apartment to look for more money or maybe even something else?"

"It doesn't seem likely, now that somebody has the money. But, as the sheriff said, it's a crime scene right now anyway, so they'll be combing through it to see if they find any clues. If anybody else does want in, they surely won't do it anytime soon, not with the police there."

"Okay. Let's go back to sleep. I'm tired." Ellie slipped her nightgown back on, fluffed her pillow, and curled into a ball. Within minutes she was sound asleep.

Harry took advantage of the clean summer air wafting through the open balcony doors to clear his head. Yes, he decided. Their plan was the best thing to do. Summer was not in danger, not with Betty and a deputy at her side day and night. As usual, he felt fortunate to have been able to talk this situation over with his wife because he, too, like Summer's parents, had an impulse to run to his niece and rescue her. His determination to toughen her up this summer had vacillated mightily upon hearing that she'd fallen on top of a dead man in a grave. It was "incomprehensible," as Ellie had said when they'd been on the phone. In spite of the macabre absurdity of the situation, Ellie loved Summer and, from a woman's point of view, always seemed to know what was right. It was time for the young woman to learn to save herself.

For the thousandth time he thought of what a great mother Ellie would have been. His heart bled for her in her sadness at not being able to conceive a child. The doctors had never been able to figure out why, but Ellie was barren. He thought he'd be a good dad, too, partly because it would make his beloved so happy. They had considered adopting, but always waited to see if they would have their own. Now that they were getting older, reality dug in like a dagger, stabbing deeper and deeper into their unbidden knowing with each year that went by. A family was not in their future.

Thank you, God, Harry prayed, as he so often did, *for giving us each other.* He wrapped his arm around his sleeping wife's waist, and fell into restless twilight slumber.

13

"Are you feeling better, Summer?" The sheriff, she noticed, had become more informal, no longer calling her "Miss Krause." It made her feel comfortable, more herself, to be addressed by her first name.

"Yes, thank you."

After showering thoroughly; washing her hair; cleaning and filing her nails; and donning jeans, a light sweater, and her tennis shoes; she'd joined Betty in the lobby by the fire. There wasn't any furniture there yet—Betty told her that was coming in the morning—so they bundled up with pillows and blankets on the soft Persian carpet. Betty had made hot chocolate, like the sheriff ordered, and the drink soothed Summer. In fact, she thought it would put her right to sleep. She'd been so exhausted she fell onto her bed fully clothed; but, when she closed her eyes, the eyes of that ghastly dead man stared right at her. Consequently, she got up and padded across the ballroom to the mystery apartment, now unlocked, to see what was happening in there.

Sheriff Kowalczyk and Deputy Bush rummaged through the place. Although the lights had been turned on, they shed little illumination, casting a spooky glow. The lawmen used their flash-lights to investigate each item they picked up and looked over. Dust flew off everything they touched.

"Here we go," Betty said, coming into the room with an armful of lightbulbs. "These will work a lot better than those old ones from the '20s. We can use these in the lamps that aren't on yet and turn off the overheads. Then when they cool down we can replace them, too.

"Oh, hi, Summer. Couldn't you get to sleep?" Betty's voice belied her concern.

"No, too curious, I guess," Summer fibbed, not wanting to reveal her cowardly visions. "How can I help?" She looked around, taken aback by the spectacle before her. One enormous room contained a small kitchen with ancient appliances on the back wall, a bedroom section with an opulent canopied bed at the center of the far wall, and a sitting area with overstuffed furniture near the front windows. More furniture and accoutrements filled the room. The canopy over the bed hung in tatters at one post, and the upholstered furniture had busted out of its seams in spots. A blanket of dust covered everything, as if protecting this secret dwelling from the outside world. The room not only looked but smelled like it had been closed up in an era long gone by.

Summer stepped into the middle of the apartment and turned from side to side, trying to take it all in.

"It's amazing, isn't it?" Betty asked while changing a light bulb in a floor lamp in the sitting area. She switched it on and a bright circle of light warmed the space. She moved to a table lamp by the bed.

"Yeah," Summer agreed. "Who on earth lived here?"

"Wish we knew," Betty said, turning on more welcome light. "The sheriff has figured out the place wasn't broken into. The locks are intact. Your Uncle Harry had a locksmith get him inside, but they hadn't changed any locks yet. Whoever came in here tonight had a key that worked. A very, very old key."

"Whoa. That's weird. I think I heard him swear right before leaving, so he might have run into something or had a hard time with something as he hurried out."

"Hm-m, so he may not have known his way around all that well," the sheriff interjected while nosing into a closet. He pulled a string to turn on a hanging lightbulb overhead, looked up and down, and whistled. "Look at this. Ladies, come here and take a look-see." He stepped out of the closet so the women could crowd in.

Summer felt like she'd stepped into a musty wardrobe that could transport her to the magical realm of Narnia, like in her favorite childhood books of fanciful flight. This, however, was a closet that would lead to the bootlegging, jazz-crazed, speak-easy-loving, adult world of the "Roaring '20s." She and Betty stood there in their casual 1960s jeans surrounded by sequined and beaded shifts, fur stoles and coats, bowed and feathered hats, and silk caftans and scarves. Not a pair of slacks, and certainly not a pair of jeans, in sight.

"Wow. Women used to dress like this." Betty pulled out a beige linen dress, dull from age, mid-calf length with a drop waist. "This must've been her daytime attire, as casual as she ever got. Probably what she cleaned house in."

"I doubt she cleaned her own house."

"Pfft. So true."

For the second time that night, Summer's mind became lost in memories of her grandmother's stories of her Flapper life in Chicago in the early '20s, the over-indulgent years of her youth. Now Summer understood. This was what it had been like. It brought her earlier imaginary vision in the ballroom to life, when she'd been doing the Charleston herself.

She fingered a shiny red shift embellished with layers of scallops embroidered with crystal beads on the short skirt. Carefully taking it off its hanger, she held it up to herself and looked in a mottled mirror on the closet wall. The dress would be too short for her, of course. It would be above the knee on a short woman while it was high thigh length for her. Still, she could imagine how girly-girl she'd feel in a dress like this. She put it back on its hanger and hung it up.

"Did you see all these shoes?" Betty asked.

Summer turned around to a row of shelves that held twenty-five or thirty pairs of every kind and color of pump she could imagine, each pair neatly arranged together. Betty stood on her tiptoes to stretch her arm up to pick a sparkly pink pump that had fallen over on a high shelf. Looking inside the shoe, she said, "Whoever she was, she wore a six and a half. Petite lady." She reached up to replace the shoe when Summer stopped her.

"Wait. There's an opening in the wall up there."

"Where? I don't see it."

"You're too short. Being tall does have its advantages sometimes. It looks like somebody shoved that pair of shoes over and slid open a little door. There's a hole big enough for that sack of money."

"Let me see." Deputy Bush came up to the closet door and motioned for them to get out of the way. The sheriff followed, but seeing that he was short himself, he let his tall deputy investigate. Bogey Bush took his flashlight and peered inside the hole. "It's a safe. The door slides open. It's empty now. Summer's right. It would've been a perfect hidey-hole for that money."

"So," the sheriff said, "not only did our dead man have a key to this apartment, he knew where to find the safe and he knew the combination. Furthermore, he knew that stash of money was there." He pointed to the empty safe. "That explains why it looks like nothing else was taken. We've found other valuables, like jewelry, and he didn't touch them. He may not have even known they were there. He only had one goal in mind: get in and out as quickly as possible with that money.

"This apartment hasn't seen the light of day for forty years. The dust alone tells us not a living soul has spent any time up here. Thousand-dollar bills haven't been printed since the 1930s. What in blazes does all of that tell us?" He scratched his head in quandary.

"Somebody somehow inherited a key and information about that safe," Deputy Bush said.

Summer had a thought and went to one of the two front windows, pulling back the frail, dusty curtain and looking out. "What about that boy?" She pointed to the Midstate Theatre, which from this location sat closer than from her bedroom. "Maybe he saw something."

The deputy came to her side and looked across the street. "Tommy," he said. "You saw him, too?" He turned to Summer and the intensity of his brown eyes, "bedroom eyes" Charlotte called eyes that color, made her knees weak. He was about six inches taller than she was, so he must be six-foot-three or -four, she figured. Like her dad. Her mom was only five-foot-three, so always had to cock her head way up to look at her husband. But Summer had long been able to raise her gaze ever-so-slightly to look her dad in the eyes. Like with this Deputy Bogey Bush.

She forced herself to focus. "Yes. I saw him out there smoking not long before I heard the intruder. Maybe he saw a light or something."

"I'll talk to him today." The deputy explained to the sheriff about the teen who liked to smoke on the roof of the theater by the marquee.

"Well," Betty said, yawning like a lion, "I'm beat. I'm going to bed."

"Me, too," Summer agreed, not able to squelch her copy yawn. Suddenly, she felt like she'd hit the proverbial brick wall.

As Summer nestled into her comfy bed, she relaxed for the first time since she'd been home in her own bed a couple of nights earlier. This hick town had turned out not to be as boring as she'd expected, even if it did send her to an early grave. She wasn't the only one who'd endured being in that pit with a dead person. Deputy Bogey Bush had to climb down there to retrieve the body. She and the deputy had something in common, it seemed, even if it was something gross. And he would be sleeping right in the room next door. She'd never slept so close to a man like him. Sure, he was sexy, but he was unnerving, too. She still didn't know much about him. So, she decided, she'd simply put him out of her mind and go to sleep, even if he would be on the other side of that wall.

There were a million reasons he wasn't her type: small-town boy, shaggy hair, brusk, maybe even rude sometimes. Oh yeah, odds were he was a ladies' man, too. He was old enough to probably have had plenty of nookie. A guy his age should be married. What was wrong with him that he was still single? No, she wouldn't let herself give one moment of thought to a "cad," as her former jail-mate and teacher-in-the-ways-of-the-world Carla the Cynic labeled most men. That Deputy Bogey Bush was probably one of them, too.

Her waking, conscious mind did a fine job doling out rational orders but after she drifted off to sleep her dream mind had no qualms about disobeying and conjuring up forbidden fantasies about that imagined cad on the other side of the wall.

14

The ear-piercing whir of a siren jolted Summer awake.

Fire. It must be fire.

The siren was so close it felt like it was right above her head on the roof.

She jumped out of bed, raced to the window, and looked out. On a sunny Saturday, people were casually walking and driving around town as if nothing was happening. Cars stopped at the red light without a concern in the world. Women looked at dresses in Linton's store window as if deaf to the blare. Kids rode their bikes down the sidewalks, and a lineup waited for a drink at the fountain in front of the bank. A number of people headed for the Model Restaurant down the street in one direction and to the bakery two doors down from the B&B in the other direction.

Yet, the siren shrieked.

As she ran to her side window to check that direction, the whir began to wind down, like an opera singer losing her voice decibel by decibel. Thankfully, silence finally ensued.

Why hadn't anyone responded to the warning siren, which had to be the signal for fire? Oh, she got it: It must be some kind of drill that everyone in town knew about, so they weren't surprised. She wondered how often that blasting noise would be tested. Not often, she hoped.

She'd had a hard enough time sleeping through the night,

what with a stupid train barreling through town and blowing it's whistle at 2:00 a.m. How could these people live like this?

Fifteen minutes later; still bleary eyed but dressed in shorts, a sleeveless blouse, and a pair of sandals she hoped could survive the day; she left her room. Focused on her growling stomach, she missed the man coming out of his room and bumped right into him.

"Oh, I'm sorry," Deputy Bush said as he instinctively reached out to steady her.

"It was my fault," she insisted, shaking her head. "Sorry, Deputy Bush." The rush she felt upon being so close to this manly man shocked her.

They backed away from one another, where Summer had a better view of his casual clothes, a short-sleeved pull-over shirt that emphasized chiseled arm muscles and those jeans that clung to long, lean legs. She saw him looking her over, too. Nervously, like a couple of kids caught looking at a dirty magazine, they both looked away.

Remember, Summer reminded herself, *I don't even like him.*

"Please," he said, motioning to the stairs, "call me Bogey. Everybody does when I'm not at work."

"Oh, sure." She scampered down the stairs, uncomfortable not knowing what to say and then coming up with, "Boy, that siren was something else. Was it a drill?"

"No. That's the noon whistle. It blows every day."

"Every day? Why?" She didn't mention she was shocked to learn she'd slept until noon. She hadn't realized it was so late in the day. There had been no nightmares about the dead guy in the grave. She'd slept like a log after her second attempt at rest.

They reached the bottom of the stairs and he came to her side.

"To remind people it's time to break for lunch," he said, answering her question.

"Oh, how... quaint." Other words; like parochial, outdated, and dumb came to mind; but she thought it best to keep those thoughts to herself. "It sounded really close."

"It is. It's on the roof at the other end of this building." He pointed. "It blows for fires, too, but three shorter blasts instead of one long one. And on rare occasion when we have one, for tornadoes, too."

By then they'd stepped through the archway leading from the back hallway into the lobby of the B&B. Summer gasped. "Look at this." The place had been transformed. Beautiful furniture, new and antique, filled the room, beckoning any traveler to sit and stay.

"Good morning, my children." Betty greeted them from a ladder where she hung a painting of an old mill. "How do you like it?" The painting straight and secure, she hopped off the ladder and swept her arm to indicate the entire room.

"It's fantastic," Summer admitted. "Absolutely beautiful."

"Betty, you've done a wonderful job here," Bogey said, broad hands on slim hips as he looked around. "Was this all stored at Morse's?" he asked, referring to the furniture store down the block.

"Yup. They've been great about this. Their movers brought it all right down the sidewalk this morning and helped me set it up. We tried to be as quiet as possible. Everybody needed their sleep after last night."

"Well, you didn't get much sleep," Summer noted. "I'm sorry I didn't wake up in time to help." She really wasn't all that sorry, but knew it was the right thing to say.

"Oh, don't worry about that. I needed this to get my mind off our little adventure in the cemetery. I was so wired about that and excited about this I couldn't sleep anyway. There's more to come and lots to do, so I still need lots of help. But everybody's on lunch break right now, including us. Come on." She turned on her heel and went through the door adjoining the café, which wouldn't be open until the following Friday, the same day as the open house for the B&B.

"I made us sandwiches for lunch." She took a platter of egg salad and chicken salad sandwiches out of the refrigerator. "Plates are up there." She pointed to a shelf and Bogey got down three plates. "Pop's over there." She motioned for Summer to get bottles out of the Coke machine.

Summer went to the big red box, lifted the lid, and found that coins weren't necessary for this machine, as it sat in the kitchen and wouldn't be accessible to customers. "Everybody want Coke?" she asked, noticing the choices were Coca-Cola, Sprite, Vernor's Ginger Ale, Faygo Redpop, and Faygo Orange Pop, all Michigan favorites. Never mind that the machine said "Coca-Cola" on the front.

Betty agreed to a Coke and Bogey wanted a Redpop, so Summer pulled out three cold bottles, opened them on the opener on the side of the machine, and carried them over to the table in the café where they set up. The W.B. Café was an adorable restaurant, with a black-and-white checkered tile floor like in Summer's bathroom, a tin tile ceiling like in the lobby, and sturdy wood tables and chairs that looked like restored antiques. Red-and-white checkered tablecloths covered the tables, and a matching ruffle lined the tops of the windows in front.

"While we eat," Betty said as they settled into their chairs, "we have some updates for you, Summer." She took a big bite of an egg salad sandwich and a gulp of pop before continuing. "Our police are done in the apartment, but the state police are sending a couple of detectives from Detroit to look it over this afternoon. After that, there'll be more for us to do in there. Harry wants everything catalogued and stored, but he wants us to wait until he gets here to get started. The mystery of the murder has yet to be solved, that's for sure. Last night they came up with more questions than answers. They said I could go ahead as planned with the furniture in the rest of the place today, seeing that the apartment is the only crime scene."

Betty filled Summer in as they ate, saying she'd slept a few hours after she and Summer left the apartment to go to bed. But, she woke up too curious about what might be going on to get back to sleep.

"Bogey was leaving to go feed his horses at six o'clock," she said, nodding at him, "when I went back in. The sheriff had me stay out of the way this time, but I hung around until the furniture men came at eight."

"Yeah," Bogey said, "and then I came back here and crashed until noon. I don't remember the last time in my life I slept until noon. That would be never, actually. Anyway, we went through the whole place. Nothing indicates that the man stayed there for any length of time. Like Aleks suspected, it looks like he was in and out with one goal in mind."

"'Aleks' is Sheriff Kowalczyk," Betty explained to Summer.

"Oh, sorry," Bogey said. "We're pretty informal around here and use first names. Anyway, seeing that most people in town don't ride their bikes around with bags of money in tow, we don't think anyone else is in danger. The murderer is probably long gone, which is why the Detroit police are looking into this case. There could be a connection there."

Betty carried on the story. "They think it's an old Purple Gang thing." Her fascination with that idea shone in her bright eyes framed by their red cat-eye glasses. "They were a Jewish gang from Detroit in the 1920s and '30s and '40s, but hung out in this neck of the woods to evade police down there. We suspect they supplied illegal booze to our very own speakeasy upstairs. So that's the most logical explanation for all that money. Nobody else around here would ever have had access to all that loot."

"They were a ruthless bunch of hoodlums," Bogey said. "Most were killed in gang wars, some are still in prison, and I hear that one of the leaders is now a respectable old businessman in California. Go figure. They did run a big business for a long time, though, especially after hooking up with Al Capone and his Chicago gang. The Purples easily got booze from Canada right across the Detroit River, and delivered it to Capone. So, the possibilities about what went on here are endless."

"Yeah," Betty said, "Aleks says it could be some descendent discovered the secret of the hidden money up here and had an accomplice, maybe even another family member, who offed him to take all the money himself. Isn't it amazing that something like that happened right here in our little town?"

Summer gulped down the last of her sandwich so she could answer. "I can't believe it. Uncle Harry and Aunt Ellie will never believe this."

"We don't know any of that for sure," Bogey said. "But no matter what, something strange went on here last night. We'll figure it out if it's the last thing we ever do." He didn't waver in his determination to solve this mystery, which appealed to Summer, even though she was determined to dislike the guy.

"The truth is," Betty said, "this will only help the B&B. A reporter from the *Bay City Times* was here this morning. Somebody from the *Detroit Free Press* will be here in a little while. It's free advertising for the B&B."

"I'm glad something good will come out of this," Bogey said as he stood up. "Thanks for lunch, Betty. I wasn't expecting that. I'm going back to the farm to change into my uniform. We're all working extra hours, and our two part-timers are taking on full-time loads for now. Fitz has come back full-time, too. So, if you need anything one of us will be close at hand. And Aleks'll be back in the apartment this afternoon with the state police. I'm staying here for the next few nights after my shift is over at eleven. You shouldn't need to worry. You'll be good and safe."

Summer watched Deputy Sheriff Bogey Bush's backside as he strolled out of the café, those long jeans striding along with unwavering confidence.

"He's single, you know."

"What?" Summer wasn't sure she'd heard Betty right.

"Single as in not married, in case you're interested."

"Pfft. I am not interested."

"Sure, kid. That explains the look on your face while you watched that hunk of a man saunter out of this room." Betty rose and picked up their plates. "You might be able to fool yourself, but you can't fool me."

Summer looked at Betty as she disappeared into the kitchen, looked at the door through which Bogey Bush had disappeared, and popped up out of her seat.

"I'm not interested, really I'm not," she insisted as Betty filled the sink with soap and water, and plopped the plates in. "I mean, of course I looked at him. Who wouldn't? But, but, um, he's not my type. I mean, he lives here, in West Branch. I'm leaving in two months. I live in Traverse City." Betty lifted a wet hand out of the dishwater and pointed to a dishtowel on the counter. Summer picked it up and dried the plate Betty rinsed and handed over. "Besides, I'm sure he'd never be interested in somebody like me any more than I'd be interested in somebody like him." She realized she was drying the plate so hard she might break it in two.

Betty squinted at Summer. "Uh huh. Well, not that you're interested or anything, but his family was forced to sell their farm when the state decided they want to extend Interstate-75 all the way up to Mackinaw City, and they want it to go right through the Bush farm, which has been in their family for as long as anybody can remember. Bogey and his parents fought those bastards tooth and nail; they even went to court. But in the end, the government won. Mr. and Mrs. Bush have already moved to where Bogey's sister lives. All the animals on the farm here were taken up there, except for Bogey's horses. He won't give them up, but doesn't know yet what he's going to do. He has to be out by the end of the summer. Then their beautiful farmhouse and big red barn will be bulldozed so the interstate can go through.

"Everybody in town feels horrible about it. There wasn't anything anybody could do. 'Progress,' the government called it."

"That's horrible," Summer conceded. "Do you think he'll move away, too?"

"Not that you're interested or anything..." Betty grinned... "but I don't know." She shrugged, not able to speculate any further. The dishes done, she drained the sink and dried her hands on a dishtowel.

"He got an ag degree from State," Betty continued unbidden, "then the Army sent him to that Vietnam. Then he came back here. As for his love life, all I know is the gossip about a woman who works at Jerry's Joint, a bar. They dated for a couple months, then he discovered she's a real nut case. He's been trying to get rid of her ever since, but apparently she's quite a leech." She pulled a pack of Winstons and a matchbook out of her shirt pocket, lit up, and took a puff. "I have no idea why a thirty-year-old stud like him hasn't been caught by some chickadee and wrangled into marriage. Maybe the right chickadee hasn't come along... until now."

Betty snapped her dishtowel at Summer's fanny, howled with laughter at the resulting yelp, and sashayed out of the kitchen.

Summer sighed. "I am not interested in him," she insisted, although the image of that man striding out the door would not vanish from her inner sight.

15

Summer ambled down Houghton Avenue on her return from mass on Sunday morning. Receiving communion, familiar and calming, gave her a remote sense of belonging to something bigger than this town, bigger than herself. The congregants had been welcoming, and at the reception line after service the priest shook her hand warmly and reminded her about the schedule for confession. *Ha.* As if he inherently knew she needed to confess her sins.

The afternoon and evening before, after lunch with Bogey Bush, she and Betty had arranged furniture and unpacked accessories for the lobby of the B&B, and the rooms looked fantastic. Summer felt good about that. Betty's taste for paintings and vases and books was impeccable. Decorating gave Summer an excuse to ignore the reality of what she was being forced to do otherwise. She and Betty ended their Saturday by sitting on the new couch and eating popcorn in front of the fire.

Now on Sunday morning, Summer enjoyed walking through town. The place didn't look so foreign to her anymore, although it still wasn't anything like home. The summer sun bathed her in warmth while a few fluffy clouds lolled about in a blissful blue sky. Peace enveloped her in the quietness of inactivity because of businesses being closed on the day of Sabbath. A couple of gas stations and restaurants would open at noon, but other than that the town would remain still. Certainly no alcohol would be sold on a Sunday. Only the cars coming and going from various churches passed along the main road.

Her walk gave her time to think about the events of the last couple of days. After homily, the priest had announced that the sheriff had asked all the preachers and priests in the county to announce there would be a town meeting this afternoon at three o'clock, after people had time to go to church and have Sunday dinner. There didn't seem to be any lingering danger after Friday night's murder, the priest said the sheriff wanted him to say, but townspeople had a right to know the status of the investigation.

Townsfolk would naturally be interested in knowing about the strange, cryptic incident that had occurred in their own bailiwick. But for Summer, having come face-to-face with death and danger in an earthen grave, this was as personal as it could get. She burned to solve this mystery involving old thousand-dollar bills, a fat dead man, and a gang of 1920s bootleggers. Not able to conjure up what she could possibly do to fulfill that desire, for the time being she had no choice but to settle for teaching children, serving food, and cleaning toilets. The very thought made her shudder.

This wasn't the life she envisioned in her childhood fantasies about being a grown-up. How could she ever have imagined this? She walked on, amused by the recollection of her little girl dream about being a horseback-riding ballerina when she got "big."

Her mind came back to the present when she saw something unexpected up ahead. From two blocks away she could see someone standing in front of the B&B with two bicycles. From one block away, she could see for sure that it was Betty, having already changed out of her church dress, and donning pedal pushers and a short-sleeved blouse. She attended the Episcopal church in the other direction and had obviously beat Summer home. Close up, Summer could see that the bikes were brand-spanking-new Schwinns, one yellow and one green.

"Come on," Betty hailed as Summer approached. "Get out of that tight dress and let's ride."

Summer grinned, ran inside to change, and was back within minutes in Bermuda shorts and a tee shirt. "Betty, where'd you get these bikes?"

"Your Uncle Harry had them brought over from the hardware store yesterday. See? He's not such a bad guy. Come on, pick the one you want. I've got something to show you."

Summer hopped on the yellow one because her shorts were yellow, pink, and white plaid. She got back off, raised the seat, and got on again. "Where're we going?"

Betty took off on the green bike, going east down the sidewalk. "This way. It's a surprise."

Summer had no choice but to follow. After two blocks they turned left, crossed over a creek, went two more blocks, and turned right. There on the left side of State Street stood a very large, two-story, brown-brick building with wings on either side.

Betty stopped and slid off her seat, standing with the bike between her legs. Summer did the same. "That's the school," Betty said, pointing. "It's a quick ride for you each morning. Tomorrow you'll go in the big doors there in the center, and up the stairs. The principal's office is right there. Remember, her name is Miss Campbell. Your classroom is on the far side of the building, downstairs, the kindergarten room. Every kid who lives in town went to kindergarten in that room. It's an old school, kindergarten through twelfth grade. Farm kids in the country go to one-room schools spread out throughout the county until seventh grade, when they get bussed here. But, your little Head Start kids will be bussed in from all over Ogemaw County. They're not just town kids. For some of them, the bus ride alone will be a big adventure."

Summer stared at the formidable building, trying to take it all in. *Breathe,* she reminded herself. *Surely this won't kill me. If I could survive cavorting with a dead man, I can survive being with a bunch of children. Can't I?*

"That's okay, kid, you don't have to speak. You'll need to find your voice by tomorrow morning, though. Come on, I have more to show you." Betty turned left and they rode down a street named Sydney. Pedaling slowly, Betty said, "Pretty houses, aren't they?"

"Yeah. Beautiful," Summer admitted. "They remind me of some of the neat old houses in Traverse City."

"West Branch started out as a lumbering community, like Traverse City, right at the height of the Victorian Era. That's why there are so many Queen Anne and other Victorian styles, and the houses are so well built. They knew how to make them last in those days.

"With the railroad coming right through town, timber was big business around here. That is, until too much timber was gone. By then, though, families were entrenched in the area, with lots of farming, and oil was discovered. The town kept on going. The speakeasy and moonshine helped the economy, too, right when they were needed."

Casually they rode on. At one house; a small, blue, craftsman style home; an elderly woman sat on her porch, writing in a notebook. Betty waved, so Summer did, too. The woman waved back. Once past, Summer turned to get another look, and the woman looked up at her. Probably in her sixties, she had poufy snow white hair, stunning features, and cute granny glasses. Summer thought her beautiful.

At the end of Sydney Street, the cyclists came to N. 4th Street and Betty stopped, putting one foot down to steady herself on the bike. Summer followed suit.

"The lady back there," Betty said, cocking her head, "her name is Hazel Hazen. She's a very successful, famous romance novel writer. Have you heard of her?"

"Ah, maybe. I think Charlotte sent one of her books and it's in my room right now."

They got back on their bikes, turned right, and slowly rode side-by-side as they talked.

"She's the town's main claim to fame. She goes to Florida in the winter, but she's here seven months out of the year. I don't know her very well but everybody says she's nice, considering she's rich as Midas and nobody is sure why she wants to be here."

"Does she have family here?"

"Not that anybody knows. Some women speculate she likes it here because it's quiet and she can concentrate on her writing."

"That makes sense."

"I guess. I've never read one of her books. Not my type of thing. I like stab and slab murder mysteries. Oh, sorry. I didn't mean to remind you of your, um, incident."

Betty sped up and they passed small houses until reaching the end of the pavement where it butted up to a dirt road. They took that dirt road. After a few minutes Betty stopped and hopped off her bike. "We'll have to leave these here." They leaned their bikes against a tree and followed a footpath into the woods. Before long, they came upon a dilapidated, abandoned cabin in a clearing.

"We won't go inside. It isn't safe anymore. But this was where 'Injun Joe' lived. Or, at least, that's what we called him when we were kids. A Chippewa Indian and his family lived here. I don't know what ever became of his family, but he lived here alone for a long time when he was really old. He's dead now. But when I was young I used to sneak back here all the time, I was so fascinated with him. I don't know if he ever knew I was hiding in the woods. Probably.

"I wanted you to see this so you'd know what this town is like. Mr. Schubert from the meat market used to give him free food every week. The adult townspeople would come back here to check on him. Doctors took care of him and didn't charge. You'll find all kinds of people in West Branch, Summer. Kind, warm, snobby, fun, lonely, religious, and rebellious. But in the end, we stick together.

"That means you'll have all kinds of kids in that class of yours. No matter what, you'll need to find a way to stick with them and help them stick together. Around here, each other is all we've got."

"I'll try." Summer wasn't sure what that little lecture had been all about or if she could even begin to measure up to those expectations.

16

Summer and Betty rode their bikes down N. 5th Street back toward the main street, and came upon a beautiful two-story home on a large tract of land. Apple and pear trees stood in rows at one side of the house next to a fenced area containing chickens, a horse, and a cow. That fence butted up to the creek, which they'd crossed over on the other side of town and which meandered over here. A huge garden was at the back of the house and lush flower gardens adorned the front yard.

"Wow, a little farm right in town," Summer noted.

"Yeah, two blocks from Houghton. Here's the greenhouse and flower shop..." she pointed to the other side of the street and then back to the right... "and that road leads back to an old mill on the creek. There used to be a lumberyard right here. That's an old potato barn." The long wood building stood next to the railroad tracks. Hobbling their bikes over the tracks, Betty pointed out Rau's Tavern on Houghton Avenue, then they stopped and she pointed across the main street at an old timey train depot, now a barber shop. "That was the passenger depot. A block further down is the freight depot," she explained. Summer could see the rundown building in the distance. "And past that is a cattle corral. The train has always been important to the town. It used to transport people and lumber; now it's farm produce and cattle mostly. You'll hear the whistle at two every morning. It might wake you up, but I've always found it to be comforting."

"Yeah, it wakes me up."

"Don't worry, you'll get used to it.

"Well, I'm starved. How about you?"

"Yeah, I could eat. I can always eat."

The easiest thing to do was stop at the Model for the restaurant's pot roast Sunday special. When they finished the juicy roast with vegetables, mashed potatoes, and rolls, Betty explained that Harry had an account there and they could charge whatever they wanted, until their own café opened. Then they could eat for free at their own café. Harry also had accounts at almost every other store in town, so anything Summer needed she could charge, seeing that she didn't have access to any money except what little might have been in her purse.

"Your uncle said you can get whatever you need as long as you don't buy a car," Betty noted, amused. "I know you might think it isn't fair that you're not being paid to do your job at the B&B, but remember you're in a room that could have been rented out all summer starting next week. Plus, you'll be eating for free. And your uncle is covering your incidentals. So you really are working for your room and board. And, he got both of us those fabulous bikes. We've got it made, kid." She winked, stood up, threw a dollar bill on the table for a tip, and said, "Put it on our tab" to the cashier as they headed out the door.

Summer thought it best not to mention her new convertible back home. That, in her opinion, was having "it made."

They got back on their bikes to join the crowd for the town meeting at the Community Building, only a block away. Half the town seemed to be there. Almost every seat was taken and a number of people stood around on the sides of the room. Summer and Betty squeezed their way into a couple of empty seats in the back.

Sheriff Kowalczyk started by pointing out that there had only been one killing in town before, that anyone knew of anyway, back in 1878 when a sixteen-year-old bartender at the Ogemaw Hills Hotel shot and killed an infamously incorrigible woodsman. The drunkard leapt over the bar and attacked the young man when the lad refused to serve him. Determined to be a justifiable shooting, no charges were ever filed.

Then the sheriff explained what they knew so far about the recent murder. He asked that anyone who might know of a connection to that apartment or to a man who looked like the "deceased," please come talk to him. A sketch of the deceased, provided by the coroner, would be in the *Ogemaw County Herald* the next day for all to see.

When someone asked what would happen to the deceased's body, the sheriff said it would be buried in the township cemetery out by Ogemaw Springs. A stone with "unknown" would be placed on the grave, unless someone identified the body within the next few days.

"There's a potter's field out there," a man beside Summer said.

Betty leaned over to Summer and quietly explained, "Ogemaw Springs is where the town was at first, in the mid-1800s. Then it moved into our little valley here."

When the sheriff was telling the crowd to remain vigilant on the side of safety, even though he thought there was no threat, a rough-and-tumble galoot in the back hollered out, "Aw, sherff, ya know ya don't need to worry 'bout us. Most of us hunt. We know how to use our guns." That elicited nods from around the room.

A man in a button-down shirt and tie took that opportunity to stand up with a reminder. "There's an NRA meeting Wednesday night at the shooting range behind the hotel. Everyone's invited." That drew more nods.

"The shooting range is right here in town?" Summer whispered to Betty.

"Sure. I'm going. Wanna come?"

"Um, I'll see." She didn't see. She knew she wouldn't be going.

By the time they returned to the B&B, stored their bikes in the barn out back, and went inside, gloom had come over Summer like a black storm cloud. No matter how nice this Sunday had been, she could no longer avoid the fact that the next day was Monday, the day she had to go work with children at the school. She begged off when Betty invited her to join in doing some more accessory arranging in the lobby, and went to her room. Plopping onto the bed, she napped fitfully until seven, when Betty hollered up the stairs asking if she wanted to eat. She joined the innkeeper in the closed café where they finished off what was left of the chicken salad from the day before, with the addition of a bag of potato chips. Summer politely declined Betty's invitation to watch the TV show *The Fugitive* in the innkeeper's apartment.

Summer felt like enough of a fugitive herself.

Irritable and nervous, she went back to her room and attempted to read the book Charlotte had packed. Wouldn't you know, it was a romance by Hazel Hazen. A picture came to mind of the attractive white-haired woman she'd seen while riding bikes with Betty. The best-selling author was West Branch's claim to fame, Betty had said. It didn't matter. There was no way Summer could submerge herself in *Once You Have Found Him*. She doubted that teaching Head Start would help her find a "him."

She went to bed early enough, about ten, to get a good night's sleep before having to get up at six-thirty, but had a fitful time falling asleep. Fear of the next day roiled in her belly.

Her Uncle Harry might have a good heart for giving her a new bike, but she sure did hate his guts for making her go back to school.

17

Her nerves crisscrossed like a jumble of electrical wires, zapping energy every-which-way through her body.

Summer gave up trying to sleep and got up to look out the window at the clock hanging from the second story of the bank. Ten-forty-five.

The windows of the second story over the bank had the shades drawn, but bright light could be seen around the edges. Earlier Betty had explained that was where the telephone operators worked at their switchboards, seeing that West Branch was the last town in the state to use operators instead of the new-fangled rotary dial phones.

Summer remembered when she was a little girl and they had operators in Traverse City. Once when she was four years old she'd picked up the phone and the operator had come on with the usual, "Number please."

"Would you please tell me the story about the three bears?" she whispered into the clunky, black receiver, not wanting her parents to hear. She'd been warned many times that she could only use the phone in case of emergency. Well, she figured this was a sort of emergency. She was so bored she couldn't stand it.

The operator had chuckled and accommodated her with a brief rendition of Goldilocks' adventures with the bear family. Summer thanked her and hung up.

Figuring a number was needed in the title in order for an operator to tell a story, the next night she called back and asked for the story about the three little pigs. That operator had been so gruff, telling her to get off the line, she'd hung up in tears. She never asked an operator for a story again.

Longingly, Summer looked out at those windows across the street, wondering if someone up there might be willing to talk to her. Considering their jobs, those women must have all kinds of stories to tell. Who knew what all they heard over those telephone lines?

Sticking her head out her bedroom door, total solitude awaited. She couldn't waste any time, she figured, because Bogey Bush would be done with his shift at eleven, so she only had about twenty minutes before he came up to his room.

Just enough time.

She threw on a sweater over her nightie, left her room, and tiptoed barefoot across the ballroom floor. Drawn by that haunting apartment, she felt compelled to accommodate the other thing niggling at her mind, the thing that kept her awake as much as the fear of teaching. She needed to look inside that apartment one more time, as it was, frozen in the 1920s. Soon it would all be taken apart and the aura of the Golden Age would be gone. Four B&B guest bedrooms and bathrooms would take its place.

Even more pressing for Summer was her need to get a feel for who had lived there so long ago. After touching the woman's clothing and seeing her personal items, the mystery behind the former resident gnawed at Summer.

Had she been a gangster moll? A wife? A mistress? Had she been happy there?

Most intriguing was the question of where the woman might be now.

Summer had been told to stay away, like she'd been told to stay away from the telephone as a child. Yet, as if of its own will, on this night her hand inched toward the apartment doorknob like it had inched toward that telephone way back when. What stories might lie within that large room? The tip of her finger grazed the antique brass fixture and a spark caused her hand to snap back.

Not to be deterred, she tried again. This time, her palm encircled the knob.

"It's locked."

Summer hurled herself into the door from fright, banged her head, and crumbled to the floor. Holding her hands up in self-defense, she expected to see a ghost.

Bogey reached down to help her up. "I'm sorry," he said, again sounding more amused than sorry, like he had when she'd first met him. "I didn't mean to scare you."

She took his hand and let him pull her up, leaving her standing within inches of him. She backed away.

"Oh, um, I just, um…." She pointed at the door. "I just…." Try as she might, she couldn't spit out a cogent sentence.

"You just wanted to see that apartment again before they take it apart. I know. I feel the same way. But Aleks had the locks changed and locked it up so whoever had a key can't get in again. Not that we think any other intruders will be trying that, but he's being extra cautious."

Summer studied him as he spoke, noticing his shoes in his hand. She pointed at them. "That's why I didn't hear you."

"Oh, yeah, I take them off so I won't wake you up when I

tromp up those stairs. Especially tonight. You need your sleep for your big day tomorrow."

"I know. But I couldn't sleep."

Ushering her across the ballroom, he said, "Tell you what, how about a glass of milk? I was thinking of going down for one myself."

"Whiskey might be better."

He chuckled. "I don't have any of that. It's milk or nothing."

"I guess milk it will have to be."

She considered going back into her room to get dressed, but he went straight to the stairs so she gave up on the idea. After all, with a sweater over her nightwear she was more covered up than usual.

They didn't talk as they went down the stairs, or in the lobby as they passed through, or in the kitchen as Bogey poured two glasses of milk. They were seated at a table in the café before he said, "Here's to a good night's sleep before your first day of school tomorrow." He raised his glass in a toast.

"Ugh. Don't remind me." She clinked glasses with him anyway, and watched as he chugged the cool, white liquid. She sipped at hers.

She'd only finished half her glass by the time he drained his. Setting his glass down, Bogey looked at her, startling Summer with the intensity of those bedroom eyes of his. Her resolve to dislike him shattered and fell away with the ache in her body to experience his touch. That look in his eyes: was it longing for her? Was he as attracted to her as she was, reluctantly, to him?

Abruptly, he stood up and as crusty as a mean, old nanny demanded, "Drink up. You need your sleep."

Like a scared, docile child; she gulped down the last of her milk; and watched as he went to the kitchen to put their glasses in the sink. He turned off the lights and went through the B&B lobby. Wordlessly, she followed while he led the way upstairs. Merely nodding good night rather than saying it, he went into his room and shut the door.

Summer's resolve to dislike Deputy Bogey Bush hardened into a stone wall she vowed never again to climb.

18

"Are you the chick that fell in the grave with the dead guy?"

What? Summer couldn't believe she'd heard that coming from a mere waif of a mousy girl who couldn't be more than seven years old, one who, unfortunately, didn't wear shoes. She also emitted a pungent odor. How did someone so young hear about her wallow in a grave?

"Ever'body dies." This came from a chubby ragamuffin who looked to be about four.

"Did it give you the heebie-jeebies?" Another little girl wanted to know.

"Hey, you did the *Monster Mash*." the waif said, doing the dance that went with the popular song. That got a big laugh and a few kids joined in the silly dance.

"Yeah, you were a 'graveyard smash.'" Summer couldn't see who'd said that, but it was another crowd pleaser. More of them did the mash dance.

"Ew-w-w. Did you touch his dead eyeballs?" The little girl who asked that question looked stricken with terror at the thought.

The dancing stopped as the gang considered dead eyeballs.

"My grandpa died-ed. He was old and smelled funny." A scrawny boy smiled broadly, exposing a missing front tooth. Clearly, he was pleased with himself for eliciting giggles from some of the girls.

"Okay, okay," Summer said, holding out her hands in the universal gesture for "stop." "Nobody here is going to die any time soon, so let's drop it."

"You never know," the chubby ragamuffin mumbled in warning.

Desperate to move on, Summer said, "How about I read a story?" She went to the bookshelf and ran a finger across the spines of the colorful children's books.

"No." The shoeless *Monster Mash* waif who'd called her a "chick" crossed her arms over her concave chest and thrust out her lower lip in defiance. The child wore a rag of a dress and her bare feet were filthy.

"What do you mean 'no'?" This Head Start teaching thing, after only fifteen minutes in the classroom on the first day, proved to be even worse than Summer had feared, especially seeing that the lead teacher hadn't shown up. The principal, the one and only Miss Campbell, was in her office now trying to call the missing miscreant, which left Summer all alone with twenty-four little urchins.

Maybe I should have stayed in jail. Carla the Cynic had nothing on this gang.

"We say the Pledge of 'legiance first," someone informed her.

"Oh, of course. Okay, everyone stand by your desk and face the flag for the 'Pledge of Allegiance.'"

Each student had a desk with a cardboard name tent on it supplied by Miss Campbell so that as soon as they walked in on the first day they would know where to sit. The desks were the old-school wooden kind with a slanted top; an ink well that hadn't been used in years; and a slot underneath the top for books and supplies. The front of each desk had a bench seat attached for the next person up; all the desks in a row were connected by long wood runners. The kids clamored to their spots, some of the smaller ones needing help from older ones. Before long, everyone stood by a desk, put their right hands over their hearts, and turned to the corner of the room where an American flag stood. Obviously, they knew the drill.

"I pledge allegiance to the Flag of the United States of America, and to the Republic for which it stands, one Nation under God, indivisible, with liberty and justice for all."

Whew. That went okay. Summer looked at the clock. 8:16. Four hours and forty-four minutes to go.

The kids stood there, some shifting from foot to foot, waiting for her to do something. This was one tough crowd.

"Storytime now?"

"Nah, we stretch first," someone kindly assisted her.

"Then the caf'teria lady brings our milk and peanut bunner sammiches."

"Ah, okay," Summer said, recalling that Mrs. Campbell had told her the kids got a hearty morning snack because some hadn't had breakfast at home.

"Then us big kids do 'rithmetic while the little kids count." A boy pointed to the circle of numbers embedded in the floor by the room's large bay window.

"Then us big kids help each other with spelling while the little kids learn to write their names. I'm a good speller. I could win a spelling bee."

"Then we have recess, then circle reading, *then* storytime."

"Then lunch in the caf'teria. Yay."

"Then nap time on our rugs and then we go home."

"Ah, I see. Okay then, we start with stretching." Frantically, she rummaged through her memory bank to come up with an activity from her childhood that would include stretching.

"Wait. You forgot to tell us your name," the barefoot waif said, swiping her dirty hair off her forehead and rolling her eyes as if this teacher was the biggest ignoramus on the planet.

"Oh, sure." Remembering what Miss Campbell had told her about how real teachers used their last names with a title but volunteers used their first names with a title, Summer wrote it on the blackboard. "My name is Miss Summer. You can call me Miss Summer." She dotted the "i" with enthusiasm.

"That's a weird name."

"How come you ain't Miss Winter?"

"Or Miss Spring. Or Miss Fall?"

Summer lost track of who said what, but they got a big chuckle from the gang. Four-to-seven-year-old humor was, she could see, as base as it gets.

"Do you have a boyfriend?"

"Um," Summer hemmed and hawed, doing her level best to garner control, "let's not get off track. It's stretch time. Right? Let's do *I'm a Little Teapot*." She stood straight with her hands in front of her, thrilled that this memory surfaced.

"I bet she doesn't or she'd say yes."

"How come you don't have a boyfriend?"

"Don't you wanna get married?"

"My sister got married 'cuz she's having a baby."

Ignoring the barrage, Summer started to sing. "I'm a little teapot short and stout...."

Mercifully, that reined them in. "Here is my handle, here is my spout...." Everyone made a handle with one hand on their hip and a spout with the other hand raised up to the side. A couple of younger ones were a beat behind, having to copy the older kids, who looked bored, but everybody finished the song. Summer had them run through it a second time, seeing that she had nothing else to offer for stretch time.

That over with, Summer asked, "How many of you were in Head Start last year?" All but five of the two dozen raised their hands. No wonder they knew the routine, next to Summer knowing zilch.

The door opened and Miss Campbell came in. An athletic, middle-aged woman, the furrow on her brow didn't encourage Summer.

"Children," she said, "get out your drawing paper and draw Miss Summer a picture of yourself with your name on it, so she can get to know you. You older students help the younger ones write their names."

Dutifully, the children each reached under their desk, took out a piece of paper and a small box of crayons, and began to draw. No one asked the principal if she had a boyfriend.

"Summer," Miss Campbell said in a low voice, "I need to talk to you in the hall."

Terrified, Summer followed her into the hallway.

"It seems that Mrs. Lane, the woman who was lead teacher for this program last year and was supposed to do so again this year, has run away with a truck driver. It also seems that she absconded the Head Start funds. I just got off the phone with her husband, who is beside himself. Now, don't you worry, we'll find funding somewhere. There's no way we'll let these kids down at this point."

Miss Campbell had no idea that funding wasn't even a flicker of concern in Summer's mind. What she dreaded most was what the principal might say next. Sure enough, the woman said it.

"So, I need you to hang in there with them today while I make calls to find a new lead teacher. It might be hard, because during summer break most of our teachers either farm or go to the lake or go on vacation. But I promise I'll find you at least a good parent volunteer."

"Oh, Miss Campbell, no. Absolutely not. I don't know anything about children." Panic rose in Summer's voice.

"It's okay. They're good kids. Well, for the most part. I'll check in as often as possible for the rest of today. And I'll have my secretary, Beatrice, come in, too. By tomorrow someone else should be here to help. Together, Summer, we can do this."

"No, no, no, no, no. I cannot do this."

Miss Campbell put her hand on Summer's arm. "We never know how strong we are until we're put in a situation where we need strength. I have faith in you, Summer. You're stronger than you know."

"No, I'm not," Summer moaned as the principal walked away.

Summer turned back to the classroom and looked through the door window. There they were, some still drawing, some making paper airplanes and zinging them at each other, and one standing and singing a song as if on stage.

The clock on the wall said 8:29. Four hours and thirty-one minutes to go.

Jail looked better and better by the minute.

19

"It's been the worst day of my life. And I've been in jail and fallen into a grave with a dead man. Did you know that children never stop talking? And they say the grossest things. Where do they get that stuff? They were utterly fascinated with the fact that I've been in a grave with a dead man. They even did the *Monster Mash*."

Betty chuckled until Summer gave her the evil eye. "Oh, sorry," Betty said, smoking a Winston and sipping on a cup of coffee while they waited for hamburgers at the Model Restaurant.

"I spent all day trying to get the little monsters to pay attention and do their schoolwork. Managing bathroom breaks alone is a major challenge, reminding everybody to wipe and wash their hands. And little boys aren't very good at remembering to zip up their pants. One informed me that his dad forgot to zip up once and he saw daddy's pee-pee. The little girl who came up with *Monster Mash* kept calling me a 'chick.' She didn't even have any shoes, poor thing. They've collectively decided there's something wrong with me because I'm not married. One wants me to come over to meet her uncle. 'Maybe he'll marry you,' she said. 'My mom says nobody wants him 'cuz he's lazy. Maybe you can have him.'

"When the little suckers finally left—after what felt like eighteen hours—Miss Campbell told me she wants me to watch for two of the children she fears are abused at home: the *Monster Mash* girl with no shoes and a really sweet, quiet little boy. Like now I'm the abuse police. Who would do that to their own child? Or any child? I know nothing about any of this.

"God save me. I can't go back there tomorrow. I can't do that 'stick together' thing you talked about. I'm outta there." Summer sulked as she sipped her Coke.

"And into jail," Betty reminded her.

Summer sighed loudly, frowned dramatically, and visibly caved in to accepting her fate.

"Did Loretta, that's Miss Campbell, did she find somebody to help out?" Betty asked.

"Maybe. She said, there 'might' be someone there tomorrow. Big whoop," Summer added sullenly. "I can't believe I have to do this. I'm not a teacher. I'm not a mother. Sure, I have lots of little cousins who run around at grandma and grandpa's house, but I don't pay any attention to them. They annoy me. I'm not good with children. In fact..." she looked off, distracted... "I'm not good at anything."

"What does that mean?" No reproach was evident in Betty's husky voice as she asked the question. She merely wanted to know.

"Look at me. I'm a colossal failure next to everybody else in my family. By the time she was my age my mom had saved lives as a nurse in the war, she'd been married and widowed, she killed a German soldier who tried to kill her and Uncle Harry, and she was pregnant with me. By my age my grandma had been the toast of the town in Chicago, a high-living Flapper, then married to grandpa, and was pregnant with my mom and Uncle Harry. She even had babies in a big way, twins. Then ten more. Hail Mary,

I don't know how she did it. And now grandpa is governor and my dad owns a big winery. And my mom runs her family's businesses, all those companies and stock and bonds and investments and stuff. I can't even begin to imagine ever doing that. She's the most successful business person of everybody in the family. One of the most successful women in the country, according to business magazines.

"And here I am. I went to art college in Chicago for one month and was so homesick I came home without even telling my parents I was coming, so they couldn't try to talk me out of it. The only 'job' I've ever had is working at the winery with my dad. Uncle Harry says Dad lets me do whatever I want, so that's not like a real job. That's true. But I can't do anything else. I have no brain for business. I have no talent, at least nothing other than drawing dumb pictures and painting. I'm a giant compared to most girls. All my girlfriends are married or getting married, and I can't even get a boyfriend."

Summer's blue eyes became liquid pools as she struggled to keep them from overflowing.

Betty leaned into the table and pointed at Summer with her cigarette. "You know what I hear you saying?"

Summer, sitting directly across from Betty, leaned in, too. "What?" she asked, anxious to hear the older woman's sage advice.

Betty paused, took a puff of her cigarette, and in an exaggerated shrill snapped, "Waa, waa, waa." Then she turned serious. "Listen, kid, when you've been pregnant at age fifteen by a boy you madly love, and your parents send you away to an unwed mothers' home in Detroit all by yourself, and they force you to give up the little boy you fell in love with while he was still in your womb, and you come home to find that your boyfriend's family has moved away and you have no idea how to find him, then you'll have a right to complain. When you join the Army right out of high school and get sent to war, and you try to stay in the Army but they politely ask you to leave because you've turned into a drunk, and you come home and can't find a job, and you live in poverty fighting your alcoholism every single day of your life, when all those things have happened to you, then you'll have a reason to whine.

"But I've got to tell you, girl, the fact that you're filthy rich, you're gorgeous, and you have every opportunity in the world, but you still can't get your life together, isn't cutting it." Betty pointed at Summer one final time with her cigarette, then violently stubbed it out in the ashtray.

"Here you go," the waitress interrupted, delivering two juicy hamburgers with sides of fries. "Anything else?"

"No, I think this will do," Betty said, friendly as could be. She took a big bite while Summer sat and stared at her.

"Come on, chow down," Betty suggested, winking at Summer assuredly. "These burgers can't be beat." She continued to dig in while Summer remained motionless.

"I'm so sorry. All that really happened to you?"

"Yup. Now eat up. It'll make you feel better."

Summer picked up her food even though she'd lost her appetite. She took one tiny bite, and then another. That's all it took to prod her appetite into revving up. She finished off her food at the same time Betty did.

They said no to the waitress's inquiry about dessert. Betty tossed a dollar bill on the table for a tip and charged the rest to the B&B account, and they left the restaurant. As they strolled east on Houghton Avenue, looking in store windows and enjoying the pretty summer evening, Betty said, "Do you have any concept of what a hero your Uncle Harry is to a lot of people?"

"Yeah, I guess. He fought in a war."

"Not that war, it's the one he's been fighting ever since that makes him a very special man in the eyes of the many people he's saved."

"Saved? From what?"

"Alcoholism. He helped set up a lot of AA groups, Alcoholics Anonymous, all over the northern part of the mitten, and in the U.P. In fact, I think he started some down south, too, in the Carolinas or something."

Summer knew Betty referred to the northern part of the lower peninsula of Michigan, the part shaped like a mitten, and the upper peninsula of the state. Seeing that her Uncle Harry and Aunt Ellie owned B&Bs in North and South Carolina, that made sense, too.

"That's where I met him," Betty said, rummaging into her purse to come up with a pack of Winstons and her lighter, "at an AA meeting here. He attends meetings whenever he can, wherever he's at." She lit up, inhaled deeply, and blew a plume of smoke into the air.

"I never knew about that," Summer said. "I knew he drank too much right after the war, but he's always said once he met Aunt Ellie he knew he couldn't do that if he wanted her to stay around."

"He had a problem, like so many of us, that no amount of money can fix. Earlier I said you've had every advantage because you're rich. Truth is, that was unfair. Money doesn't help with everything. Being beautiful doesn't, either. Some things take determination and desire. Succeeding at life takes determination and desire, no matter how much mullah a person has. I don't think it's easy for any of us, not even you, with all that dough, and with those legs that go all the way up to your neck, and with a big family that loves you. I'm sorry if I was too rough on you." She smoked as she spoke, swirling her cigarette hand around in-between inhalations.

They'd stopped in front of the jewelry store. Summer wasn't interested in the rings, statuettes, and jewelry boxes in the window. She gazed at Betty.

"No, you weren't too hard on me. I need to stop whining about my life, don't I? Even if I did fall into a grave with a dead guy." She offered a crooked grin.

Betty smiled. "Tell you what: I've changed my mind about dessert. I need a Dilly Bar. How about you?"

"Yessiree. I'm always up for a Dilly Bar."

They turned around and walked in the direction of the Dairy Queen, three blocks west. After snarfing down a chocolate Dilly Bar and going home to the B&B, Summer knew there had been a shift in her life on that night. Betty was right. She was acting like a baby. If her mom could do what she did in the war, killing a man to save her own life and others'; and her Uncle Harry could fight alcoholism all these years, helping so many people; and Betty could go on with her life after suffering the tragedy of having her baby taken away from her; then Summer would be damned if she'd let a roomful of little moppets get her down.

She would indeed return to the school bright and early the next morning. She might not be any good at this teaching thing, but come hell or high water she would try. After all, if she couldn't handle them, she'd never be able to handle anything.

Summer fell into bed too exhausted to even think about the

handsome deputy who quietly came in after his shift at eleven and went to bed in the room right next door.

20

At seven forty-five Tuesday morning the clouds parted, a golden beam of light shone down from the heavens, and God delivered an angel to the kindergarten room at West Branch School. Summer arrived fifteen minutes early, but the golden-haired saint already had those little devils well in hand as they scuttled into the room.

Before she even entered the classroom Summer could hear a big, booming, feminine voice. "As you come into the room, children, check your shoes. If they need to be cleaned, go to the boot scraper outside the front door."

A boy dashed out of the classroom and into the hallway, bumping into Summer. She watched as he went out the front door and scraped the soles of his shoes on a thin brass rail near the ground. He cleaned off manure, she realized. He must have done farm chores before coming to school, and he was only five or six years old. He finished and ran back inside.

While she observed the boy, Summer listened to the big voice in the room: "In a nice orderly line you will come up to the desk…" Summer followed the boy in and the woman waved at her as she continued giving orders. "…and get a toothpick. The first five of you will go to the trashcan and clean under your fingernails. You older kids help the younger kids count to five. The rest of you will wait in line for your turn at the trashcan."

Summer stood there stupefied as every child followed directions with the precision of an obedient army platoon. The woman, a cheerful-looking person in her thirties with rosy cheeks and pink lips, rushed up to Summer.

"Hi. I'm Angela Fitzgerald. Loretta called yesterday and said you could use some help. I'm so sorry about what happened to you." Turning to some children coming in the door, she demanded, "Over here. Get your toothpick." They came over without question and took a toothpick from a box on the teacher's desk, and she motioned them to get in line. She turned back to Summer. "Falling into that grave and then this with all these little hooligans. Two of them are mine, by the way."

She held out her hand for what resulted in a warm, firm handshake. Summer wanted to kiss her.

"Thanks so much for coming. You're a godsend. I have no idea what to do here."

"Okay," Angela addressed the children, "you five at the trashcan, go to the bathroom and wash your hands. No lollygagging. Come back in two minutes. Next five, trashcan."

She turned back to Summer. "Don't you worry. I volunteered last year with Helen, Mrs. Lane, the one who ran away. I swear, I always did think she was a flake. Anyway, you and I will get everything set up this morning. I can only stay for a couple of hours before the baby wakes up." She pointed at a stroller Summer hadn't noticed at the side of the room. "Then I'll need to go home to feed the little one."

"Wait. You said 'Fitzgerald.' You're not the deputy sheriff's wife are you? She had a baby a few days ago."

"Oh, that was last Friday." She waved a hand in dismissal. "Number nine. It isn't like I don't know the drill. I do get tired, but

I'll be okay for a couple of hours. I live right across the street, so this is easy-breezy. My mother even lives next door, in case I need anything." Turning away again, she hollered, "You five, bathroom. Next five, trashcan."

In less than fifteen minutes all the children had cleaned up. Without being told, they stood by their desks.

"Say 'good morning' to your teacher, children," Angela reminded them, cocking her head at Summer.

"Good morning, Miss Summer," they bellowed.

"Good morning, students," Summer ad libbed. "Now say 'good morning' to our assistant teacher today, Mrs. Angela."

"Good morning, Mrs. Angela," most of them said, but one husky little boy was out of sync with "Good morning, Mommy. Oops, I'm sorry," he tittered. "I mean, Mrs. Mommy."

Not able to decipher his gaffe, his brow furrowed in puzzlement when some of the other students giggled.

His mother laughed, a rich, jolly sound. "Good morning, everyone."

The children stared at Summer for an instant before Angela whispered to her. "It's pledge time."

"Oh, yeah. Thanks." Loudly, mimicking Angela's firm voice, she looked at her students and said, "Now we'll say the pledge." She put her hand over her heart and turned toward the flag, giving a quick private thanks to God for sending Angela the angel her way.

The morning flew by, and by the time Angela wheeled the baby stroller out of the room and said goodbye, Summer actually felt like she might be able to survive. In two short hours of watching Angela handle children, she'd learned to be firm but kind, always fair, and specific with directions and timing. Most importantly, she'd watched the mother's confidence in herself and her lack of fear of the little whippersnappers. Summer vowed to herself that she'd work on that because, as she'd learned the day before, the buggers would eat her alive if she didn't.

Angela had said, "Even if you're terrified, don't let them see your fear. This is the most demanded acting job in the world."

At the end of the school day, after everyone left and welcome stillness fell over the classroom, Summer walked around looking at the pictures taped to the wall, the drawings the principal had the children do the day before with self-portraits and their names. Next on Summer's list would be to learn all their names by heart. The name tents on their desks helped, but she wanted to know who they were without prompts. Their self-portraits ranged from squiggly to adorable to quite accurate.

An idea hit her. Each day she would pick a name out of a sack and sketch a portrait of that child. They would tape her sketches to the wall next to their self-portraits, and at the end of the summer take them home. If nothing else, Summer was a good artist and could give the children at least that.

Miss Campbell interrupted her reverie, tapping on the window of the open door. "Sorry to intrude on the quiet," she said, coming in with a shoe box in her hand. "This was always my favorite time of day when I was teaching. The solitude when another day of doing a good job was done."

"I'm not doing a very good job."

"Nonsense. You're doing great. You're still here." The woman had a ready smile.

"Now, these are for Stella." She opened the box to reveal a pair of girl's white tennis shoes. "We buy her some every year. These should fit, but if there's a problem, let me know and I'll exchange them."

"Okay. I'll give them to her first thing in the morning."

"Thanks. You have no idea how encouraging that is," the principal said as she walked to the door. "That means you plan on coming back tomorrow." She turned toward Summer and let loose with that smile again. When she walked away, the sound of her footfall echoed off the walls of the long, tiled hallway. Summer inhaled deeply, once again soaking in the bliss of peace and quiet.

If only it could stay like this.

21

Summer rode her bike back to the B&B after school feeling lighter than before. The day had been, as one of the kids said, "hunky dory."

Betty asked how her day went and she happily said it went okay. It was then that Betty burst her bubble by reminding her it was time for her chambermaid training. The B&B had booked its first guests for the weekend, including her Uncle Harry and Aunt Ellie, so it was time for Summer to learn how to change beds and clean bathrooms.

"Wouldn't you know," Summer groused. "One gift from heaven today, and one from hell."

Betty showed her where to find the linen closet first, and they took fresh sheets and towels up to Bogey's room. This part, Summer decided, wasn't so bad. Being in the room where a big, handsome man slept, even one she didn't like, gave her a heady feeling. He had few things in the room but the pleasing masculine scent of Old Spice lingered. He'd made the bed and hung the towels. Betty demonstrated how to strip the bed and remake it with square corners. She also showed Summer how to turn a pillowcase inside-out to easily slide it onto a plump pillow. They took the dirty linens down to the laundry room at the back of the building, and Betty showed her how to start the washing machine.

"I've done this before, you know. I do know how to do laundry," Summer insisted.

"Good. 'Cuz you'll have a lot of it to do this summer."

Next, they went to the supply closet to retrieve the new supplies: a bucket, bright yellow rubber gloves, a toilet brush, sponges, rags, and Comet cleanser. This part of the job was disgusting, as far as Summer was concerned. But she soldiered through and for the first time in her life cleaned a toilet. At least Bogey was neat and his bathroom wasn't grody.

"There," Betty said when they were done. "Now you need to do your room." She patted Summer on the shoulder and deserted her, fleeing down the stairs.

Summer stood in the vestibule, cleaning bucket in one hand and toilet brush poised in the air in the other, like the Statue of Liberty lifting her torch with its flame. If cleaning toilets would lead to her liberty, she'd clean the crappy toilets. Her yellow rubber gloves, she noticed, provided the most interesting fashion statement she'd ever made.

"My life just gets better and better," she moaned as she went into her room to clean her own bathroom for the first time in her life.

Betty invited Summer into the café for supper that night, for healthy salad, gooey homemade pizza, and Coke. The women were chowing down when Deputy Bogey Bush came through the door from the lobby of the B&B. Summer quickly wiped a glop of cheese off her chin in an attempt to be presentable.

His brown deputy's hat politely in hand, he said, "Good evening."

"Hey, Bogey," Betty greeted. "Come on, have some supper with us."

"Oh, no, Betty, I can't keep taking advantage of your generosity like this. I only wanted to check to make sure everything is okay this evening."

"Nonsense. Come on. I made way too much. We can't possibly eat it all. You can take a break for supper, can't you?" She patted the back of the empty chair next to her at their square table.

"Well, okay. Thanks. It looks delicious." He placed his deputy's hat at the empty spot on the table and sat next to Betty, which was directly across from Summer. She regaled herself for the catch in her breath at the sight of him. His hair slicked back for work, his uniform clean and crisp, his body sexy as hell... *Okay,* she admonished herself, *don't go there.*

Betty went into the kitchen to get him a plate and silverware, and in her absence Bogey looked intently at Summer. "How's Head Start going?"

"I'll be honest, yesterday was hell. But today Angela Fitzgerald came to help, and that made all the difference in the world."

"She's great," he said as Betty handed over everything he needed to dig into fresh salad and homemade pizza pie, which he did with relish.

"I thought you might like an update on the case," he said in-between bites.

"Have they figured it out?" Betty asked, excited at the prospect.

"No, nothing like that. But we know more than we did before."

"Wait. Let me get you a pop," Summer said. She flew into the kitchen and came right back with a frosty bottle of Faygo Redpop having no idea why she'd bothered to wait on this guy.

"Thanks," Bogey said, taking a sip. "Well, it's like this. I talked to Tommy, the boy who smokes by the marquee." He pointed in the direction of the Midstate Theatre. "He's out there every Friday and Saturday night after work. He did see what he thought was a flicker of light in the apartment that night, not long before I came along and reminded him to go home. At the time he thought you…" he pointed at Betty… "were in there. Now we're thinking it was a flashlight used by the very alive man who was soon to be deceased.

"As for the money, the state police in Detroit say the money very well could have come from the Purple Gang. They robbed banks in Detroit and in small Michigan towns, and got big bills like that. And Al Capone and his gang in Chicago robbed banks and could have used that cash to pay for illegal booze. During Prohibition the Purples brought alcohol over from Canada and drove it to Chicago in cahoots with Capone."

"How long did prohibition last?" Summer asked.

"It started in Michigan in 1917, before the other states because Henry Ford wanted a sober workforce. It was 1920 everywhere else, until 1933. We've been speculating about the gang connection, and everything we're learning from Detroit and Chicago substantiates that. Alphonse Gabriel Capone, also known as Scarface, was at the height of his power during prohibition with his gang, the Chicago Outfit. The year before the end of prohibition Capone went to federal prison for tax evasion. His gang stayed intact but lost a lot of its power after that. Detroit's Purple Gang was at their peak during prohibition, too, run by four Jewish brothers, the Burnsteins. By the 1930s that gang had a lot of infighting, so their demise was close at hand.

"Because of the old money and the apartment being next to what was once a speakeasy, it seems likely that our case is part of prohibition and bootlegging. Maybe gambling, too, because that went on in so many of these places. Seeing that the Purple Gang liked to hole up in this neck of the woods, the possibility of a connection to them seems even stronger.

"Unfortunately, who stole the money now, all these years later in 1965, we have no idea. Our next step is to talk to the older folks in town, to see what they remember. We don't know how forthright they'll be, however, if they were participating in illegal activities, even if it was so long ago. But we'll try.

"The sketch of the dead man is being passed around the police forces in Detroit and Chicago in case the guy's been in trouble before and somebody remembers him.

"That's as far as we got." He shrugged apologetically as he finished his last bite of pizza. He didn't object when Betty put the final piece onto his plate.

"It seems odd," he said, pizza in hand as he considered his thought. "A Jewish gang from Detroit and an Italian gang from Chicago doing business together. In the 1910s the Purple Gang was no more than a bunch of teenaged thugs, but prohibition allowed them to organize and go bigtime. The same is true for Capone. At first the Chicago and Detroit gangs were at odds with each other, but eventually they teamed up, which benefited everybody. Both gangs ran underground enterprises so extensive the police are still uncovering them today.

"The Purples were into racketeering, extortion, bootlegging, drugs, gambling, prostitution, kidnapping, robbery, you name it, they did it. They were brutal men. Murder, torture, even killing as a joke, that was all common practice. A number of Detroit police officers were on the take, and even some politicians were suspected. The gang made a fortune, most of which is either spent, hidden away, or lost in the wind. Good old American enterprise, I guess." With that proclamation, he polished off his pizza.

"You know a lot about this," Summer admitted.

"You should see the stack of mimeographed copies of old newspaper articles and police reports we got from Detroit. There's lots more. I haven't even scratched the surface."

Summer found it fascinating that such scoundrels might have been connected to this boring little town. Wonders never ceased.

"Well, thanks for supper, again," Bogey said as he stood and secured his hat on his head. "Back to work. This is the last night I'll be staying here. I understand Harry and Ellie are coming to-morrow."

"Yes," Betty said, lighting up an after-supper cigarette. "It's been such a relief having you here, Bogey. Thank you."

The deputy nodded, touching the brim of his hat. "My pleasure. Good night, ladies."

"Night," Betty said.

"Good night," Summer repeated, sadness sweeping through her at the thought of that man's absence in the nights to come. *That's ridiculous,* she reminded herself as she attempted to sweep her sadness out of her mind. *I don't even like the guy.*

Do I?

22

Even though rain pelted down, Wednesday turned sunny for Summer when once again Angela Fitzgerald greeted her in the classroom. Betty had taken pity on Summer and driven her to the school in her Beetle, but not all the children were so fortunate. About half the class came from the countryside and rode the bus, so they stayed relatively dry. But many a soaked little body drudged into the building, the kids who lived in town and walked to school, some from all the way on the other side of town.

Angela had left her baby at home with her mother, and she and her boys had raincoats and umbrellas. But, although most kids had on at least a jacket of some kind, more than one child came with no protection from the weather whatsoever. Summer counted four, all boys. There seemed to be an attitude amongst some parents that boys are, or should be, tough and can take anything thrown their way, even buckets of water.

"Okay," Angela said as she and Summer assessed the situation, "the first thing we'll do today is get the saturated ducks as dry as possible. I'll tell you what: how about I take the wet ones into the hall and you start class with the dry ones in here?"

Relieved, Summer agreed. After all, she had not one clue as to what to do with a gaggle of drenched little people.

As they divided up the group, Stella, bare feet and all, came in, soaked to the bone, her tattered dress so thin it clung to her body like mottled skin. On this day Summer wore a pair of slacks, a blouse, and a soft summer sweater. All of that as well as a full-length raincoat and, yes, her galoshes. And an umbrella to top it off. Her sweater was long, down to the tops of her legs. With her height, it was a good foot longer than Stella's short dress.

Summer took the waif aside, knelt down to her level, and asked, "Stella, would you mind if we took off your wet dress and I gave you my sweater to wear? It would be like a dress on you. And once we get your feet dry, I have some tennis shoes for you, too, from Miss Campbell."

The girl studied Summer's face, clearly analyzing what had been said. She looked doubtful. But she quickly did an about-face and said, "Sure. Why not?"

Summer told Angela the plan and the mother agreed that would work. She'd already sent the older of her sons back home across the street to get dry tee shirts for the unfortunate boys. "There are sports programs here right now and the baseball coach is one of Fitz's best friends. When my Jerry gets back he can go find him and we'll have him take the boys to the locker room where they can wrap up in towels while their underwear and pants dry. They have a washer and dryer down there."

Angela dubbed the wet boys "the flying ducks," which they loved, and had them wait in the hallway, where they dripped like melting ice. Switching their initial plans, Angela stayed in the classroom to lead the pledge while Summer took Stella into the girl's bathroom. Summer shucked her sweater, noticing that Stella had started to shiver.

Summer took a deep breath and took the plunge, stripping off the child's paper-thin frock and throwing it in the sink. Only a scanty pair of panties remained on the little girl's body. Summer took hands-full of paper towels and dabbed at the girl's frail frame.

"Stella," Summer said kindly, "what's this?" She pointed to a small round scab on Stella's clavicle. Looking more closely, she could see numerous scars where there had been similar wounds.

Stella shrugged. "I dunno."

Not willing to press it at that moment while she had the girl practically naked, Summer swathed the waif in the cotton sweater, which came down to her ankles.

"Wow, this is warm," Stella marveled. "You sure you wanna let me wear this? I might ruin it."

"I'm sure. I trust you not to ruin it. And if you accidentally do, it'll be okay." The sleeves hung like limp knee socks past Stella's hands, so Summer rolled them up. "There. Now, only one more thing. I need you to take off your underpanties so we can have them dried in the dryer in the locker room." No female should ever wear wet underpants, which invited urinary tract infection.

The girl shrugged again, reached up under the sweater, and took off what amounted to a rag. She tossed them into the sink with her dress.

"I'll be right back. I gotta pee," Stella announced.

Their business done, Summer wrapped up Stella's clothes, if they could be called that, in paper towels and handed them over to Angela. Her son had returned and the coach had arrived. Without explanation, Angela handed over the sopping wad to the coach and the bear of a man didn't flinch. Apparently, people who worked with youth were used to this kind of thing.

"I hear there are some flying ducks here," the coach boomed. "Fly this way." He led the frolicking flock of boys down the hall toward the gym.

Eventually everyone dried out; and the morning snack of peanut butter and honey sandwiches, and pint cartons of milk, was delivered by the cafeteria lady. After that Summer was able to deliver lessons in spelling and reading before lunchtime in the cafeteria. So much time had been spent, however, getting the kids ready to learn she wondered how teachers ever got any teaching done.

Stella seemed proud of her sweater-dress and spent the day sticking up her feet to look at her new shoes. Summer, on the other hand, spent the day worrying about the child's scars. Miss Campbell said to watch for signs of abuse. What were the signs? Had Stella done something to hurt herself? Children did play hard and injure themselves all the time, didn't they? Summer herself had been a reckless tomboy when it came to playing outside. Scraped knees, scratched shins, and bruised arms were standard in her childhood. But she'd never seen anything like Stella's small, round scars.

One more mystery piled onto the stack of mysteries in Summer's life. Who, if anyone, had hurt Stella? Would she ever be able to get that Bogey man out of her mind? Who had lived in the enchanted apartment? And, who on earth was the dead man in the grave and what was all that money about?

Mysteries never ceased, it seemed, in West Branch, Michigan.

23

"Charlotte!" Summer's hand flew to her chest in surprise. She'd been sitting in a wingback chair by the fireplace in the lobby of the B&B waiting for her Uncle Harry and Aunt Ellie to arrive, but she'd had no idea her best friend, and aunt, Charlotte would be coming, too.

"See-saw," Charlotte squealed as she rushed in and reached up to grab Summer in a hug. "See-saw" had been Charlotte's nickname for her niece ever since they'd been eight and six years old, and played on a teeter-totter together. Summer liked Charlotte to hop her butt off for a second when she hit the ground so that Summer, up in the air, would get a jolt, bouncing her off her seat. She had to hang on tight not to fly away.

"I had no idea you were coming." Summer looked at Betty. "You knew, didn't you?" Betty nodded, grinning. "I wondered why you wouldn't tell me who I had to clean that second room for."

"I heard about that," Charlotte said, a pout on her generous lips. "I think Harry is positively wretched for making you clean and things." She shook a finger at her much older brother.

"Never mind about that," Summer said. "I'm so happy you're here. You won't believe everything that's been going on in this place. I can't wait to tell you all about it."

Charlotte's eyes widened like an owl's. "So I've heard. We'll have to hide under a blanket with a flashlight tonight while you give me all the gory details." She alluded to another of their childhood adventures.

"Hi, Aunt Ellie," Summer turned to her beloved aunt who had been patiently standing awaiting her turn.

"Hello, sweetie," Ellie said as they embraced. She stood back with a hand on each of Summer's shoulders. "For the record, I don't think Harry is wretched at all."

"Um, girls, I'm standing right here," Harry reminded them. "I can hear everything you say about me."

Summer turned to her uncle. "Hi, Uncle Harry." She still couldn't decide between love and hate for him, so hesitated on a hug. He remedied her dilemma by throwing an arm around her shoulder and giving her a sideways squeeze.

"Well, girls, what do you think of the place?" He beamed with pride as Charlotte and Ellie looked around.

After twenty minutes of touring the premises, and a preponderance of "oohs" and "aahs" from the newcomers, Harry and Ellie settled into the guestroom downstairs while Summer helped Charlotte carry her numerous bags upstairs where she took what had been Bogey's room.

"Wait until you see my veil," Charlotte cooed. "Here's a sample of the lace." With a dramatic flair, she swept the three-by-three foot square of fabric out of one of her three matching pink Samsonite suitcases.

Summer fingered the delicate lace. "It's gorgeous." Taking it in hand, gently she draped it over Charlotte's head. The intricate white design atop Charlotte's dark hair made a romantic picture. "It couldn't be more perfect."

"I know. Isn't it wonderful? We found it in a small fabric shop in Charlevoix, of all places."

Summer knew Charlotte's agonizing ordeal of finding the perfect wedding dress all too well, having traveled with her and her grandmother Meg, Charlotte's mother, to Chicago to search for the ideal gown. When none materialized after three harrowing days of pounding the pavement from bridal shop to bridal shop, it was decided that the only thing to do was have one made to Charlotte's specifications. The seamstress in Traverse City, a consummate professional by all accounts, had already had her patience worn thin with Charlotte's changes. But, it did promise to be an exquisite gown. The mundane popular styles of dirndl or bell skirt, or A-line skirt falling from an empire waist, would never do for Charlotte. She'd been watching Disney movies all her life and nothing would suffice except a Cinderella-style ballgown, with layer upon layer of lace-edged toile for the skirt and a scoop-neck top with lace cap sleeves. Summer agreed that the lace veil would indeed top it off perfectly.

As maid of honor, along with an ensemble of six bridesmaids, Summer would be wearing a tailor-made, full-length, sleeveless, pink lace shift with a satin ribbon sash. The fittings had been mind-numbingly boring for Summer. She and Charlotte had a rare squabble about high heels, as Summer never wore them and refused to squish her feet into them for the wedding, no doubt only to tower over her partner groomsman. Her aunt had finally relented, reckoning that no one would see the bridesmaids' feet, anyway, in their long dresses. So true, Summer thought.

The entire wedding planning debacle had left Summer promising herself that if she ever did miraculously find a man to marry someday, she would insist they elope.

"Lookie here," Charlotte said, pulling a big, bulky scrapbook out of the suitcase. She sat down on the edge of the bed and opened it. "I've put together samples of everything for the wedding. The newspaper clipping with our engagement picture, one of the invitations, the invitation list, a picture of St. Francis, a picture of mom and dad's yard where we'll have the reception, and a drawing of the reception dinner layout. I've got pictures from bride magazines, fabric samples...."

Summer sat down beside Charlotte so she could see. "That's amazing. You're the most organized person I've ever known. This'll be a wonderful memento of your big day. You'll treasure it for the rest of your life."

Lovingly, Charlotte ran her hand across a sample of the toile for her gown, her rock of a diamond engagement ring catching light from the window and spraying sparkles across the wall. "I know. I love Bernard so much. I know we'll stay married forever and ever."

Charlotte's fiancé, the son of the biggest real estate mogul in Traverse City, seemed like a nice guy. Summer liked him. "I'm sure you will," she said.

Then a brainstorm struck.

"Hey, how about this?" She went on to explain her big idea.

Charlotte clapped happily and readily agreed. "Oh, See-saw, this'll be so much fun."

Summer wasn't sure of much these days, but she was sure of this. In fact, it might be the best idea she'd had since...She couldn't remember the last time she'd had a good idea, all the more reason to be pleased with herself for her ingenuity on this one.

24

Harry O'Neill couldn't be more stunned.

He'd come to West Branch expecting a moody, wrothy niece who hated his guts for making her be here. After all, she'd not been able to contain her contempt for him a week ago when he dropped her off in this "Podunk." At the very least, he expected her to be mortified after having fallen into a grave with a dead man.

Instead, she was positively giddy. Oh, she'd been noncommittal when he and Ellie first arrived, but now at the supper table she seemed to be a very happy young woman. Two things buoyed her spirits: the scheme she and Charlotte had cooked up, which would occur the next day; and excitement over scavenging through the mystery apartment, which they would begin as soon as Sheriff Kowalczyk finished his run-down of what the police had done to search the originating scene of a crime.

Harry, Ellie, Summer, Betty, Charlotte, and the sheriff all sat around a large table in the café. The new cook for the café, which would open the day after next, Friday, the same day as the open house for the B&B, had provided them with a scrumptious meal of meatloaf, scalloped potatoes, and green beans. Joey, the cook, was a war veteran like Harry. Thin as a rail, no one would ever know he could cook up a storm.

Joey had already cleared their dishes off the table so the sheriff could lay out faded blueprints of the apartment, which Harry had been given upon buying the building. Sheriff Kowalczyk tapped the diagram of the closet on the blueprints. "This was the hardest part to investigate. We didn't want to disturb anything, but we had to check out every bit of space. So, we carefully removed the clothes, section by section, to make sure we would put them back where we found them. We scanned every inch of the walls and ceiling and floor, and that safe was the only hidden structure in there. We also removed everything in the cupboards in the kitchenette and bathroom, and again nothing unusual was found.

"Well, I guess that depends on your definition of 'unusual.' Somebody lived a very cushy life in that apartment. Obviously a woman, as you'll see when you go through everything."

All eyes stayed glued to the large diagram in front of them. They all looked up when Joey came up with a coffee pot in hand.

"Another cuppa Joe, anybody?"

"Yes, thank you," the sheriff said, pointing to his empty cup. Joey filled the sheriff's cup, and Betty nodded for more, too.

"We took pictures of everything before going through it." He handed Harry a large envelope. "Here are copies. I think you'll find that we left everything the same as we found it. We checked windows and doors to make certain none had been pried open. They had not. Whoever our dead man is, he had a key." He paused to sip his coffee. Finding it satisfying, he sipped again. "We went through paperwork, books, things like that, but nothing gave up any clues about this case. We dusted for fingerprints and found nothing.

"So, the bottom line is we have no idea who was in that apartment, where the money came from, why on earth the man chose to ride a bicycle into the cemetery at night, and who killed him and why. There are lots of theories flying around about the Purple Gang, but at this point that's pure speculation. We have no proof.

"Therefore, the apartment is released to you to do with as you wish." The sheriff reached into his pocket, produced three new keys, and slid them across the table to Harry. "But because this is an unsolved murder, we ask that you contact us should you run across anything that looks suspicious. At this point, we welcome any piece of information that has even the most remote possibility of helping us solve this crime." He polished off his coffee and stood up.

"Thanks, Aleks, for taking such care with the place," Harry said. He stood to shake the sheriff's hand. "We'll be vigilant, I promise." He pulled a keyring out of his pocket and twisted one new key onto it to join half a dozen others. He handed the other two new keys to Betty, who pocketed one and handed the other over to Summer. "Who's ready to go take a look?"

Everyone scrambled to their feet, anxious to see the puzzling apartment. The sheriff wished them well and left. The rest of the crew went upstairs to finally get a gander.

When he and Ellie peeked into this part of the building before, there were no lights. Now, with the lights on, Harry couldn't believe his eyes. Enchanting didn't cover it. Enigmatic didn't cover it. Magical offered a mere start.

Harry felt like he'd traveled back to the "Roaring '20s" on a time machine. He looked at Ellie and it was obvious she felt the same way, with her eyes wide circles and her mouth a gaping oval.

"Who on God's green earth lived here?" Ellie wondered as she slowly turned full circle to take in the whole place.

"That's what we've been asking ourselves all week," Betty answered.

"There's been a lot of head scratching over that one," Summer said.

"Ho-ly mo-ly," Charlotte added, otherwise rendered speechless.

Betty produced a large pad of paper and a handful of pencils. "These are for writing down what we find. A sort of inventory. The sheriff says there's jewelry that looks expensive in a jewelry box on the dresser." She looked around, spotted the dresser with a box on top, and pointed. "We might find other valuables, too. So, we need to keep track."

"Some things," Harry added, "we need to write down and then stack together to be stored away in boxes. All the knick-knacks together, for example, and dishes together…"

"Look at this." Ellie had gone to the jewelry box and pulled out a long strand of pearls. She raked her hand through the jumble of baubles in the box. "This is full of diamonds and pearls. The real thing. There must be thousands of dollars' worth of jewelry in here."

"Our lady apparently was a woman of means," Harry said.

"Or, she grew up poor as a church mouse and became a beautiful woman who escaped poverty by becoming a gangster moll," Charlotte said as she went over and peeked into the jewelry box. Summer couldn't resist taking a look, too. Once they ogled the jewels, they went to the closet, where they spent more time conjuring up tall tales about the "moll" who'd worn all those jewels and clothes than they did cataloging anything.

Summer eventually wandered out into the main room and gravitated to a bookshelf. She grabbed a rag to dust them off, then studied the titles.

"Our 'lady,' gangster moll though she may have been, liked

to read the good stuff. We've got Dumas, Wharton, Fitzgerald, three Brontës, Hemingway, Barrett Browning, Twain, Stein, Austin, Shelley…" She sat on the floor and began pulling books out and thumbing through.

"We'll put those in our library downstairs," Harry said.

At nine o'clock, after half a dozen stacks of belongings had been piled in the center of the room, Harry declared it to be quitting time. "We have another job to do tomorrow," he reminded everyone. "Friday we'll be busy with the open house. Come Saturday we can go at this again. But now we need some shut-eye."

Reluctant to leave but knowing it was necessary, especially considering their plans for the next day, everybody exited the apartment. Ellie took the jewelry box to have its contents appraised. Harry locked the door behind him and left the apartment to its moll ghost.

25

As he sat on the side of the bed in the downstairs guestroom, taking off first his shirt and then his shoes and socks, Harry couldn't help but hear the pitter patter of not-so-little feet in the rooms overhead. His younger sister and his niece were scurrying from bedroom to bedroom up there, no doubt gossiping and plotting like a couple of twelve-year-olds at a pajama party.

"They certainly seem to be having fun," he said. When he got no response, he turned toward the bathroom behind him.

"Oh my holy stars," he moaned at the site of his sexy wife, standing there as she was in a black negligee so skimpy it left nothing to the imagination. Her lush dark hair had been tied back earlier. Now it laid in tussled waves about her shoulders. Her lips had been painted a luscious deep red.

Languidly, she stretched her arm up onto the bathroom doorway, a gesture that hoisted up her transparent garment even higher on her plush hip. The dim light from above the bathroom mirror behind her cast an angelic halo around her body. An angel she was not, at least not on this night. Many such nights had taught him that.

He moaned again.

"It's time for us to have our own kind of fun," she teased, striding toward him and crawling onto the bed like a preying panther. "We need to initiate this B&B, like we have all the others."

Harry didn't give his sister and niece another thought that night. In fact, he thought of nothing at all. He merely laid back and silently reveled in being ravaged by a wild beast of a woman, one he was lucky enough to call his wife. A domesticated wife, at that.

No one would ever know that behind closed doors their love life was anything but tame.

Deep in the night, Harry awoke. Nothing had roused him except his own thoughts.

He gazed at his wife, her beautiful features outlined in the dark. She slept soundly, quietly, allowing his musings full freedom. Ellie needed children. So did he, not only for himself but because it would make her happy. They shared passionate lust and romantic love; they adored their family and friends; they were successful professionals; they contributed to their community; they were devoutly religious and attended church regularly. The gaping hole in their lives was their lack of a chance to give parental love. He knew they would be good parents. Well, he supposed every parent thought that before the kids actually arrived. But Ellie and he could handle whatever came their way.

He was forty-three; she was thirty-nine. They'd always hoped for their own. There had been three miscarriages, two when she was in her twenties and one in her early thirties. Each time, their hearts had been broken. They agreed that with each conception a place had opened up in their hearts for that child. When the child was lost that place remained in their hearts. They loved and missed each child that never made it into their arms. They had often discussed the joy they would feel someday in the far future when their lives on earth would end and they would finally be able to embrace their lost children in heaven.

Even in the face of such painful loss, they kept hoping for a viable pregnancy that would go full term. But Harry knew it was time to admit that would never happen. It was time to consider other options. It was time to share their otherwise blessed life with posterity by finding other children to embrace.

Softly, he touched his wife's shoulder, the feel of her skin filling him with love for the beauty of her soul. There was so much more to their relationship than physical intimacy. There was a deeper, more binding emotional intimacy, as well. Theirs was the stuff of fairytales, and Harry O'Neill was man enough not to be ashamed of that. Bringing a child or children into their lives would only deepen their connection, of that he felt certain.

26

Stella stared at Summer in disbelief, the child's penchant for distrust plastered across her wan face. The rest of the children seemed quite excited, as Summer had hoped. After everyone had scraped their boots if need be, cleaned their nails, washed their hands, and said the pledge, Summer had announced that special guests were coming and this would be a very special day.

The morning ritual had become much easier after only a few days of direction from Angela Fitzgerald. The kids caught on to the routine and hardly needed coaching anymore.

But it had already been a testy morning, with Stella showing up barefoot, her three-year-old sister Gloria in hand. She'd stuffed toilet paper into the toes of her new tennis shoes and the little one wore them like a clown with floppy clodhoppers. Stella explained that Wilma wasn't home and she wouldn't leave her sister alone, so she had to bring her to school. She'd fixed the shoes because Gloria had complained that her feet were cold.

When Summer asked, "Who is Wilma?" the child looked at her like she was daft.

"Wilma," she said, "is our mom. But she doesn't like us to call her that 'cuz she doesn't want her boyfriends to hear us say that. We stay in the back room when they come, so they won't hear us, anyway." She rolled her eyes in disgust.

Saddened, although no longer shocked, Summer rushed the

two girls to the principal's office where Miss Campbell quickly assessed the situation and gave the shoes back to Stella. With the patience of a saint, she asked Stella if it would be okay if her secretary, Beatrice, took Gloria into town to get her a pair of shoes that fit just right.

Stella had eyed Beatrice suspiciously, deciding the plump woman looked okay. She agreed. Gloria got swept away and Summer dashed back to her classroom with a shod Stella in time to join Angela and the class in saying the "Pledge of Allegiance."

For the thousandth time, Summer wondered how real teachers did this every day for nine months straight, and years on end. She counted down the days like a soldier in boot camp.

Right on cue, Uncle Harry, Aunt Ellie, and Charlotte entered the room. They'd come early with Summer to set up projects for the children in other rooms. Summer had called Miss Campbell the night before to get permission to use the home economics room and wood shop.

The children's heads spun around and their small bodies quaked in anticipation of what the guests might be doing there. All except Stella, of course, who would, as usual, pass judgement once she'd analyzed the situation.

"Children, I need three volunteers to write our guests' names on the board," Summer said. Three hands popped up and she invited them to the blackboard. "Each one of our guests will tell you how to spell their name."

"I'm Mr. Harry," her uncle said, waving at the class. Half of them waved back. "My name is spelled…."

"I can spell that one." One of the boys at the board interrupted, wrote it correctly, turned to the class, and bowed.

"Excellent," Harry said, shaking the boy's hand, which made

the kid beam with pride as he swaggered back to his seat. "I'm going to take you boys to the wood shop where we'll be making something very unique with wood."

"Yeah." "All right." "Groovy." Most of the boys fidgeted excitedly in their seats like bobble dolls on the dash of a car traveling over a pot-hole-riddled road.

"I'm Mrs. Ellie." Ellie waved, too, and more kids responded this time. She spelled her name and the girl wrote it down correctly before returning to her seat. "I'm going to take you girls to the home economics room where we'll bake wedding cupcakes."

The shrill of gleeful high-pitched little girl's voices vibrated in Summer's ears.

A boy raised his hand. Summer nodded to give permission for him to ask his question. "Do us boys get to have some cupcakes, too?"

"Oh, yes," Ellie said. "We'll make enough for everyone."

The lad nodded his approval.

"And I'm Charlotte. My name is hard to spell, so let me help." She went to the front of the class, the scent of Shalimar perfume following in her wake, and smiled at the remaining boy, who stood there holding a piece of chalk poised an inch from the surface of the board. Charlotte wore a short, white dress that hugged her curves and pumps that added to her aura of sophistication. A small, white silk scarf circled her neck with the tie pulled to the side to hover pertly above her shoulder. Her dark hair was teased into a perfectly poufy flip.

"What's your name?" Charlotte asked her scribe.

"Ah, L-Larry."

"Thank you for your help, Larry."

Summer watched as seven-year-old Larry fell head over heels

in love with stunning Charlotte. He blinked up at her in awe and wrote each letter carefully as she spelled out her name. Not constricted by proper teacher behavior, she grabbed him for a hug when he'd finished. "That's perfect. Thank you."

Poor Larry, Summer thought. He was toast. He'd harbor that crush for years to come. Charlotte might have ruined him for a real girl, like an awkward teenager, in the future.

Larry blushed but couldn't suppress a grin as he returned to his seat.

"While the cupcakes are baking," Charlotte said to the class, "I'll show you girls my wedding scrapbook, because I'm planning my wedding and getting married real soon."

That garnered approval from the girls and disinterest from the boys, except Larry, of course. But most of the boys were ready to go to the shop.

The morning proceeded beautifully, gifting Summer with a sense of relief that her plan had actually worked. She never knew for sure with kids.

27

After lunch in the cafeteria, everyone gathered back in the classroom. The boys had sanded blocks of wood and painted their first names on them. Furthermore, they'd made one for each girl, too. Even Miss Summer and Mrs. Angela each got one. Everyone could use their wood nameplates on their desks or take them home to display as they wished. The boys' pride in their masterpieces showed in their smiles. They had learned how to sand rough wood to make it smooth, paint it, and clean up afterwards. Harry always had construction supplies in the back of his truck, so he'd had everything they needed.

Many of the girls giggled as they presented their creations. One little girl wore the "bride's veil" over her hair, the large swatch of lace Charlotte had brought. Each girl had taken a turn wearing it as they looked at the scrapbook while waiting for the cupcakes to bake. There was a white "wedding cupcake" for everyone, plus extras for Miss Campbell, her secretary Beatrice, and Stella's little sister Gloria. Miss Campbell and Beatrice had brought Gloria back in a new pair of tennis shoes and a new summer sweater over her ragged dress. They stayed to join the class in enjoying the treats.

The cupcakes had ended up with every configuration of decorating imaginable, with a lopsided mound of vanilla frosting atop each one. Ellie borrowed the ingredients from Joey the café cook and from the bakery next door, and these small missies had stirred and decorated with wild abandon. Like Harry, Ellie had guided them through cleaning up, a considerable task.

Every kid got a paper plate and napkin, and gobbled down their cupcake, after which Mrs. Angela sent them to the bathrooms for another round of handwashing. Before Stella left the room, Ellie called out to her. Summer watched as the girl readily came to the woman's side without a trace of her usual suspicion of adults.

"You're a good baker," Ellie said. "Your cupcakes were so pretty. You decorated them beautifully. And I noticed you did a lot of the cleaning up. Thank you for all your help."

Stella stared up at Ellie for a moment, then an enormous smile erupted across her face. Summer had seldom seen the girl so much as grin, let alone let loose with a genuine smile.

"You're welcome." Stella turned and skipped to the bathroom.

"You've made one usually sad little girl very happy," Summer said to Ellie.

"Well, the truth is you've made me very happy. This is the most fun I've had in ages. Thanks for having us. These kids are wonderful."

"Uh, would you like to come every day? You might change your mind."

Ellie grinned, then became grim. "I'm worried about Stella and her little sister. I can't stand the thought of them not being well cared for. Clearly, they are not."

"No, I'm afraid not. I don't know what to do about it, though. Miss Campbell told me to watch for signs of abuse, but I can't find anything like that. I see neglect, and that seems like abuse. But it's not enough to take them away from their mother."

Ellie stared into the hallway, her gaze following Stella's path. "Keep watching. Let me know if you find anything."

Ellie and Harry and Charlotte left to get back to the B&B. They needed to check on preparations for the big open house the next day. Angela had left with her baby boy in his stroller, after cupcake time. Miss Campbell and Beatrice had gone back to their office, so Summer was left alone with her students when the clock on the wall signaled the end of the school day.

She called Stella aside again, asking her to come to her desk. With her little sister at her side, Stella obeyed. Summer waited until the last of the other children left the room to open her desk drawer and bring out a paper sack.

"Miss Campbell and Miss Beatrice left this for you, Stella. They wanted you to have a new sweater, too." She pulled out an adorable cotton sweater, much like the one Gloria wore, only bigger. Summer wondered how much of her own money the principal spent each year on needy students. This was one student in one class; during the school year the whole building would be full of kids like this. Summer held up the sweater by the shoulders to help Stella put it on.

The girl's eyes widened. Her body tilted toward the inviting garment. She put her hand out to touch it, then snatched it back.

"I can't have no new sweater."

Summer had observed Angela correcting children's grammar in a gentle way. Instead of admonishing them, she would repeat what they'd said using correct grammar. Summer did the same.

"You can't have a new sweater? Why not?"

"I can't bring back the one you gived me yesterday when it rained." Stella's head fell to her chest and she wouldn't look at Summer as she spoke. "I told Wilma you letted me borrow it and

I had to bring it back, but she said she ain't gonna let you be no Indian giver. She wore it when she left last night."

Summer held back tears and cleared her throat before she could speak. She wouldn't even attempt to repeat what had been said in order to correct the grammar. She certainly didn't want to reinforce "Indian giver" by repeating it.

"That's okay," Summer said. "Your mo... Wilma can have it. But if you don't take this one, Miss Campbell's and Miss Beatrice's feelings will be hurt. It made them feel good to make sure you have a sweater, too, and if you don't take it they'll feel bad. Please take it. It'll make them very happy."

Stella looked up and the intensity of her piercing gray eyes belied a mind that had been forced to mature far beyond its years. She knew this was charity and wasn't sure she liked it. On the other hand, she must be tired of being cold.

She turned around, stuck her arms into the sleeves, and wrapped the sweater around her body. "Thank you," she said solemnly. "Will you tell Miss Campbell and Miss Beatrice I said thank you?"

"Of course."

Stella nodded matter-of-factly, took her sister's hand, and left the room.

Resisting tears all the way home, Summer pedaled her bike like a maniac to get downtown to help with preparations for the big celebration.

Thoughts of children were pushed to the back of her mind when she and the rest of the crew became buried in getting ready for the B&B open house the next day, as well as the opening of the café. Summer wouldn't think of Stella and Gloria again until she fell into bed, totally exhausted. She wondered what kind of bed, if any, those little girls had to sleep on. She prayed to God they slept well at night, seeing that their days with "Wilma" were not good.

She thought again of her own parents, on vacation in Hawaii. She'd always known she was blessed to have such good parents, but now that knowledge deepened to a new awakening of how privileged she'd always been. How could she have been so blind all her life to the plight of others? She'd only cared in a remote, impersonal way.

Now it was personal and she worried about those kids she saw face-to-face every day. Who ever would have guessed such a thing could happen? Oh, Uncle Harry, of course. This was what he'd hoped for.

Well, Uncle Harry, you were right. Now, if I can survive five more weeks of Head Start, you can be pronounced a true success.

But that remains to be seen. I might lose my mind first.

Summer's worries faded away as she fell into a deep sleep. Her dream allowed her to escape to a country road where a tall, handsome deputy with black hair pulled her onto his horse with him, and they rode off into the sunset…

28

"May I have this dance?"

Summer turned to face the bearer of that deep voice, the question taking her by such surprise she didn't answer.

"Please," Bogey said, holding out his hand.

Summer reminded herself to close her gaping mouth as she rested her soft hand in his firm one. How could she resist his request with him looking so fine in his uniform, his hat off and his black hair slicked back. He led her to the center of the ballroom.

The band played *Stranger on the Shore*, with a mellow saxophone that begged for proper, romantic waltzing. Placing her left hand on Bogey's shoulder, she felt a tingle when he wrapped his right hand around her waist, pulling her close. She recalled how women always "swooned" in old movies. She used to think that schmaltzy, but now she caught herself swooning over the feel of his strong body next to hers, the smell of his masculine Old Spice mingling with her feminine Evening in Paris to add to the appeal. He held her right hand high and swung her around in the four-square pattern she'd learned when her parents made her take social dance classes as a gangly teenager. She'd thought she'd never use those lessons, but here she was dancing away like a pro with a man who clearly knew his way around a dance floor.

The blue full-skirted dress Charlotte had brought from Summer's closet at home was perfect, the patterned fabric swirling prettily around her long legs, while her flat blue Candy shoes allowed her to feel assured of her steps. She relaxed and let herself enjoy being led around the ballroom by a handsome man. Bogey was the perfect height for her, which allowed her to tilt up her chin ever so slightly so they could gaze into each other's eyes as they spun around the room. They were too focused on each other to notice the appreciative audience their moves attracted. They turned and twirled, and Summer felt like Cinderella at the ball, dancing with the prince.

The song ended, and the others in the room clapped. Parting, the couple was taken aback by the attention. But Bogey smiled and took a deep bow from the waist, so Summer curtsied, which generated more applause.

"Bravo," the band leader said into the microphone. "Thank you Summer and Bogey for that wonderful performance."

The couple turned away from the stage to return to the side of the room when another voice screeched from the mic. "Bravo, my ass. Bogey Bush, you horndog, you need to get your sorry ass away from that rich bitch."

Shocked, Summer turned in time to see the band leader nudge a flashy broad, which was instinctively how Summer thought of her, away from the microphone. "Hey, Chastity, we've heard this before…" the band leader admonished.

Too stunned to move, out of the corner of her eye Summer saw a flash of red flying toward the stage. Oh, oh. Charlotte's face was as red as her dress.

Before the band leader could finish his sentence, Charlotte catapulted onto the stage and shoved the dame. "How dare you call her that."

"Don't you touch me, you bitch," the broad wailed.

Hands flew like the claws of fighting wildcats for the few seconds it took before Bogey got there to grab the madwoman and Harry harnessed his sister. They shuffled the women off the stage and out the door, the females spewing venom at each other all the way. At last glance, Charlotte's French twist had been pulled out of her hair and the broad's red lipstick had been smeared across her face.

Summer stood frozen on the now abandoned dance floor.

The band leader saved her, announcing, "Okay, folks, show over. We've all seen Chastity do that kind of thing before. Don't forget this is a celebration of the opening of this beautiful B&B, so let's dance." The band played *Big Girls Don't Cry* and the floor filled with dancers while three elder ladies hustled up to Summer and escorted her to the side.

"Don't worry, dearie. That poor Chastity does that all the time. She calls everybody that nasty name." The lady was short and squat, with a frazzled gray bun in her hair. Her flowered housedress had been fancied up with a short string of imitation pearls.

"I heard her do it once to a clerk at Gus' Pantry." The second lady wore a suit that appeared to be at least twenty years old. The jacket was unbuttoned over a blouse, so that fit okay, but the skirt cinched her in so tightly it was a wonder she could walk. "She was upset," the lady continued to say, "because the line wasn't moving fast enough. The poor clerk burst into tears. I hit Chastity with my purse, I was so mad. Then she called me that name, too."

"No wonder she has problems, her parents saddling her with that horrible name." The third lady stood tall, her skinny form swallowed up in a belted dress with a gathered skirt.

They tittered.

"Yeah. She's anything but."

"That poor, nice Deputy Bush had no idea what she was like when he came back here."

"That's right. He only dated her a few times before he got to know her, and he broke up with her."

"Yes, and from what I hear he did it as gently as possible. But she isn't the type to take anything kindly."

"Oh my, yes. Remember when Bobby what's-his-name broke up with her? That was before Deputy Bush came back. Why, she stalked Bobby all over the place. He moved away."

"Married a girl from Ohio."

They crinkled their noses, as if moving to the state on Michigan's southern border was tantamount to living in the Siberian Desert.

"We've got to get home; it's late," the short lady said. Summer glanced at the clock on the wall. It was 7:37. "We'll thank Betty when we see her at Creative Arts." Summer had never heard of that, but nodded knowingly. "Please tell your aunt and uncle we had a great time. We love the place. This has been a wonderful open house."

"And extend our greetings to that Charlotte. She's our kind of gal."

"She's a real pip."

Summer smiled. She liked these old ladies. "Goodbye. I hope to see you again."

They moved on and Summer looked around the ballroom. The mayor and his wife were there, as well as her priest, the Episcopalian priest and his wife, doctors and their wives, a number of store owners, lawyers, doctors, farmers, and others she didn't recognize. Earlier Hazel, the white-haired romance novel writer, had been there, and Summer found her to be delightful, although she hadn't had much time to talk to her. Summer had spent most of her time running up and down the stairs replenishing the refreshment table. Angela Fitzgerald and her husband, the nighttime deputy sheriff, had been there, too, with the principal, Miss Campbell. Summer would have known "Fitz" anywhere seeing that his two sons in her class were carbon copies of him, all of them looking like kin to Hoss, the actor Dan Blocker, on *Bonanza*.

At the moment, people danced; they ate cake; they drank punch; they laughed. No one seemed traumatized by what they'd seen. Therefore, she decided there was no reason for her to be embarrassed.

West Branch was teaching her a lot of lessons, the most frequent of which was "go with the flow."

She sure did like the flow of dancing with Bogey Bush.

29

Ellie and Betty couldn't stop laughing. Harry's rendition of Chastity's "brouhaha" and Charlotte's wildcat response, which they had missed, had them rolling. Harry said it was lucky their parents spent so much money sending Charlotte to finishing school, so she'd know how to brawl like a lady.

Charlotte sat there prim as could be, unfazed by the razzing. Her French twist was back in place with nary a stray hair. There remained no sign of her recent catfight.

"Well," she said, taking a ladylike sip of her hot chocolate, pinky finger in the air. "I wasn't about to let that 'bitch' say that to my See-saw. Besides, she spoiled the mood. Everybody could see that Summer and Bogey were having a moment."

All eyes riveted to Summer.

Summer, Charlotte, Betty, Ellie, and Harry sat in the closed café, its shades drawn. It was ten o'clock. Joey the cook had gone home, having worked a long day with the successful opening of the café. They had cleared and cleaned the ballroom for an hour after the end of the open house, but decided to leave the rest for the next day. They were beat, retreating to the café for a quick rundown of the event while having coffee and hot chocolate before hitting the hay.

"We were not 'having a moment.' Geez, Charlotte. We were only dancing. Like everybody else. No big deal."

"Uh huh. I've got eyes. That was a moment to beat all moments."

Everyone jumped when Bogey appeared at the door leading to the B&B lobby. "Sorry to interrupt," he said, coming up to their table. "I, well, I wanted to apologize for Chastity. I'm so sorry she interrupted your open house. She does that kind of thing a lot." Hat in hand, he did indeed look contrite.

"Apology accepted only if you join us," Harry said.

"Coffee or hot chocolate?" Betty wanted to know, getting up to head to the kitchen.

"Thanks. Ah, hot chocolate, I guess. But I can only stay for a few minutes. I have to get back to work, especially since I already took a break to stop in during the open house." He sat down and glanced at Summer.

Their eyes met, no words needed. They had indeed been "having a moment" while they danced. Now his deep brown eyes and her buoyant blue ones locked, the meeting of earth and sky.

All other eyes glommed onto the look between them.

"Here you go," Betty said, breaking the spell by bringing a full cup to Bogey. She sat back down. "I'm sorry I missed Chastity's show. That girl needs help."

"Well," Bogey said, running a finger around the rim of his steaming cup, "I don't know how much help she'll be getting tonight. We arrested her. She's in jail."

"No kidding?" Betty said.

"Has she ever been arrested before?" Ellie asked.

"No, but she should have been. She harasses people. Aleks and I have always given her a break, hoping she'd get help. A few months ago he even suggested a counselor in Bay City, but she wouldn't hear of it. Tonight he'd had enough. When I took her in for a good talking to, he locked her up. I agree; we had no options left."

"Do you think that'll help her get over you?" Harry asked.

"Oh yeah, it already seems to be working. Right now she's calling me every name in the book. I'm the biggest S.O.B. who ever lived." Bogey shook his head.

"Damn," Betty said, "Aleks and his wife will have to listen to her rantings all night long."

"I think that's what made Aleks hold off on arresting her in the first place. They don't want to be stuck in the same building with her," Bogey speculated, referring to the fact that the sheriff and his wife lived in the house that also served as the county jail.

"We may have had a little more excitement than we anticipated," Ellie said, "but things worked out great on our end." She pointed to Betty and then to herself. "We were swamped in the lobby, greeting people and booking dates. Three hundred and ninety-seven people signed the guest book. Considering that only two thousand people live here, that's great. We've got three wedding receptions and a family reunion lined up. Our guestrooms are full up for Old Fashioned Days in August. And we have a dinner for Harley Davidson riders during the Jack Pine Run this fall."

"And lots of inquiries for future events," Betty added.

"Betty," Harry said, "your idea of having the band was brilliant. It showed people what could be done in the ballroom."

"Thanks. It did work out well. But wait until you hear this: Our booking for the next month is the most interesting of all. It's a guy who was here after reading about us in the *Detroit Free Press*. Tell them, Ellie."

"He's a movie producer. He's small time, he said, but he does movies about historical events. He's working on one about the rise and fall of the Purple Gang, and came to look the place over. He said we have perfect settings for some of his scenes. He'll be here with his assistant starting on Monday. Next week his entire crew will come in. The producer and his assistant will stay here at the B&B the whole time, but their crew will need to bed down at the Tri-Terrace Motel on the other side of town. The producer figures it'll take them a month, until mid-July, to get all the shots they need. Most of the movie is set in Detroit, but because some of the 'Purples,' as he called them, hung out around here, they'll use our building, some street scenes, and the courthouse."

"Yeah," Betty added, "the courthouse in Detroit where the real trials of some of the gang members were held has been torn down. So ours will be used as a stand-in."

"Don't they have to get town council permission to do all of this?" Harry, ever the businessman, knew all about permits.

Ellie nodded. "I suppose. But he and the mayor talked for an hour down here in the lobby. The way the mayor was smiling, I think they worked that out. The town will benefit, and people will probably have some fun in the process."

Her Uncle Harry looked at Summer. "I'd say this stay in West Branch has turned out to be a lot more exciting than I ever expected. Maybe I should make you go back to boring Traverse City."

"Not a chance," Summer said. "I'm in for the duration." She couldn't hold back a glance at Bogey.

The deputy smiled and drank down the last of his hot chocolate, and stood up. "Well, I've got to go. Congratulations on your success. This place is a great addition to the town." He put on his hat, nodded, and went out the way he'd come in.

"Sure," Charlotte chided. "Nothing going on there."

"Oh, shut up," Summer quipped.

"Hey, Summer," Betty said, changing the subject, "how was school today? You made it through a whole week."

"It was good today. They were still all atwitter over yesterday. They love their nameplates, and wanted to know if we could make more cupcakes on Monday. Larry asked if Charlotte could come back."

Charlotte grinned and held out her hand to admire her engagement ring. "I hope my fiancé doesn't get jealous when I tell him I have a new boyfriend."

"It sounds to me like you're doing a great job with those kids," Harry said to Summer.

"I don't know about that. I wouldn't survive at all if it weren't for Angela Fitzgerald. She's a true angel.

"Some of the kids are great, with good parents, I'm sure. They simply don't have much money. But a few are in bad situations. Stella had on her new tennis shoes and sweater that Miss Campbell bought her, but with that same ragged dress she wore all week. I fear it's the only one she owns."

"We've been thinking about that," Ellie said, indicating herself and Harry. "Those thousand-dollar bills the mystery man dropped in the alley: they're all dried out and in a lockbox in the bank. What would you all think if we donated them to the school, not only for teachers and supplies, but for a slush fund for Miss Campbell when she sees a child who needs necessities?" She looked earnestly from person to person as she spoke.

Everyone readily agreed. Somehow, there seemed no better place for illegal Purple Gang money. Little did those hoodlums know that someday they would be helping needy children from the very town they helped corrupt.

Summer fell into bed exhausted yet happy. It had been one heck of a day.

30

Summer stretched, yawned, and snuggled back into her covers. Maybe it was time to get up, but her body didn't care. Her dreams about dancing with Bogey Bush had been too fantastic to give them up for the real world. She snoozed for twenty more minutes before her eyes opened again, first one and then the other.

The curtains undulated in rhythm to the gentle breeze at the open windows. Muted rays of sun filtered in through the diaphanous fabric, illuminating specks of dust frolicking in the air. Pink and yellow and pale green colors alternately dotted the wall with the changing of the traffic signal, dim in daylight. She'd come to feel soothed by the sound of the train roaming through town at 2:00 a.m. each night, waking her only long enough to offer security in its predictability. Now, at whatever time it might be in the morning, the sounds of automobiles on the street and people on the sidewalks conjured up a sense of belonging.

Summer quite felt like she might still be dreaming.

Her stomach growled. Except for hot chocolate before coming to bed, she hadn't eaten since lunch the day before, she'd been so busy working at the open house. Realizing she was starved, she threw back the covers and hopped out of bed. Within ten minutes she was dressed and out of her room. Peeking into the ballroom, she was surprised to find it completely cleaned up. It must be later than she thought.

Betty was on the phone in the lobby and waved as Summer passed through on her way to the café. There she asked a waitress she'd never met for two fried eggs, two pieces of toast, three pieces of bacon, hash browns, orange juice, coffee, and a donut. The young woman looked at her in surprise, or maybe it was adoration, and said, "Coming right up."

Summer hadn't forgotten that she was supposed to be helping in the café, but nobody had said anything since it opened and she wasn't about to jog anyone's memory. Especially her Uncle Harry's.

Twenty-five minutes later, stuffed, she went upstairs to the apartment, where the day would be spent sorting again. Harry sat at the small dining table looking through stacks of papers and Ellie rifled through dresser drawers. The curtains had been taken down and the windows opened, so plenty of air and light filled the room.

"Oh, Summer, come here," Ellie said. "Look at this underwear. It's so unusual."

Summer went over to the large dresser and Ellie handed her the most delicate personal garments she'd ever seen, including some satiny tops with thin straps and lace. "Wow, these are so pretty."

"I think it's called a chemise," Ellie said. "My mom said they didn't wear bras back then, lucky dogs. 'Brassieres' were around but didn't become popular until the 1930s. These things that we wear today…" she pushed up her boobs, obviously ensconced in a pointy bra… "didn't come into being until the 1950s. In the 1920s if a woman did wear anything it flattened her chest because that was the fad."

"There's nothing like that here."

"Uh uh. This girl let her puppies roll. I'm jealous. As for these bottoms," Ellie said, holding up a few pairs of what looked like underpants that matched the tops, "I don't know what they were called."

Ellie pulled out more similarly made garments, some sexy satin and some comfy cotton.

Summer ran the dainty items through her hands, trying to imagine the petite woman who'd worn them. Once again, she longed to know what had happened to her. What would make her leave all this behind? Especially all that money.

"Look at these," Ellie cooed. "Wow." She fingered a pair of black silk nylons. "I love the seams up the back. That's so sexy. Wish we still had that today. Here are some garters that held them up."

Summer peeked inside the drawer to see a stack of elastic garters, most with ruffles around the edges.

"Summer," Harry said, interrupting the women's admiration of underwear from the 1920s, "would you mind going through the clothes in the closet? When Charlotte gets up she can help. Make a list of what's in there, but don't pack them up yet. We have to decide what to do with them before we know if they need to go in boxes or stay on hangers."

"Sure." Summer took a notepad and a pencil, and went into the closet, pulling the string to turn on the overhead light. The musty smell from a few days ago had abated, what with the closet door being left open and the windows being opened for the first time in years. She stopped and inhaled deeply.

"Huh, this is strange," she said, stepping out of the closet. "Ellie come in here and tell me what you smell."

Her aunt did as requested and without hesitation said, "It's Chanel No. 5."

"That's what I thought. Imagine, after all these years."

"Check out the medicine cabinet." Harry pointed to the bathroom. "Look at what I found in there."

They went to the door he indicated and opened it to discover a charming room with a pedestal sink, porcelain clawfoot bathtub, and toilet with a wooden tank high on the wall. A chain hung down from the tank for flushing. They opened the cabinet door to a lovely display of antique perfume bottles. Shalimar, Chanel No.5, Arpege, Evening in Paris, Yardley's Lavender, and more.

Ellie took down the Chanel No. 5, dabbed some on her wrist, and took a whiff. "At least forty years old, and it still smells good. That's definitely what we smell in the closet. Must have been her favorite."

Summer tried to remember where she'd smelled that before, but nothing came to her. So many women still wore that iconic perfume, it could have been anywhere.

They went back to their tasks, and Charlotte eventually joined in. In the closet, they decided it would be easiest to describe the dresses in categories, seeing that types of clothes had been hung together. There were sections for nighttime party dresses and gowns, daytime dresses and suits, coats and furs, loungewear, and stay-at-home dresses. Normally, the latter would have been called housedresses, but these were notches above anything so mundane. Charlotte took the party dress section and Summer tackled the loungewear, and they listed each item with a short description and the designer's name on the label.

At one point Charlotte whistled. "This baby is so transparent it almost looks like a nightgown. But I'm pretty sure she wore it out in public." She held up a black lace number that would make most women blush. Apparently, their woman hadn't been the blushing kind.

As Summer finished listing a lavish Egyptian-style caftan, she had an idea. "Hey, Harry, Ellie." She poked her head out of the closet. "Maybe that movie producer could use some of these clothes as costumes for his movie."

Harry looked at Ellie, and she nodded. "Good idea," he said. "So, we'll definitely leave them hanging until he sees them."

Back to work, Summer's hand brushed against an item unlike the others. She pulled it out. Rather than a garment, it was a zippered garment bag. She took it down and carried it out into the room. Draping it over the back of an armchair, she pulled down the zipper then took the dress out, carefully laying it on top of the bag. Sunlight from the nearby window struck the fabric to grace it with an ethereal glow.

Summer gasped. "It's a wedding dress," she whispered.

A gorgeous ivory-toned satin-and-lace gown, it was sleeveless with a dropped waistband. Three tiers of scalloped lace on the skirt fell to ankle length. From the back of the waistband, a long satin panel made up a train.

"Holy moly," Charlotte rasped, having come to her side.

Ellie and Harry gawked, with nothing to add.

They all knew what this meant.

The tailor's label still pinned to the nape of the neck, the dress had clearly never been worn. Their mystery woman had planned on getting married and had not.

"Somebody broke her heart," Summer said softly.

Silence filled the room as that sunk in.

"It breaks my heart." She swiped at tears.

"It's so sad," Ellie noted, blinking to fend off her own waterworks.

"I can't imagine," Charlotte said with glistening eyes.

Protectively, she wrapped her right hand around her engagement ring.

Harry remained silent for many long, measured moments. Eventually he said, "This is all the more reason for us to solve these mysteries. If we find out who this woman from so long ago was, it may help us solve the mystery of our recent murder. Or, if we solve the murder first, it may help us find out what happened to our girl here."

"Yes," Summer agreed, still staring at the enchanting yet melancholy wedding dress. "We've become so intimate with her, she's become part of us. She's like family. We have to do everything we can to take care of her, even if we are forty years too late."

31

"Are you gonna marry Deputy Bush?"

"No. My goodness, no. Whatever made you think that?"

"My mom said you two were dancing all lovey-dovey." The chubby ragamuffin said "lovey-dovey" with a trill of his voice and wiggle of his body that made the other kids laugh. Summer didn't recall his name. She looked at his nameplate.

"No, Hector, we were only dancing. We are not getting married."

"Why not?" a girl named Annie queried.

"Because I don't want to marry anyone right now."

"Why not?" Annie asked more insistently.

All eyes stared at Summer, waiting for an answer.

"We need to move on to arithmetic. Get out your books."

"My uncle is still available," a girl offered, "if you can get him off our couch."

"No thank you. Now, on with our lesson...."

"My grandma says you gotta know how to make pie to get a man."

"Nah. Ya gotta comb your hair and wear red lipstick. You can't look cruddy."

"Ya gotta get all lovey-dovey." Hector trilled and wiggled again going for a second laugh with the same lame act. He got it.

Summer couldn't miss Angela tittering behind her hand. The

mother of nine enjoyed the pickles Summer got into with these kids.

"Arithmetic," Summer insisted.

"Geez."

"Okay."

"Bor-r-ring."

Although the day got off to a rough start with all that marriage chatter, Summer's good mood couldn't be shaken. The day before, Sunday, they'd gone to mass followed by a private dinner in their café, which was closed on the Sabbath. Ellie whipped up a yummy chicken casserole. They spent an hour scavenging through the apartment again before it was time for Harry, Ellie, and Charlotte to leave. The best part of the day, however, had been the evening, when Bogey stopped by and Betty left them alone to talk.

Normally, Bogey didn't get off work until 11:00 p.m. Seeing that Summer had to get up so early each morning for school, there was little chance they would see each other during the week. But he didn't work on Sundays, so could stop by.

Sitting on the couch in front of the fire in the lobby, Summer told Bogey about what they found in the apartment, relaying the story of the wedding dress. He listened with keen interest, and they speculated together about the possibilities of what might have occurred so long ago, not able to come to a solid conclusion.

He ended the evening by telling her she was beautiful and kissing her hand. Although it wasn't a real kiss, he did ask her out for horseback riding on Sunday. She figured that was a good start.

Now on Monday morning in her classroom, she felt as if the glow of her private time with Bogey still emanated off her. The munchkins seemed to be able to see it.

Hoping to distract them, and herself, she had to admit, from thoughts of marriage, when they finished arithmetic she announced her plan to sketch one child per day. The room was abuzz with approval.

She drew a name from a brown paper bag she'd prepared beforehand, and a shy boy named Kenny was the pick of the day. Summer had hardly heard him say a peep and he'd never looked her in the eyes, so she was glad to have a chance to interact with him. He was the other child, besides Stella, that Miss Campbell wanted her to watch out for in case of abuse.

While the others paired up for arithmetic and counting, she took Kenny aside and had him sit on a stool by the window. She sat on a stool facing him with a sketch pad and charcoal pencil in hand.

"Okay, Kenny, if you sit as still as possible and look out the window, this will only take a few minutes."

Summer found the boy to be not sullen and not happy, but unreadable. Unlike most five-year-olds, he showed little emotion in class, dutifully following orders but giving up not one clue as to how he felt about them. It made her think a lot of emotion might be bottled up inside the lad.

She concentrated on her work, finding it easy to draw his curly brown hair and darling features. Within a few minutes, she had a good rendering of him.

"Here you go, Kenny. What do you think?" She turned the sketch pad around so he could see it.

Slowly, as if not sure he wanted to see, he turned on his stool and looked at it. His eyes widened slightly for an instant. He shot Summer a glance, the first he'd ever given her, and quickly looked back down at his likeness.

"Do you like it?" she asked.

"Yes."

He sounded sincere and his response pleased her so much she had an urge to ruffle his unruly hair. But, of course, she didn't know if he'd like that or if it would scare him half to death. So, she kept her hands to herself, something she constantly told her students to do.

"Here," she said, tearing the sketch off the pad at the top, and handing it to him. "Let's go hang it on the wall by yours."

When the two drawings hung side-by-side and they stood there admiring them, Summer saw one corner of his mouth arch up, almost a grin. He reached out to touch the edge of the paper but pulled his hand back.

"Hey, that's nifty." Stella had left her seat, a breach of the rules, and come up behind them.

Kenny looked at Stella and Summer realized he seemed uncertain around most people, but not this girl. "Yeah," he said to Stella, "that's me."

"You look good, Kenny," Stella reassured him.

He nodded, but Summer's attention became drawn away by a room that had gone topsy-turvy, like a broken dam. Now that one student had broken away, they all did. Summer gave up and let them break for recess. As usual, Kenny trailed behind while most of the class bounded outside like monkeys.

"Come on," Stella said, coming back for him. She grabbed his hand and they took off.

Something tugged at Summer. She'd missed something with Kenny and had no idea how to figure out what it was. That child held secrets inside, confidences she needed to know to be able to help him. How she might unlock those secrets she did not know. But she refused to give up until she could make that child smile.

32

Deep in thought, Summer took Sydney Street as she rode her bike home after school. Even though there was a shorter route, truth was she wanted to see Hazel again, the romance novel writer. She found everything about the woman to be intriguing.

As luck would have it, Hazel sat on the porch of her blue craftsman-style house. She sipped from a straw in a tall glass.

"Come on up," she said, waving Summer up to her porch.

Struck again by the woman's beauty, with her white hair and stunning features, Summer parked her bike and trotted up the porch steps.

"Sit here," Hazel said, pointing to the rocker next to hers as she set down her glass and stood up, "while I go get you a glass of lemonade."

Hazel disappeared into her house, and Summer took a chair and rocked. The scent of lemon and lilacs filled the air, the aroma of the fruit drink sitting on the table and the lush bushes bordering the porch combining to please her senses. It was a pretty summer day. Summer let herself relax and enjoy it. Shortly, Hazel returned with a glass of lemonade and handed it over.

"Here you go. You deserve it after a long day with all of those children."

"Thank you." Summer drank through the paper straw and

marveled at the flavor of the cool liquid trickling down her throat. "Oh, that's good. That's the best lemonade I've ever had."

"I make it myself. The secret is a boatload of sugar." Hazel winked behind her granny glasses and imbibed herself.

"So, you know about my stint as Head Start teacher."

"Of course. Everybody knows. We also know you got stuck all by yourself when that silly Mrs. Lane stole the money and ran away with a truck driver. I'd bet my last dollar she'll come back with her tail between her legs, begging her husband to take her back."

"Do you think he will?"

"Probably. He always has before. But you don't want to talk about that, do you?"

Summer studied Hazel before answering. How this woman could read her mind, she did not know.

"No, I don't. I've been wondering if you lived here in the 1920s. You would have been… what? In your early twenties? You know all about the apartment, no doubt, what with the robbery and murder and all. We've been going through it and are curious about who lived there. I'm wondering if you know."

Hazel drew her eyes away from Summer, took a sip of her drink, and looked out at her small front yard, her eyes taking on a faraway gaze. Summer could see her going back in time, reliving days gone by.

"I'm sixty-five," Hazel said as she came back to the present. "I was born in 1900, so, yes, I was in my twenties during the '20s. Why are you so curious about who lived in the apartment?"

Summer told her about what they'd found, clothes and jewelry, except she omitted the story of the wedding dress. That felt too personal and too sad to share.

"My uncle found lots of papers but nothing with a name on it. There were newspaper clippings, mostly from the *Detroit Free Press*, about social events. And magazine articles she'd torn out and saved, mostly about fashion. But nothing that left clues about who she was."

Hazel looked out across her lawn again as Summer spoke, rocking and sipping her lemonade, taking it all in.

"The lilacs are especially fragrant this year, don't you think?"

Summer paused to adapt to the abrupt change of subject. "Yes. They're beautiful."

"It depends on our spring weather. If we get both rain and sun, they bloom magnificently.

"Now…" Hazel looked at Summer… "as for who lived in that apartment, I don't think people in town knew anything about that. People enjoyed the speakeasy here. We came here for it. We were from Detroit and went to lots of speakeasies there, too. My favorites were Tom's Tavern and Tommy's Detroit Bar. We drank. We smoked. We danced. There were plenty of people who followed the law and didn't partake, and there were those of us who lived for the bootleg gin to flow.

"I was young. Times were wild. Women had new freedoms. I admit, I had the time of my life."

"You said 'we.' Were you married?"

"Oh, no. I had a boyfriend. We were both from Detroit but were up here often. Then when he and I…" she took a deep breath… "when we broke up, I eventually bought this house and one in Florida for winters. The crash of '29 had happened, the 'Roarin' '20s' were over. I wanted to start a new life.

"When I started writing I put that history behind me. I still go to my place in Florida every winter, but West Branch is my home.

"And, yes, I was married, to answer what I suspect was your next question. He was a wonderful man. An insurance agent. Howard Hazen. My married name really is Hazel Hazen; it's not a nom de plume, like most people think. We met in Florida but Howard loved coming up here in the summertime as much I did. Unfortunately, he died young, only forty-five when he had a heart attack. We'd only been married a few years. I was thirty-five. I never married again."

"I did wonder. I'm so sorry that happened to you."

"So am I."

Summer sipped her drink, not knowing what more to say about such a tragic loss. She never knew what to say about death, so decided to go back to their former topic.

"Hazel, if you spent so much time in speakeasies, you must have met men from the Purple Gang. We think our robbery and the murder are related to them."

"Probably," Hazel agreed matter-of-factly. "They did run a lot of booze, and there was gambling, too. So that makes sense as the source of all that money I heard about that was stolen."

"What were the gang members like?"

The elder woman chuckled. "Well, I was young and impressionable. I thought them dashing and fascinating and… rich." She looked away again, pulling pictures out of her mind. "They wore tailor-made suits and fancy fedoras and shiny leather shoes. Their shirts and pocket handkerchiefs were white, and their ties were flashy. They were dark-haired and brown eyed, being Jewish after all, and ruggedly handsome. They had gorgeous girlfriends and threw money around like water. They'd started out as a bunch of street thugs who met in school before dropping out. They ended up being some of the most brilliantly devious businessmen gangsters you could ever meet. At that time in my life I couldn't imagine anything more exciting."

"Was your boyfriend a member of the gang?"

"Oh, my, no. 'Membership' wasn't for him."

"What did he do?"

"He ran his own business."

Summer had a much better picture of what the gang had been like, but still had no clue about the apartment. Yet, this Hazel herself was a delightful acquaintance. Summer certainly had never known a writer, especially a famous one.

"I have one of your books. I haven't had time to read it, but I hope to start it tonight. It looks good."

"Ah, when you finish that one I've got thirty more you can borrow."

"You write a lot."

"Yes. I suppose it could be said that I prefer living in my fantasy world to the real one. Except for my lilacs." She pointed to her bushes. "It's nature that always draws me back."

They smiled at one another, and finished their lemonades.

"Well, I have to get to the B&B," Summer announced as she stood up. "We have a movie producer and his assistant coming in this evening. He's going to use some of our settings for his movie about the Purple Gang."

Summer could have sworn she saw Hazel's chin quiver. "That's interesting," she said.

"Yeah, I'll keep you updated, if you don't mind my coming by every now and then."

"I don't mind at all. I'm done writing by this time of day. I enjoy the company. I enjoy your company."

Summer smiled. "Me, too. I've enjoyed getting to know you.

Well, I have to go. I'm the B&B maid. I've got to get rooms ready for those guests."

"Part of your punishment for dallying in a fountain, no doubt?"

"You know about that?"

"Oh, my dear, everyone knows about that. Phyllis at the hardware store has a cousin whose friend works at the sheriff's office in Traverse City. Don't worry about it. I, of all people, have no right to judge someone else's youthful foibles. We're kindred spirits, as far as I'm concerned."

"Thanks. That helps."

Summer waved as she rode away, happy to have an intriguing, if mystifying, new friend. As she turned the corner onto N. 4th Street, she stopped on the little bridge to look down over the rail. The clear creek water below ambled its way to the east as thoughts swirled through Summer's mind. She mulled over Hazel's story and became struck with the realization that the woman had been transparent in some ways, answering some of Summer's questions, and quite oblique in other ways, avoiding the question about whether or not she knew who'd lived in the apartment next to the speakeasy.

One more mystery to add to the pile.

33

"Perfect. All of it. Jillian, agree?"

Movie producer Monty Miles talked in snippets. It annoyed Summer.

"Uh huh," his assistant Jillian demurred, nervously chewing on a cuticle.

She hardly spoke at all. That annoyed Summer even more.

"Love the ballroom. The lobby. We'll use both. And the vestibule. And Jillian's guestroom."

Betty said, "Good. We're happy to have Mishigamaa Movies here. We've discussed the price of renting the whole place for a month, so I have a letter of agreement to that effect. Let's go down to my desk and get that signed."

The four of them stood in the ballroom, with movie-worthy romantic light from the opulent chandelier washing over them. As exciting as it was that a movie would be shot here, Summer was ready to wrap-up this tour so she could go to bed. As usual, she had to rise and shine early in the morning for school.

"Wait. The apartment. We haven't looked at it," Monty said, pointing with his long bony finger at the locked door on the far side of the room. Everything about the man in his mid-thirties was long and bony. "Jillian read about it. In the paper. She's my researcher."

"Oh, no. We're doing inventory in there. We did find some

clothes you might want to use in your movie, and I'll bring them out to show you tomorrow, but otherwise the apartment is off limits. Sorry." Betty's raspy voice remained firm. She wasn't going to kowtow to this guy, even if he was some kind of highfalutin' moviemaker.

"But… but I want it."

"I'm sorry, Mr. Miles. It's not available." Betty stood her ground.

The innkeeper headed out of the room, but Summer caught Monty looking back at that door. How did he know that was the door to the apartment? She'd read every newspaper article about their robbery and the murder, and none described the location of an entrance to the apartment. Something was off about this man. She didn't like him. It sounded as if Betty didn't, either.

"Jillian," Monty quipped. "Bed. See you tomorrow."

The chubby body of the assistant, who looked to be in her early thirties, noticeably relaxed at the command. She hustled into her room, the one next to Summer's, the one Bogey had occupied, and then Charlotte. Summer would have sworn Jillian felt relieved to escape the presence of her boss, quickly closing the door behind her and clicking the lock.

"Well, I have to get up early, so I'll turn in, too." Summer nodded at the remaining guest. "Mr. Miles, I'll see you tomorrow. Good night. Good night, Betty."

"Night," he said absent-mindedly as he and Betty started down the stairs.

It was ten o'clock, time for Summer to be in the land of Nod, but the meeting with Monty and Jillian had been so unsettling she didn't feel ready to close her eyes. She didn't know what she'd expected out of movie people, but it hadn't been what she got.

Maybe she'd expected a producer more like a handsome movie star, Paul Newman, Rock Hudson, or Troy Donahue. This guy was more like Boris Karloff. *Creepy. Spooky. Malevolent.* In his clipped vernacular.

He made her uncomfortable, in any case.

Needing time to wind down, she got ready for bed and looked around for the book Charlotte had packed for her. Finding it still in her suitcase under a *Cosmopolitan* magazine, she picked up *Once You Have Found Him* by Hazel Hazen. The blurb on the back promised a frolic into heartwarming romance. Not long ago Summer's response to that would have been "ick." Now she sat up against her pillows, opened the book, and began to read.

Catriona didn't want to fall in love. Really, she didn't. Lord Laird Logan was all wrong for her....

Before she knew it, she heard a car stop and someone get out on the street below. She went to the open window, looked down, and there stood Bogey by his cruiser.

"I saw your light," he said, trying not to be too loud in deference to the late hour. "Are you okay? It's eleven o'clock."

"Oh, my, I lost track of the time. I'm reading a really good book, by Hazel."

Hands on his hips, he smiled up at her. "Okay. As long as everything is okay."

"Yeah. I'm fine. I'll go to bed now."

Bogey didn't move, staring up at her.

She stared back.

"Good night, Bogey."

He hesitated. "Good night, Summer."

Sharing another "moment," as Charlotte had called it, Bogey eventually gave in, nodded, and got back into his car. Summer knew he needed to get back to the sheriff's office to end his shift and hand the cruiser off to Deputy Fitz, who would be starting his overnight duty.

Summer didn't leave the window until Bogey's car disappeared from sight.

Was it Hazel's influence with her "lovey-dovey" writing, as her student Hector would call it, or was the attraction so strong no outside influence was needed? Summer could feel herself thaw out—hell, heat up—over the idea of falling in love. Had she truly found *him*? Or was she lost in a fictional love story? If she was, she didn't ever want to find her way back to reality.

34

Kenny looked up at Summer with his big eyes encased in thick, black lashes and said, "Miss Summer, will you take me home and be my mommy?"

Reality struck like a slap in the face. Tears stung Summer's eyes, making her acknowledge that life as she knew it did not exist for all children. Her breath caught in the back of her throat. She hadn't expected this when the five-year-old came to sit beside her on the bus. He'd always been so quiet and reserved. Posing that question must have taken all the nerve he could muster.

It had been a fun day for the class, visiting a fish hatchery twenty miles outside of town. The best part for the kids was having lunch at a restaurant along the way. Most had been to the hatchery before; Summer was one of only a handful who had not.

She put her arm around the boy's shoulders, instinctively wanted to protect him. Yes, if things were different she would take him home and be his mother. If she was married and if she liked children and if there was so much as a remote hope of ever getting married.

"Kenny, do you have a mommy at home?"

With an expression that could only be described as lamentably grim, he shook his head.

"What happened to her?"

"She died." His voice cracked with emotion.

"Oh, Kenny, I'm so sorry. I didn't know that. When did that happen?"

"Last year."

"Do you live with your dad now?"

"Yeah." Gloom oozed out of his voice.

This must be why Miss Campbell had asked Summer to watch for signs of abuse for Kenny. Did his father abuse him now that the mother was gone? Had he abused him while she was alive? Had he abused her? Summer's suspicious mind made a giant leap to: had his abuse killed her?

Summer squeezed Kenny's forearm as a gesture of understanding, only to be shocked to see him recoil in pain. For the first time, she noticed he always wore long-sleeved shirts, even on warm days. *How could I have missed that?* she berated herself.

"Kenny, let me see what's wrong with your arm."

Obediently, he stuck it out. She unbuttoned the cuff and rolled up the sleeve of his shirt.

There Summer discovered a swollen, red, jagged lump the size of a ping-pong ball, that appeared to be incredibly painful. She was no doctor but thought it looked like a broken bone that had never been set. She rolled the sleeve back down.

"Kenny, do you have any other places that hurt?"

He nodded, looking at her intently again with those enormous, pleading eyes.

"Okay, honey, as soon as we get back to the school we're going to go see Miss Campbell. She'll help us go to a doctor to fix your arm and anyplace else that hurts. We'll get you all better. Okay?"

"My dad won't like it."

"Let me worry about your dad. I promise I won't let him hurt you." Summer had absolutely no idea how she would keep that promise. Call the sheriff? Run away with the child? Shoot that dirt-ball dad? Whatever it took, she would do it.

Kenny clung to her hand as they got off the bus in the school parking lot. Summer called Angela over and said she had to go to the principal's office with Kenny. The mother immediately grasped the meaning of this and said she'd take care of the rest of the crew.

Within twenty minutes Kenny, Summer, and Miss Campbell were in the emergency room of Tolfree Hospital. The doctor, a large man with enormous hands, talked to Kenny kindly as he gently poked and prodded. Kenny shivered with fear, even though the room was warm, but let the doctor examine his entire body.

When done, the doctor had a nurse help Kenny dress while he called the two women out into the hall. Another nurse appeared, and he told her to call social services and the sheriff. Understanding the gravity of the situation, the nurse hurried down the hall to do as instructed.

The doctor turned to Summer and Miss Campbell. "His arm is broken, probably a couple of weeks ago. We'll put him out and reset it. There are at least ten bruises on his body. They look like punches and slaps. I'm turning this over to law enforcement and social services. His father needs to go to jail."

Miss Campbell remained focused and solemn, but Summer gasped. "Oh my, why didn't I see this sooner? That poor boy."

"You didn't see it sooner," the doctor said, "because men like this are masters at hiding their brutality. And children are afraid to tell for fear of more beatings."

"How did his mother die?" Summer wanted to know.

"Supposedly, she fell down the stairs and broke her neck. We never believed that. We did everything we could to try to prove it was murder, but to no avail. There wasn't enough evidence to charge the man or to take his son away from him."

"That's why they told me," Miss Campbell said, "to watch out for Kenny. It's such a blessing, Summer, that you found this. Kenny's aunt and uncle, his mom's sister and her husband, have wanted Kenny ever since his mom's death. They're wonderful people. We've had them thoroughly checked out. They've gone to court but there was no legal way for them to get him. Now we have the evidence they need." She patted Summer's hand in assurance.

"I have to get back in there," the doctor said. "We'll start surgery as soon as the sheriff comes to witness the injuries and take photos. Do you want to stay with Kenny while we get him ready for the operation?"

Both women said, "Yes."

By eight o'clock that evening, with the shades drawn and the lights dimmed, Summer and Betty sat in stiff chairs at Kenny's bedside. Once Betty came and the principal knew Kenny was okay, she left for a school board meeting. Betty had heard about Kenny's surgery through the proverbial grapevine, and showed up to offer support.

Kenny had awoken a few times since the surgery, which the doctor proclaimed to be a complete success, but dozed most of the time. A clunky white plaster cast encased his forearm. Summer held his hand.

Looking at his innocent face and fragile body, she couldn't imagine how any parent could do this to their child. She'd said that before, but now she understood it firsthand. Now she knew the horrific agony some children live through. She knew the injustice of mistreating those who are so young they have no choice but to trust adults. She knew that men like Kenny's father deserved to hang. Anger, horror, disbelief, acquiescence, and resolve all mingled in her mind, leaving her ravaged with sadness and emotionally drained.

Sheriff Kowalczyk had taken photos, and then left to find the dad and arrest him; a social services worker had come and filled out a bunch of forms; the judge in town had already declared the child to be a ward of the aunt and uncle. An official adoption would be allowed. They lived a couple of hours south and were already on their way. A lawyer in town who represented the aunt and uncle, a Mr. Genks, waited for them in the hospital lobby.

Thrilled that the boy would go to people who loved him, at the same time Summer couldn't stand the thought of him being taken away from her. She had become his protector. His friend. And he had become hers. She felt profoundly honored that he had trusted her with his secret. Closing her eyes in exhaustion, she laid back her head and closed her eyes.

"Where's my son?"

The man's menacing voice echoed down the long, sterile hall. Summer's eyes flew open. Betty had already jumped to her feet by the time Summer could get up. Both women stood like sentries at the side of Kenny's bed. The boy awoke and in fear clung to the back of Summer's belt. Summer had never seen or heard Kenny's father before, but there was no doubt this was him.

"Where's my s-son?" the voice slurred.

"Mister, you must leave the building." Summer still couldn't see him but could tell that a brave nurse confronted the oaf.

"Go to hell." The clang of a metal tray or bowl hitting the wall rang out.

"I said get out."

Hail to that nurse, Summer thought. She was one feisty woman.

The surly bulk of a drunk appeared at the door.

"Get out of here," Betty seethed.

"Mister, I've had the sheriff called." The nurse was at his heels, pulsating with anger. Summer could picture her as a fearless Viking warrior woman, metal helmet on instead of a white nurse's cap.

"Get outta my way. I want my boy." The brute faced off with Betty, who stood closest to the door. The stench of stale booze followed him into the room.

Betty took one look at him and threw an upper cut, slugging him squarely underneath his chin. In his drunken stupor, that was all it took. He went down like a felled tree.

Three nurses congregated around the unconscious body. No one bothered to kneel down to check on him. One tunked his side with the toe of her white nurse's shoe.

"Damn." Sheriff Kowalczyk popped up at the door. "We've been looking everywhere for him. What happened?"

"Aw, nothing, really," the Viking warrior nurse said. "He's so drunk he fell down. He'll be okay. Take him away."

It was then that Summer saw Bogey. He nodded her way, then helped the sheriff drag Kenny's dad out of the hospital and into a cruiser, on his way to jail.

Kenny's stronghold on Summer's belt relaxed, and she sat down beside him on the bed. He was finally awake enough that she could explain that his aunt and uncle were coming for him. It gratified her to see his eyes brighten at the news.

"Do you like them?" she asked.

"Yeah. They were my mom's best friends. They love me and want me to live with them. They told me."

A nurse brought him supper and he ate rubbery, gelled food like a champ.

Shortly afterward, a sweet-faced woman and pleasant-looking man rushed in. The reunion between them and their nephew, their soon-to-be adopted son, stripped away any fear Summer had for Kenny's future.

Betty nodded at Summer. It was time for them to leave. Betty went to the bed first and said a sweet farewell. She took out a pen and signed his cast. She handed the pen to Summer.

Summer's heart filled with emotion when her turn came. She went to his bedside and gently laid a hand on his.

"Kenny, it's time for me to go, too. It's been an honor being your teacher. You are one great boy. I know you'll be happy in your new home. Goodbye." She signed his cast, "To a great boy, Love, your teacher, Miss Summer." She kissed his brow.

Kenny threw her a big smile. "'Bye," he said.

There it was, what Summer had waited for, that smile. She was ecstatic for him and, irrationally, at the same time felt a heart-wrenching loss. She had fallen in love with this child.

Kenny's aunt and uncle thanked them profusely, and the two women left. Outside the room in the hallway the lawyer, Mr. Genks, stood looking in the window at the family scene before them. "Don't worry about Kenny," he said. "His new parents are great people. He'll be a much loved little boy."

Summer nodded at the lawyer, and smiled at the nurses who'd come to their aid and covered for Betty.

Outside in the parking lot, Summer said, "You've got one hell of a swing there, Betty."

Linda Hughes

"Well, yeah, truth is I always wanted to do that to my old man. It feels good to finally get it out of my system."

35

"Betty, would you like more lemonade?" Hazel picked up the pitcher that sat beside her. The card table she'd brought out to the porch was covered in a creamy lace tablecloth and the drinkware was crystal.

"Yes, thank you." Betty skootched her glass over and Hazel filled it.

Hazel had arranged her porch so she and her guests could gather together for conversation. They had already told her the saga of Kenny, and the three women had kvetched about how terrible some parents were.

Now no one spoke for a few minutes, instead sipping their drinks, with Betty also smoking, and enjoying the peacefulness of the gentle rain that pitter-pattered around them. The light shower fell straight down like drips from faucets, seeing that there was no breeze, which added to the pleasant warmth of the afternoon.

Eventually Betty looked at Hazel and said, "I'm so glad you invited us over today. I needed a break. That movie producer, Monty, is driving me nuts. His demands are ridiculous. He's got equipment scattered all over the lobby, and his 'people' are constantly coming in and out. I asked Aleks to check him out and the guy does make legitimate movies, mostly historical, documentary type things used in schools. He does real movies, too, like this one about the Purple Gang."

Hazel paused, considering that, and said, "So, the movie is about the life and times of gang members, up until their demise. Is that it?"

"It's hard to tell," Summer said. "Conversations with him are like talking to a record that skips essential words. He's not very verbal. He says he sees things visually instead of with words."

"No," Betty interjected, "he says, 'Visually. I see. Pictures. Not words.'" Her brusk staccato delivery made her two companions laugh.

"Doesn't it seem oddly coincidental that he's making a movie here about the gang suspected of being linked to your robbery and the murder?" Hazel reiterated what Summer and Betty had been noodling over all week.

It was Friday afternoon, and it had been a hectic week at the B&B with Monty and Jillian bustling around picking out precise settings for movie scenes, and endlessly hassling Betty and Summer in the process. Since the happening with Kenny, school had gone well and Summer fell into a routine of waitressing in the café for a few minutes each morning to help out during crunch time before she had to leave, teaching at Head Start from eight o'clock until early afternoon, stopping at Hazel's for a short break, housekeeping at the B&B, supper with Betty in the closed café (Joey always left them something), and evenings of sorting through the apartment with Betty. And amongst all that, juggling Monty's demands.

"Water." "Pop." "Snacks." "Got cookies?" Everything he demanded he could get for himself.

In order to get a break, Betty had hired one of the switchboard operators who worked for the telephone company, which was housed in the upstairs of the bank across the side street,

North 3rd Street, from the B&B. From her side bedroom window, Summer could see through the windows of the telephone company office, with the backs of the operators sitting in their tall chairs and their hands busily plugging and unplugging telephone lines. The operator Betty hired worked a shift at the phone company that ended at three in the afternoon, so she would be covering the B&B lobby and answering the phone until seven at night each weeknight. That was the only time Betty had away from the building, except Thursday nights from seven to nine when Summer covered for her while she attended her weekly AA meetings. Betty had told Summer and Hazel that until the B&B got up and running full speed she couldn't hire more help. Being so confined to the place, she especially appreciated the invitation to take a break on Hazel's porch.

"Aleks wonders that very same thing," Betty said in response to Hazel's question about the odd coincidence of a movie being made about the gang, in their town, at this time.

"And so do we," Summer added.

"If I were writing this into a book," Hazel said, "I wouldn't believe that's a coincidence. I'd say this Monty has something up his sleeve."

"We think so, too, but we can't find a thing to prove that," Summer lamented. "I confess, when I clean his room, I snoop as much as I dare. I haven't seen anything but movie stuff—scripts, notebooks, and photos of settings—stuff like that. He's such a slob, though, I could be missing something. And Jillian's room doesn't have anything except her suitcase, piles of scripts, and a box full of old newspaper articles and reports and books on the Purple Gang."

"We gave them some of the clothes from the apartment, for

movie costumes," Betty explained. "I thought Monty would be grateful, but he keeps grumbling about wanting into the apartment. I have no intention of letting him in there. Everything of value is gone, like the jewelry. Harry and Ellie took that to be appraised. And the money, of course, is gone, we know not where. There's some beautiful antique furniture, but Monty could hardly carry that away by himself. There's nothing else of great value, so I'm not afraid of him stealing. I simply don't want the creep in there."

"The place has become almost sacred to us, as if a family member lived there and we need to protect her somehow," Summer added. "Did I tell you about the beautiful wedding dress we found? It had never been worn. Our girl planned on getting married but didn't."

Hazel's eyes misted and her voice became soft. "That's so sweet, the way you feel about 'her.' No, you didn't mention that you'd found a wedding dress."

"It's fabulous. We'll show it to you sometime. But I don't want Monty the monster seeing it." Betty stubbed out her cigarette in the crystal ashtray on the table. "I swear, he's up to no good. Keep looking when you clean his room, Summer."

"I will. Let's hope I don't get caught and land in jail, again."

"Aleks would never arrest you," Hazel noted. "And that hunk of a deputy would rescue you and set you free if he did. How's that going?"

"How's what going?"

Hazel and Betty shared a look of disbelief.

"I was in the ballroom that night you two danced. Don't act innocent with me," Hazel teased.

Summer smiled. "We have a date this Sunday, his day off. We're going riding. He still has two horses on the farm and I miss mine terribly. I usually ride almost every day in the summertime. So, we'll see how it goes...."

Now Hazel and Betty grinned at each other.

"Uh huh," Betty said, "we'll see."

"And you'd better let us know, young lady. I need some juicy bits for the story I'm writing."

"Oh, pfft, you," Summer sluffed them off, embarrassed. Although, she secretly hoped Hazel was right and there would be some juicy bits to the date.

"Summer," Hazel said, "I don't know much about your family. I know quite a bit about Betty's family because she's from town here." Betty shook her head knowingly. "Even though we hadn't got to know each other before, I'd heard a lot about them.

"But other than Harry and Ellie O'Neill, and the fact that your mom runs the family business and your granddad is governor, we don't know much."

"Ah, well, my family history is fodder for some juicy stories. I don't know if you could even write it all up. My great-grandpa who is a hundred and three years old had a terrible first half of his life. I guess he had to live a long time to make up for it. His first wife was a horrible, evil woman, a murderess. But they didn't know for years what she'd done. I can't believe her blood flows in my veins. She spent the last fifteen years of her life in the asylum in Traverse City."

"Oh my, that's awful," Hazel said. "I guess if I wrote that up I'd call it *Secrets of the Asylum.*"

"Yes, that's it. My great-great-grandparents had a horrible time, too. Nobody knew about all their tragedies until my mom came home from the war and lived on the island for a few years, where they'd lived. They were immigrants who were duped and abused and, well, you get the picture. My mom kept uncovering more and more secrets about them, too."

"Ah, *Secrets of the Island*," Betty suggested.

"I might steal that," Hazel said, lifting her glass in acknowledgement. Betty clinked glasses with her.

"I suppose we all have secrets," Summer said, hesitating. "Hazel, I asked you before if you knew who might have lived in our apartment during the '20s. You didn't really answer my question."

"Ah, I've 'foiled' the case, as they say in murder mysteries." Hazel's eyes twinkled. "You caught me. It's true, I intentionally didn't answer your question."

She still didn't answer the question, so Summer asked again. "And? Who lived there?"

"Give me a minute." Hazel rose and went into the house.

"What on earth?" Betty queried.

Summer shrugged. "I don't know."

The elder woman returned with a well-worn hatbox overflowing with frayed pictures, yellowed newspaper articles, and wrinkled notes.

"I found this today," she said, laying it on the table. "I'd forgotten all about it. Then when I remembered I wasn't sure I still had it. So I rummaged through an old trunk and, lo and behold, there it was. Take it. See if it helps you figure out what went on in that place of yours."

With the hatbox secured in the basket of her bike, Summer rode home that afternoon fully aware that Hazel had not answered her question… again.

36

Summer, Betty, Bogey, Aleks, and Joey sat in the closed café, Hazel's hatbox in the center of their table. Everyone shuffled through the items for a third time, stopping to read, and then passing their find along.

Joey had stayed over to get ready for a big day the next day, Saturday, and had fixed supper for the two women. Summer had come to like Joey during her brief morning gigs as waitress. Stowed away back in the kitchen, customers never saw his ever-present white sailor's cap and the cigarette perpetually hanging out of his mouth. He smoked them down so low that in the end a butt looked like a jagged tooth hanging out over his lip. But the man could cook like nobody's business.

When Summer opened the hatbox, Joey became intrigued and asked if he could look, too, so that was how he joined the group. Betty had called the sheriff once they saw the contents, and Bogey had innocently stopped by for a break during his shift. So, quite a group had gathered to try to figure out what this collection of memorabilia meant.

Betty had locked the door between the café and B&B lobby in order to keep Monty out, who acted like he owned the place. Betty said, "He might want a cracker, or a toothpick, or some other ridiculous thing." They could hear him out there moving equipment and hollering at Jillian, but did their best to ignore the annoyance.

Focusing on the articles, photos, and notes in front of them, Aleks said, "It's obvious that Hazel was right in the middle of things here." He tapped one of the many 1920s photos of the ballroom speakeasy upstairs, this one with customers lining a long bar lifting their glasses for the camera. There were others of a crowded dance floor, the band, a flapper twirling her long strand of pearls, and people sitting at tables drinking. Summer and Betty kept looking for women dressed in any of the clothes they found in the closet but didn't see any.

"Yes, she was right here," Betty said. "She's never denied that."

"But she's tightlipped about what she knows," Summer said.

"A lot of these old newspaper articles about the gang are the same ones we have copies of from the Detroit Police," Bogey observed.

"Yeah, if she bothered to keep all of this about the Purple Gang, there had to be a reason." Aleks lit up a fresh Chesterfield. The ashtray on the table was full of his, Betty's, and Joey's smashed butts. Aleks blew a perfect circle of smoke into the air and pointed at Bogey with his gasper. "It's too late tonight, but we'd better have a talk with Hazel in the morning."

"Hey," Betty said, pointing to some numbers scribbled in pencil, barely legible after all these years, on the side of an otherwise blank scrap of paper. "Could this be a safe combination?"

Aleks grabbed the piece of paper and drew it in to get a closer look. "It's hard to tell, but it looks like…." Joey grabbed the pencil from behind his ear, pulled an order pad out of his apron pocket, and wrote as the sheriff read off the numbers: 6, 9, 48, 1, 7. "Or is that a four at the end?" Aleks wondered, squinting at it. "Nope.

It's a seven. Damn, Betty, you're right. That might be a combination. Let's go try it."

They all barreled upstairs. Betty unlocked the apartment door, and the sheriff led the way to the closet. He motioned for Bogey, the tall one, to try the combination. Joey handed over the piece of paper and Bogey closed the safe door, which had been left open, and tried the combination. It didn't work. He tried again. It didn't work again. One more try, and another failure to open the safe.

"Try it with a four on the end instead of seven, in case I read that wrong," the sheriff suggested.

After three tries, it was clear that wouldn't work, either. Badly disappointed, they left the apartment, Betty locked the door behind them, and they went back downstairs to the café. Aleks told Bogey he wanted to talk to him about visiting Hazel in the morning, and they left. Bogey hardly had time to throw Summer a quick wave goodbye.

Joey shook his head. "This is one mystery that may never be solved. Well, I've gotta get some sleep, what with that whole movie crew coming in tomorrow. Mr. High-and-Mighty Monty has informed me they'll be here by lunchtime and I need to be ready. La-di-da.

"There are some bakery chocolate chip cookies left, in case you want a bedtime snack. Good night, ladies." He left by the back door.

"How about it? Cookies?" Betty headed for the kitchen.

"When have I ever turned down chocolate chip cookies?"

It might have been the sugar or it might have been the unsolved mystery. Or, it might have been fantasies about Bogey. Whatever it was that bothered her, Summer couldn't sleep. At midnight she got up and looked out at the Midstate Theatre.

Tommy sat on the roof by the marquee, smoking away. He turned his head toward her, smiled upon seeing her, and waved. She waved back. The teen flicked away his cigarette butt and crawled back inside the window behind him.

Glad she'd stopped in at the McGowan Ace Hardware store a couple of days earlier to buy a transistor radio, on her uncle's charge account, of course, she tuned it to her favorite radio station, WLS 890 out of Chicago. She missed Dick Biondi, her favorite DJ, who fostered her love of rock-and-roll when she was in junior high and discovered the station. Dick, however, had moved to a station in California not long before. The new DJ was okay but, like so many teens, she missed Dick. He'd always been the first to play rock-and-roll singers like Elvis Presley and Jerry Lee Lewis, and even those rascals The Beatles.

Tonight the DJ played Elvis' oldie "I Can't Help Falling in Love," causing Summer to ache with a feeling she couldn't quite describe. A silly crush? Simple lust? Or was it love?

She didn't know.

Suddenly, she thought she heard something in the vestibule. Jillian had gone to bed an hour earlier, but maybe she needed something. Summer popped her head out her door. Jillian's door remained closed and darkness enshrouded the anti-room. She padded out and flicked on the ballroom chandelier. Nothing. Standing still, she listened.

Was that a noise in the apartment?

She went to the apartment door, skirting around lights and furniture and props that now littered the floor for an upcoming scene of the movie. She tried the handle, even though she'd seen Betty lock it. It was still locked.

Stepping back, she looked around. She must be imagining

things, she decided, probably caused by sleep deprivation. She needed rest.

Back in her room, she vowed not to scare herself like that anymore. There was nothing in the apartment anyone would want. No one was in there.

She heard the soothing whistle of the two o'clock train as she laid her head on her pillow and finally fell fast asleep.

37

"May I please see the dress?"

Summer looked up at the woman standing in the doorway of the apartment. She clutched the rope handle of another old-fashioned hat box, this one dangling at her side.

"Hazel. Good morning." Summer took measure of the situation, realizing that although this unexpected visit surprised her, it did not shock her. The pieces of the puzzle had been there, one-by-one falling into place. This was the final piece that completed the picture. "Of course you can see the dress. It's over here."

Summer had arisen early and, after a short stint helping serve breakfast in the café, decided to do more inventory in the apartment. It was only eight-thirty, and yet her dear new friend stood before her.

Wordlessly, Summer went to the closet and pulled out the garment bag. She hung it from a nail on the wall near the front window, where a picture had been taken down. Golden morning sunlight cascaded in to highlight the scene.

Without moving beyond the doorway, Hazel opened the hatbox and pulled out a satin cap with a long lace veil. She dropped the box to the floor and used both hands to place the cap on her head with the veil trailing behind her.

Slowly yet purposefully, like a bride marching down the aisle to her groom, Hazel glided across the room toward the dress that had no doubt been meant to be hers on her wedding day. A wooden floorboard creaked in protest along the way. Ironically, or perhaps intentionally, Hazel wore white slacks and a while silk blouse, her flouncy white hair somewhat tamed by the cap. Reaching the bag, she slowly unzipped it, and with the touch of one fingering fairy dust, she pulled out the dress and grazed her hands over the delicate fabric. Her cap and veil matched the dress perfectly.

Summer remained silent, letting this woman cherish her memories in peace. Or were the memories so tragic there would never be peace? Perhaps this reunion would allow Hazel to put any painful recollections to rest.

"It's beautiful, isn't it?" Hazel spoke without turning around.

"Yes. Very."

"I'm one lucky woman that I never got to wear it, even though it broke my heart at the time." She turned around and Summer found no tears in her eyes, no regret in her voice. She took off the cap with its veil and tossed it onto a dusty chair.

"You'd better call the sheriff. He and Bogey were going to come to my house at nine, but I'd rather talk to them here, so you and Betty can hear my story, too. It's a long story, so I only want to tell it once."

Twenty minutes later, the story began.

"I was a reckless, restless teenager, always looking for the next bit of fun, the next thrill. I will say, I had chutzpah. By the time I was sixteen, I had a twenty-one-year-old boyfriend who would get me into bars with him. It was in 1918 at Digby's Social Room in Detroit that I first laid eyes on Issur Aaronson. Izzy, everybody called him. Digby's was a speakeasy by then, seeing that Prohibition had started early in Michigan. I was sitting there innocently having a drink with my boyfriend when Izzy strode in, tall, dark, and handsome. Every girl's dream. So confident. He was in his late twenties, which I considered to be sexy and mature. He came in, and out of two hundred people in the room, his eyes fell on me. That was it. I was totally smitten."

Although Hazel's reminiscences started with details about an era that might not matter in solving the mystery of the robbery and murder in West Branch, Michigan, in 1965, Summer could see that everyone at the table in the apartment sat there utterly mesmerized by her telling of this tale. Sheriff Kowalczyk, Aleks, took notes and smoked one of his Chesterfields. Deputy Bush, Bogey, leaned forward studying the storyteller's face, his elbows resting on his knees. Betty relaxed in her chair, calmly smoking a Winston.

Summer didn't miss the serendipitous spectacle made by the sun shining in on the wedding dress, still hanging by the window. Hazel continued her account of what led to that dress being there in the first place.

"By midnight that night I was Izzy's new girl, a gangster's moll. I couldn't imagine anything more exciting." Hazel looked from face-to-face around the table to take their measure of shock and judgement. None was discernable.

Unabashedly, she continued, "I'd heard his name but had never seen him before. So, I knew he was high up in the Purple Gang. I didn't totally lie…" she glanced at Summer… "when I said he wasn't a mere member. He was one of the originators of the whole shebang, like a vice-boss under the four brothers, the Burnsteins, who were the leaders.

"He met a couple of the Burnstein brothers in reform school in Detroit, a sort of vocational school for boys who got in trouble.

"You do know, don't you, that this was a Jewish gang?"

Everyone nodded.

"They were Jewish. I'm Jewish. This was all happening in a neighborhood where there were Eastern European Jews who'd immigrated and didn't always know the language or American ways. They were afraid of the police, so wouldn't ask for help. I can't believe I let myself be associated with a man who did such horrible things to my own people. And to anybody else. There's no excuse for me, but I admit I was young, selfish, and stupid."

Hazel paused, looked over at the wedding dress, and sighed. Every set of eyes in the room followed her gaze. After a moment, she continued, facing them again.

"Anyway, Izzy said that the vocational school was merely an excuse to get them out of the public school system because everybody was afraid of them. At first they were coached by some men who were mob leaders; they ran errands for them. Those men did everything you can imagine the mob doing. They even ran crap games in the schoolyard during the summer.

"The Burnsteins and Izzy and their growing group of thugs also did their own things, like extorting money from shop owners and rolling drunks, that kind of thing. They terrorized the neighborhood. By the time they quit that school they had their own gang. The name Purple Gang came from them throwing dye on clean laundry when the mob was at war with cleaners who wouldn't join the mob's trade association.

"Of course, I learned about all that later. By the time I met him, the gang was a smoothly operating organization. I was completely infatuated with Izzy, even though I knew he was married. He offered me money, clothes, furs, jewelry, booze, travel, excitement, and what I thought was love. I felt certain he'd leave his wife and marry me. I suppose that's what every 'moll,' every mistress, thinks.

"We had an apartment in Detroit, right on the river, and this one here. Everything was in a bogus law firm's name, so we couldn't be traced. Or so we thought. But I'll get to that in a minute.

"It was a fairytale life at first. The gang was making money hand-over-fist. None of us could do anything to spend it fast enough. Burlap bags full of money were stored here, stacks and stacks of them all over the apartment. Hundred- and thousand-dollar bills mostly.

"There were a few scares with Al Capone's Chicago Outfit, but then the two gangs started working together. I stayed away from the business end of things, so I can't help with any information about how they operated. I truly have no idea.

"We traveled sometimes, to Miami Beach and Chicago and even New York once where we met F. Scott Fitzgerald and Zelda. He liked hobnobbing with famous people."

Summer thought of the copy of *This Side of Paradise* with Fitzgerald's florid autograph, so innocently sitting on a shelf in their own little library downstairs.

"I liked it here in West Branch. It was different: peaceful during the day. I could walk around downtown and relax without worrying about other gangs or people I knew asking questions. People here knew I was a visitor from Detroit, but there were lots of those, so I wasn't anything all that unusual. I don't think anybody from town knew a gangster owned this apartment and that his girlfriend stayed here.

"Unlike the quiet days, though, weekend nights here were a blast. We spent our time in the speakeasy. And then, instead of coming through the door between the speakeasy and apartment…" she pointed to the interior door… "we'd go out and sneak up the back stairs so no one would see us. We had our own romantic hideaway here."

"That was for the first two or three years. Then Izzy started leaving me here alone more and more. He didn't take me home to Detroit anywhere. He evaded the topic of marriage. He wanted me to dress certain ways and act certain ways, and no matter what I did, it didn't please him anymore. He questioned everything I did. He'd push me and slap me. By the time I was twenty-five years old I thought I was the most stupid, ugly, inept woman alive. Because that's what Izzy said I was.

"I drank too much. I spent too much time alone. And I was miserable, all the time thinking it was all my fault, that if I could just pull myself together I would be worthy of Izzy's love again. I'd lost all my chutzpah.

"Then one day he showed up out of nowhere and told me he wanted to get married. I was thrilled. He even brought me the wedding dress and veil." She pointed to the beautiful satin and lace gown hanging on the wall. "We were going to get married the next day and were in bed that night when…"

Hazel took a long breath and said, "May I have a glass of water, please?"

"Sure." Betty jumped up, went to the kitchenette sink, and poured a tall glass. She gave it to their storyteller and sat back down.

Everyone watched as Hazel gulped down half the water in the glass. She took off her glasses, laid them on the table, and rubbed her eyes.

"Are you okay?" Aleks asked.

"Oh my, here I am a writer. My life is made up of telling make-believe stories. But, somehow, telling my own story seems impossible. I don't know if I can do it."

38

"Take your time, Hazel," the sheriff said. "We're in no rush."

She nodded, drank more water, put her glasses back on, and said, "Okay. Here goes.

"It was the day he showed up unexpectedly and brought me the wedding dress. We were in bed that night. All of a sudden the door burst open." She pointed to the back door that led down the stairs to the alley. Her eyes taking on a glazed mien, Summer could see that Hazel no longer merely told her story, she relived it. "A woman stormed in. It was dark but I could see the shadow of a gun in her hand. I screamed. Izzy jumped out of bed, naked as a jaybird, and grabbed for the gun. It went off.

"The woman fell to the floor, dead.

"I was so confused. 'Who is that?' I kept asking. Of course, I assumed it was his wife. Ex-wife, seeing that he was marrying me. Izzy ignored me and made a phone call." She pointed to the antique cradle phone sitting on the small table of a Victorian gossip bench. "Before I knew it, two of his gang members were here helping him roll the body up into the bloody Persian carpet. They carried it down the stairs and out to a car, and drove away."

She paused and looked over at the melancholy wedding dress.

"I never saw Izzy again."

The room fell silent.

Eventually the sheriff said, "What did you do next?"

She looked at him and shrugged. "You mean besides cry?"

He nodded.

"Well, let's see…For the first few weeks I stayed here holed up in the apartment, terrified. I had no way of contacting Izzy, not even a phone number.

"At night I'd hear all the commotion in the speakeasy next door, of course, but was afraid to go in there.

"Eventually, I got cabin fever and became braver. I'd go into the speakeasy at night to drink. I begged the manager to contact Izzy for me, but he swore he didn't know how. Somebody else always contacted him, he said, not Izzy.

"I got brave enough to walk around town during the day. Everybody was so nice to me. Storekeepers were friendly. People said hello on the street. I'd see people who came to the speakeasy and they'd smile at me, like we had a common bond of sneaking into that place.

"I stopped wearing my flashy clothes and fancy jewelry. I only pulled out my furs when winter came and it got freezing cold. I clung to the fantasy that Izzy was laying low and would be coming for me soon. A year went by.

"I told people around town I liked it here so much I didn't want to be a visitor anymore, and they helped me find a house. I loved my little blue home from the instant I saw it.

"Now, mind you, I still held onto a glimmer of hope that Izzy was coming back. Truthfully, I thought he'd come back for the money, if not for me. But that glimmer faded day by day, month by month, and eventually after a couple of years that hope died altogether. I could no longer avoid the fact that I'd been abandoned. It was like a tragic scene out of a Shakespearean play.

"I took the bus to Detroit three times. I couldn't find anyone in the Purple Gang down there who would so much as talk to me, let alone help me find Izzy. I came back here each time, heartbroken."

She went on to tell how she slowly moved money out of the apartment, ending up with footlockers full of it in the basement of her small house on Sydney Street. She had no idea who paid for the apartment but figured she'd be kicked out at some point, so secured her financial future. She didn't want anything else from the place, not her clothes or the furniture or the jewelry. Nothing. It all held retched memories. But the longer there was no Izzy, the bolder she became about transferring money. It looked as if no one was ever going to come for it. Eventually, she had all of it except what was in the safe.

"I've spent a lot of the dough in my lifetime, but I still have two footlockers full of hundred- and thousand-dollar bills stored in the basement." She shrugged. "I make enough now as a writer that I don't need that 'footlocker loot' anymore. I give a lot to charities. I donate anonymously to the school. I give anonymous scholarships to kids from here going to college. I paid off my aunt's house in Detroit for her and I sent her a monthly allowance. That was until she needed to go to a nursing home. I pay for the best, of course, so she gets great care. I've given annual donations to the Shriners Hospitals for Children since the '30s. Now I give to Danny Thomas' new children's hospital, too, St. Jude. I've tried to do good things with all that mullah. I paid to keep the Head Start program going this summer, too."

Hazel smiled at Summer, drank the rest of her water, and looked around the table to see how her story was settling in. She went on to explain that a couple more years went by and she bought a place in Florida to go to during winter. It was there she met "an insurance agent of all people," and fell madly in love.

"It was real love this time," she said. "He was my rock. By being a kind, gentle man he made me realize that I'd been an abused young woman at the hands of Issur Aaronson. Unfortunately, my husband died after only a few years of marriage. I could never marry again. He was the love of my life.

"My experience with a gangster taught me that no woman should ever be treated with such brutality. That's why the heroines in my books are always strong women who determine their own fates. They don't put up with any malarkey. My husband salved my wounds and writing healed me."

Sheriff Kowalczyk nodded. "You're reminding me of what I was told by a police detective in Detroit who specializes in working with gangs. We had a long phone conversation where he explained that some kids join because they're young and misguided. Others join because they come from bad families and they're looking for a sense of belonging, a sort of family. But it doesn't matter why someone joins, when they're young it's easy for them to become so deeply entrenched they don't see any other options in life, even when they realize the gang is wrong.

"It seems the same can happen with women in bad relationships. Walking away isn't seen as a possibility."

"Yes. That's precisely the way it was. I couldn't imagine leaving Izzy. At that time in my life he was my everything. I *let* him become my everything, my whole world. I had nothing but him, even though I was raised by my wonderful aunt after my mom died when I was a little girl. My aunt was very good to me. I loved her then and I love her still, even though her mind is gone and she doesn't know me anymore. But when I was stuck with Izzy the fact that I cared so much for my aunt made it impossible for me to tell her I'd been such a fool. I felt embarrassed. Stupid. I never asked anyone for help. I certainly never went to the police to tell them about the money or the murder. I couldn't fathom doing such a thing."

The sheriff patted her hand. "Well, you've done it now. I thank you. I know this was hard for you."

Hazel took a deep breath. "Actually, it feels good to let go of it. I hope I can stay here after all this. I love West Branch and the quiet life it offers me. It's the perfect place to focus on my writing. I always say that West Branch is my North Star, my orienting point in a spinning world. From here I can always find my way. It's my home.

"But, after all these years I had no desire to come back to this apartment or remember the horrible things that happened here so long ago. However, a man has been murdered, so I finally decided I had to shore myself up and answer at least some of your questions for you.

"Now that you've heard my story, though, you see that I have nothing to offer that will help solve your case." She looked at Aleks apologetically. "I have no idea what happened to Izzy. I don't know why he suddenly asked me to marry him or who the dead woman was or how she came to be here. And I certainly don't know who took the money from the safe and ended up murdered in the cemetery. I can't help you.

"Will you need to arrest me for stealing all that money?"

The sheriff stubbed out his cigarette, his second since the beginning of the telling of the story. "Hardly. First of all, there's no way of knowing where the money originated." He shrugged with his palms up. "It was left to you. So, it's yours. Even if there were any charges to be pressed, the statute of limitations has long since run out. I'd say you more than earned that fortune.

"The fact that I have a Purple Gang member's name now helps a lot. I can pass that on to the Detroit police and see if they can make a connection to what happened here. A relative, or inheritor, or somebody connected to him who may have known about the money in the safe, and come into possession of the combination."

Hazel nodded, then looked at Summer. "You weren't surprised when I showed up here today, were you?"

"Not really. There were so many clues that I couldn't put together yet. You didn't answer my questions about who lived here. And then when you came in today and walked toward that dress, I realized you always wear Chanel No. 5. On your porch, it's mixed with the scent of lilacs and lemonade, but today I knew it belonged here, in this apartment."

Hazel smiled. "You would have figured it out eventually.

"Well, sheriff, are we done?"

Aleks pulled a slip of paper out of his shirt pocket. "I just thought of a way you might still be able to help us. These numbers: we thought they might be the combination to the safe, but they didn't work. Do you know what they are? We found it in your hatbox." He handed over the paper.

Hazel studied it. "No, I don't remember it. It doesn't look familiar. I never opened the safe. Sorry, I can't help."

"That's okay." Aleks stuffed the paper back into his shirt pocket.

"Wait," Hazel said. "Izzy sometimes stuck things in that box when he was in too much of a hurry to get to his own safe. Maybe it was his. It seems like I remember him talking to one of his wiseguys once, saying they wrote to each other in code. They were laughing that most of the guys weren't smart enough for a real code, so they simply wrote things backwards."

The sheriff whistled. "It's worth a try." He shot up out of his chair, went into the closet, and pulled the string to turn on the light, the rest of the raft at his heels like ducklings waddling after their mother. "This won't help us find the intruder, but at least we'll know how he got into the safe."

Bogey went to the tall shelf, raised his hand to turn the lock, and halted. "Ah, Aleks."

"Yeah?"

"The safe is open."

"It can't be. We left it locked. We couldn't get it open."

"I know. But it's open."

"What? No. That's impossible. How…? What in tarnation is going on here?"

The others stood jammed up behind them, having not one word to offer that would answer the sheriff's questions.

Slowly, Bogey pulled a piece of folded paper out of the safe. Opening it, he read, "You are idiots."

Gasps arose from the flock of onlookers, and Sheriff Kowalczyk said, "What in hell…?"

39

Summer figured this was as close to heaven as she'd ever been.
She and Bogey didn't discuss her stint in jail, murder, robbery, abused children, his ex-girlfriend Chastity, the batty movie-maker Monty, Hazel's amazing story, or the fact that someone thought they were idiots. They didn't talk about how scary it was that someone was getting into the apartment and the sheriff was having Fitz stationed every night outside the B&B until they could solve that mystery.

Instead, their conversation naturally gravitated toward affable topics like their mutual love of horses, and his love of farming and police work, and her love of painting and working at her dad's winery. Talking to each other turned out to be as easy as breathing.

Their date started after Summer returned from mass on Sunday. Bogey picked her up in his red-and-white 1962 Ford pick-up. He confessed that he was an "automobile aficionado" who bought the truck "brand-spanking-new" when he returned from serving as an Army Military Police officer in Vietnam.

"My truck is my baby. I make sure to feed it well, keep it clean, give it plenty of rest, get it regular check-ups, and let it know how much I love it," he'd said with a grin when she commented on its nice, smooth ride.

He'd told her not to have lunch, so the first order of business when they reached his farm was to eat. At a table on the broad porch of his lovely family home, overlooking acres and acres of farmland, now fallow, he unpacked a picnic basket that held a meal of chicken salad sandwiches with dried Michigan cherries served on slices of the bakery's French bread, Made Rite Potato Chips, and a bottle of Coca-Cola for her and one of Redpop for him.

"It's so pretty here," she commented as she chowed down. "And these sandwiches are scrumptious. Did you make this chicken salad yourself?"

He snorted. "Ah, that would be Joey's doing. That sailor can do anything in a kitchen."

"Yeah, he's amazing. I'm getting totally spoiled."

Her peripheral vision caught movement in the fenced-in meadow and she turned her head to see Bogey's golden-brown gelding prancing next to a stately gray mare. "Wow, they're both so beautiful. I tell you what: I'd like to sketch them. Would you mind if I came out some Saturday to draw? I'd love to paint them, too, but don't have all my paint supplies here. I can do that later from the sketches."

He looked at her thoughtfully. "You can come out here any time you want. Sketch. Paint. Sit around doing nothing. I don't care. Just come."

She smiled at him coquettishly. "Thanks."

They were both hearty eaters, so lunch was soon over and they were on to riding. Summer enjoyed her loveable mare, Molly. Bogey and Ranger took the lead walking down a path along the side of a field, trotting down a dirt road through the woods, and then crossing the state road to ride up to Pointer Hill, with its park and the large ramshackle barn next to it. They tethered the horses onto the split-rail fence, loosely enough so the beasts could munch on grass. Then they sat on opposite sides of a picnic table, which afforded them a view down the hill toward town.

"The first time I saw this view, I hated it," Summer confessed.

Bogey scanned the panoramic scene as if considering its merit.

"Now I think it's wonderful," she said by way of explanation.

"Good, because I love it here. I could be happy here for the rest of my life. But I'm not stupid. With our family farm being taken away, I know I'll probably have to find a job somewhere else. Aleks wants me to stay here, but I don't want to end up struggling like Fitz and Angela on a deputy's salary. Aleks is a great sheriff, so there's no opportunity there. It's time for me to set my sights on someplace else."

"Do you plan on having nine children like Fitz and Angela?" she said playfully.

"Bless them. I don't know how they do it. They're the most giving people I know. But, no, I don't plan on having nine kids. Especially if they're all boys."

"That's good, because there aren't many women like Angela who'd be willing to do that."

"How about you? Do you want kids someday?"

Summer was in some ways surprised at how quickly their conversation had dug in to become so deeply personal, but in other ways it was as comfortable as talking to a life-long friend.

"Yes. I do. The thing is, I don't especially like children." He chuckled, raising his eyebrows in deference to her candor. "I only have one brother but was raised with such a huge extended family I guess I got tired of noisy little people. But this summer has…" she looked at the sky in contemplation and then let her eyes come back to Bogey... "mellowed me. I still don't like the idea of a gang of children running around like hooligans, but I'm falling in love with my students one-by-one. I'm fascinated by them as young individuals. As I get to know them, each one has their own personality. My heart aches for some of them and swells with pride for all of them, especially because they try so hard. So, I guess I've learned that I might be able to handle a couple of kids of my own someday."

"I'm sure you will be able to."

"As long as Angela is there."

They chuckled.

"Tell me about your family," he requested. "I know the basics, of course. I know your Uncle Harry and Aunt Ellie from their visits here to set up the B&B. I know the family is rich and your grandfather is governor. And I've heard your dad runs a winery?"

A stab of homesickness hit Summer at the mention of her parents. She missed them.

"Yeah, my dad grows grapes and makes great wine. He's German and British, so he built his winery like a model of a medieval European castle. It's beautiful, out there on Mission Peninsula outside of Traverse City. The view of the bay is fantastic. People come all summer long to sit on the patio and drink wine, and take in the peace and quiet. Nice days during spring and fall, too. It's beautiful in the wintertime, but then people sit inside by this huge stone fireplace." She drew a big square with her hands. "You'll have to come see the place."

"I'd love to."

"My dad isn't my real dad." He seemed surprised by this. "My mother and real father had only been married one day during World War II when he was killed. She was a Red Cross nurse and he was a soldier; they were both in Tunisia in Northern Africa. It's a long story, but, essentially, a German soldier killed my father, tried to kill my mother and Uncle Harry, and she killed the German soldier. It's always haunted her. She doesn't talk about it, except to tell me the story one time when I was sixteen and I kept asking questions about my real father. My stepdad was there, too. He looked like a Nazi, but he was really a British spy. He helped my mom and Uncle Harry escape. When I was two years old, my stepdad came to Michigan and looked up my mom to see if she was okay, and they fell in love. So he's the only dad I've ever known."

Bogey stared at her. "Wow. That's one of those stories that if you read it in a novel you wouldn't believe it could ever be true. But I've been in war, thankfully only for twelve months, but I know very strange things can happen in the chaos.

"Do you like your stepdad?"

"Oh my yes, I love him. I don't think of him as a stepdad. He's my dad.

"My whole family is huge. I have so many cousins I hardly know some of them. Our great-grandpa—we call him Popo—is a hundred and three years old. He lives in his house on Mackinac Island. Harry and Ellie live right behind him. He's a wonderful old gent."

Bogey whistled. "A hundred and three. I hope to meet him someday."

"I'd like that.

"What about your family? How did you get named Bogey?"

"That's a story I've heard all my life. My parents' first date was to a little-known Humphrey Bogart movie in 1932, *Love Affair*. They admired 'Bogey' and thought he'd become famous someday.

Consequently..." he framed his body with his hands, "my name is Bogart James Bush.

"My parents are salt-of-the-earth folks who both come from generations of farmers. I have one sister, married with three children. They all live in Cheboygan now."

Summer had never been to that town, but knew it to be on Lake Huron, on the tip of the index finger of the left-hand mitten of Michigan's lower peninsula. It was maybe two hours away.

Bogey went on to explain that his parents had been devastated upon learning that the government would be taking their land for an interstate, but they were practical people. They'd taken the money they'd been paid and bought a smaller farm.

As he finished his explanation about his family, Bogey took Summer's hand in his. He didn't speak, choosing instead to take in her face. Summer thought she might "swoon" again, what with her whole body tingling at his gentle touch. Slowly, as if reveling in each moment of anticipation of the pleasure to come, Bogey stood up, lifting her hand so she would stand, also. They walked out from their seats on either side of the picnic table and there, with the quaint charm of Pointer Hill surrounding them, they kissed for the first time.

A car pulled into the gravel driveway not far away and parked by the obsolete well. Summer and Bogey forced themselves to part.

"Let's go back to the house," he suggested.

She nodded. They mounted their horses as a family came toward the picnic table with a picnic basket. The riders bid the family a good afternoon and headed for the farm.

With Summer's senses on full alert, the steady pulse of Molly's gate beneath her body tendered a crescendo of anticipation. Bursting with desire for another one of those kisses, Summer couldn't wait to get back to the privacy of Bogey's home.

But another one of those kisses was not to be.

As they approached the house, they could hear the phone jangling off the hook inside. Three short bursts, a pause, and three more bursts, over and over.

"That's sheriff work. I have to get it." Bogey jumped off Ranger and ran inside.

When he rushed back out after taking the call he informed Summer that the part-time deputy was busy with a wreck and there was a disturbance he needed to tend to. Quickly, they unsaddled the horses, leaving the saddles hanging right on the railing of the front porch, and Bogey opened a gate to the meadow to let Ranger and Molly run free. He and Summer hopped into the truck, he dropped her off at the B&B, and he was gone.

So much for romance, Summer lamented.

40

"Is it possible to fall in and out of love in one day?" A rhetorical question, Summer asked it more for her own sake than that of her companions. She needed to say it aloud to convince herself about the "out" part.

"Oh, honey," Hazel said, "don't say that. We told you, it isn't what it seems."

Summer, Hazel, and Betty sat in the rocking chairs on Hazel's front porch, each with a glass of lemonade at hand. Summer's bike laid on the lawn out front. It had been a good Monday at school and she'd looked forward to this afternoon break with her friends. But the news they delivered had taken her nice day and torpedoed it to smithereens.

Summer picked up the *Ogemaw County Herald* again, the weekly newspaper that reported all the local happenings, including one particularly disturbing bit under police reports. After reports of the volunteer fire department rescuing a cat from a tree, the state police giving a speeding ticket to a traveler all the way from Mississippi, and the sheriff helping a little girl retrieve a doll she dropped in the creek, a paragraph read:

Chastity Hayes was arrested Sunday night for drunk
and disorderly conduct after causing a disturbance in the

parking lot of the Elks Club. Miss Hayes was angry that a local deputy had "dumped" her.

"I can't believe they wrote up that last part." Betty scoffed as she grabbed the paper out of Summer's hand. "Don't even read it." She threw the paper down onto the floor of the porch.

"Summer, we told you: this is the third time Chastity Hayes has done this, each time with a different man. She causes commotion like this that hits the press, then she spreads around a rumor that makes it sound like she's pregnant, then when she's not she claims everyone misunderstood her. Even though that rumor is rampant around town right now, no one believes anything she says. She's a very disturbed woman. That's obvious to everyone in town. She needs help."

"She needs somebody to sit her ass down and tell her to stop lying about people." Betty puffed furiously on a cigarette. "Last week the guys at AA told me they've tried and tried to get her to join our group, but she refuses. She doesn't think she has a drinking problem. And therein lies the problem."

"Remember," Hazel said, patting Summer's hand, "the only reason we wanted to be the first to tell you was so that you wouldn't be blindsided by somebody else in town, or by Bogey, or by one of your kids in school, for goodness sake."

"I appreciate that. I'm sure somebody would have told me and I would have been devastated. Twenty-four hours ago I thought I'd fallen in love. But how can I let myself love someone who might be having a baby with another woman?"

"He's not," Hazel insisted.

"But what if he is? Chastity might have been lying before, but what if she's not this time?"

"Listen, kid," Betty said, "you need to talk this over with Bogey. I bet he'll stop by tonight. Talk to him."

"Yes, keep a level head," Hazel added, "and talk."

"I don't know if I can do that. Keep a level head, or talk about this yet. I need time to think. Right now I feel like my heart has been broken. How can it hurt so badly if I've only been in love for a day?"

"Oh love hurts, we know that," Hazel said.

Betty sang, "Love hurts, love scars, love wounds and marks…."

"Ha ha," Summer groaned. "Roy Orbison knew what he was talking about."

"Listen, nobody knows that better than us." Betty pointed to Hazel and herself. "My heart was broken in high school when I had to give up my baby, and my boyfriend disappeared."

"And mine was when Izzy disappeared, although that ultimately turned out to be a good thing. Then my real broken heart came when my Howard died." Hazel shook her head at her bad luck. "But your situation is different. You and Bogey are two decent grown-ups who genuinely care for each other. You need to talk this out. Find out the truth. Then decide what you want to do. You may not need to fall out of love at all."

Summer took in a long, deep breath. No, she didn't need to decide right now what she should do. She didn't know enough yet to know what options made sense.

"Okay. I'll try to be patient. It's so embarrassing, though."

"For Bogey, yes," Hazel reminded her. "That Chastity has targeted him for her harassment."

Her friends' support meant the world to Summer. After thanking them for telling her about this so she wouldn't be taken by surprise, she and Betty went back to the B&B and got to work.

The lobby of the B&B was blissfully quiet, with no movie crew in sight. They were all upstairs in the ballroom getting ready for a speakeasy scene to be shot that night. Summer dusted the library books, the mundane task calming her nerves. Her favorite section was that containing the books brought down from Hazel's apartment. The antique bindings, pretty lettering on the spines, even the light musty smell soothed Summer's nerves.

The solitude was broken, however, when the three old ladies she'd seen at the open house showed up, scuttling through the front door with a definite sense of purpose.

"Now you listen to us, dearie," the short one said, "we read that report in the paper and heard that nasty rumor and we want you to know that we, for one…" Summer didn't point out there were three of them… "don't believe a word of it."

"Not a word. Why, we've already heard that nasty rumor today from the grocery store clerk and the mailman and our neighbor and… well, never mind that." This came from the one who'd worn the old suit to the open house. On this day she wore a pretty dress that was right in fashion—twenty years ago. "Why that nice boy Deputy Bush would never have anything to do with that crazy girl."

"Not a thing." The short one butted in. "I mean, he might have taken her out to dinner a couple of times, but everybody needs to eat. There's no harm in that."

"No harm," the third woman, the tall one, finally got a word in.

Summer mused at how they fed off each other's sentences.

"So you can ignore that drivel and get on along with that new boyfriend of yours."

"Good luck, dearie. 'Bye."

"'Bye, Betty."

Summer hadn't noticed Betty coming into the room, protectively holding a broom in her hand as if she might at any moment turn it around and start swatting at the swarm of busybodies.

The women tottered out the door and Betty said, "Old biddies. They wallow in any drop of juicy gossip."

"Yeah, but they were trying to encourage me, in their own nosey way. It seems I have lots of friends here in West Branch." She pondered that thought as she went back to work. Books served as her friends, too. She'd been reading Hazel's book *Once You Have Found Him* and surprised herself with how much she liked it. Too bad romance apparently wasn't meant for her.

She sighed and dusted more feverishly.

41

Friends these people were not. They weren't even friendly.

Monty, who Summer had come to think of as the "monster movie mogul," and his mostly mum assistant Jillian had been nothing but a pain in the derriere since their arrival a week earlier. But townspeople were all fired up about having an honest-to-goodness movie made in their hometown. That evening the scene to be shot in the ballroom would have local residents filling in as extras. Monty had an open casting call a few days before, which she and Betty ignored. Neither of them had an ounce of interest in being a movie prop. Extras had no lines and usually milled around in the background, often not even in focus on the finished film.

Summer entertained herself by imagining Charlotte being there. With her flamboyant personality and penchant for taking over, she'd probably end up starring in the show.

The actual stars, two actors Summer had never seen or heard of, a man and a woman, were nonetheless two of the most faultless people she'd ever seen. Their hair was thick, their eyes were bright; their skin was flawless; their teeth were Chiclets; and their bodies were perfect. With their unrealistic facades and stilted stances, they looked like Barbie and Ken dolls. Both were remote, never talking to anyone but each other and Monty. Summer watched them rudely dismiss Jillian whenever she tried to pass along Monty's instructions. Only the head honcho would do for those two elitists.

Summer suspected they imagined themselves Hollywood stars. Yet here they were in the boonies, eating good-old, small-town crow. Summer hoped it would do them good.

West Branch certainly had humbled her.

To get the locals ready for their parts as extras, wardrobe and makeup were being administered in Jillian's room and the hallway upstairs. Summer elbowed her way through the fracas, hurried into her room, and closed and locked the door. She knew she wouldn't get any sleep on this school night, but hoped that at the very least Bogey would stop by during his supper break. Although not ready to talk to him, it would sooth her soul to know he cared enough to make the effort.

With her windows open for the refreshing late afternoon breeze, she could hear more noise than usual from the street below with the comings and goings for the movie shoot. She turned on her radio to be rewarded with one of her favorite songs: "Oh my love, my darling, I've hungered for your touch, a long, lonely time…." The Righteous Brothers were called the Blue-Eyed Soul Singers, and Summer swayed to their sultry sound. Their *Unchained Melody* burrowed into her core, causing her to yearn for love as never before. She plopped onto her bed and let her mind wander with the music. "I need your love, I need your love, God speed your love to-o-o me."

Would her desire ever be fulfilled? Would it be filled by Bogey, or would he indeed break her heart by needing to be with another to raise their child? Would she ever be able to settle into the wedded bliss she craved?

An insistent knock on her door shattered her moody reverie. Agitated by the interruption, she got up and yelped, "Who is it?"

"Monty. Need to talk."

"No," she whispered to herself, "we do not 'need' to talk, you bozo." She opened the door and said, "What?"

"Kids. I need some. Tomorrow. You teach."

"And…?" She was determined to force him to finish a complete sentence.

"Will you bring yours?"

"What do you mean you need them? To be in the movie? As extras?"

"Yes. Street scenes. Stores. Here in town."

"What will you give them if I bring them?"

"Give them?"

"Yes. What's in it for them?"

"Why, they get to be in my movie."

It was the longest sentence she'd ever heard him utter. She'd flustered him, which pleased her.

"How about a ten-minute roll of film of them singing a couple of their favorite songs. You can donate the film to the school." Proud of herself for conjuring that up on the spot, she added, "Otherwise, no, I won't bring them."

"Fine. Nine-thirty." He turned his back on her and huffed away, looking every inch a Boris Karloff horror film villain from behind.

Poking her head out into the vestibule, she could see that the ballroom had been set up to look like a speakeasy from the 1920s. The set crew had done a phenomenal job. Too spectacular to ignore, she went in to look it over.

"This must be what it was like," she said to no one in particular.

Jillian appeared at her side. "Yes, it was an enchanting era, wasn't it?"

Surprised at the nervous young woman's sudden friendliness, Summer said, "Yes, it certainly was. You're the researcher for this movie, aren't you? You must know a lot about the Roaring '20s and the Purple Gang." Summer didn't know why she wanted to engage this insipid woman in conversation, other than any information she could pull out of her about Monty Miles might help solve the mystery of the murder, seeing that the movie producer seemed suspicious.

Jillian scanned the room as she answered. "Yes, I know a lot." With that, she walked away.

"Thanks for the friendly chat," Summer mumbled.

Squirrelled away in the locked café for supper, Summer relayed her brief conversation with Jillian while she and Betty savored the chicken stew Joey had left for them.

"She's an odd one," Betty said. "Hey, if she's the researcher for this movie maybe she knows something about the Purples that would help solve our murder. She might not know what she knows that would help us."

"Yeah, maybe, but good luck pulling it out of her."

A knock on the door to the street caused them to look up. A familiar handsome face with slicked back black hair peered through the glass.

"Okay, I'm out of here," Betty announced, throwing a wave at Bogey, picking up her dishes, and going to the kitchen to dump them in the sink. Summer heard her footsteps in the back hallway, and the sound of her apartment door opening and closing. Bogey continued to window peep. Not ready to talk to him lest he have bad news to deliver, Summer felt she had no choice but to go to the door. After all, it might be against the law to ignore a deputy sheriff standing out on the sidewalk when he knocked.

"Hello, Bogey," she said as she opened the door a foot. She would talk to him, but would be darned if she'd let him in.

"May I come in?"

She looked back into the room as if it held an escaped convict she wanted to hide from the law.

"Um, I don't know if that's a good idea."

"Summer, you don't believe that horrible rumor, do you?"

"Is it gossip? Or is it true, Bogey?"

His pleading eyes forced her to open the door. She stepped out of the way and he stepped inside.

"It's...."

A shattering bang above their heads vibrated through the room. Terrified screams rang out and footsteps could be heard frantically scattering away from the room upstairs, the ballroom.

"Stay here," Bogey demanded as he ran to the door that led to the B&B lobby. "Lock the door behind me." He unbolted the door and vanished.

42

"You're kinda crabby today, aren't ya?" Leave it to Stella to tell it like it was.

Summer rubbed her forehead. "Sorry. I'm very tired today."

Stella had cornered Summer after coming back quickly from bathroom break. Nobody else was in the classroom except Angela and her baby in his stroller. The baby slept and the grownup shelved storybooks on the other side of the room.

"I tell you what," Summer said, bending down to face the child, "I'll do everything in my power to be more patient, because Miss Campbell and I have some exciting news for everybody. How's that?"

Stella frowned. Her definition of "exciting" might not be the same as anybody else's.

"I guess."

"Stella, what's that scab on your face?" A small round circle of dried blood dotted the skin above the girl's upper lip. The same shape and size as the scars she'd seen on Stella's clavicle, it concerned Summer.

"I dunno."

The other students poured into the room, giving Stella a chance to escape. She scampered back to her desk.

Summer filed that little scab away in her mind, to try to figure out later. Right now, she knew she'd been short with her students in the hour they'd been together that morning. She'd barked out orders and forgotten stretch time. Angela had to remind her. Even the mother looked at her sideways, as if she'd grown fangs overnight.

It had been a terrible night. The big bang in the ballroom had been a spotlight bursting. Everyone had fled to avoid shards of glass spitting in every direction. That had to be cleaned up before they could resume shooting the speakeasy scene. Filming didn't end until four o'clock in the morning, rendering sleep impossible.

And Bogey hadn't returned.

Summer sighed. She needed to pull it together. It wasn't the fault of her kids that her love life barely got off the ground before it crashed and burned.

A knock on the glass window in the door announced the arrival of Miss Campbell. Summer had come in early to run Monty's request by her, and the principal thought it a grand idea. She and her secretary Beatrice volunteered to come along to help keep the children corralled. Angela would take her baby in its old-timey black stroller, as that would look natural on the sidewalk and Monty might want it. Three of the four adults would have six students to handle and Angela would have five plus the baby. That seemed easy enough.

Miss Campbell said, "Students, I have a surprise for you today. How many of you know that a movie is being filmed in our town?"

Twenty hands shot up.

"Well, the man in charge of the movie needs children in some of the scenes he's filming today, and he wants *you* to go downtown and be in his movie."

A cheer shot up. The kids didn't seem to be entirely clear

about what that meant, but they did know they would get to leave school.

Stella remained silent, then raised her hand.

"Yes, Stella," Miss Campbell said.

"We gotta learn us some words to 'member?"

Miss Campbell looked at Summer who said, "No, you won't need to learn any words. You'll be what they call 'extras.' You'll be walking around like you usually do downtown. But you won't have any lines, words to remember."

"Let's go." Hector jumped out of his seat and headed for the door.

"Wait," Miss Campbell said.

"Aw, darn," the boy groused, plunking down in his seat.

The principal went on to explain the groups and how each one of them had to stay with the adult assigned to their group. Beatrice came in; they counted off to make groups; and they were on their way. Hand-in-hand by group, strung out like tails on kites, they walked the few blocks to town.

When they turned the corner onto Houghton Avenue, a buzz filled the air as extras, cameras, lights, onlookers, and an antique 1920s car jammed the street. Summer had to admit, as curmudgeonly as she'd been about this movie thing because she didn't like the producer, this promised to be fun. The kids certainly thought so as their little bodies revved up and they could hardly keep their feet on the ground.

They stood on the sidewalk in front of the B&B when a crew woman Summer hadn't seen before appeared to give them instructions for the children. One group would mill around by the drinking fountain in front of the bank. One group would be separated amongst adults to walk around the dime store. Another would sit with adults in the window of the café. The final group she didn't know what to do with until Miss Campbell suggested they spread out on the sidewalks on both sides of the street, because "kids always wander around down here anyway."

That settled it. A wardrobe man showed up, scanned the swarm of children, and declared most to be so "scruffy" they looked "okay for decades ago." He came up with a couple of small vests for boys and took belts off the dresses of two girls. "Females didn't wear these silly things in the 1920s," he informed them. "It doesn't much matter, though. The scenes they'll be in are filler, so quick no one will notice these miniature extras are even there." He dashed away to no doubt proffer scathing remarks to other extras who had dressed themselves.

Surprised at how organized Monty Miles was as a director, Summer found the whole experience to be delightful. Sheriff Kowalczyk, Deputy Fitz, and, yes, Deputy Bush showed up to commandeer crowds and direct traffic, seeing that Houghton Avenue had been shut down for four blocks. The atmosphere was one of a big carnival come to town. No doubt the town councilmen were at city hall counting the loot West Branch had made by opening the town up to the movie production company.

The movie crews knew right where to be and when, so the shots with the children only took an hour. The four chaperones gathered all their kids back together and stood with a large group of onlookers. As soon as she saw Monty, Summer pulled him aside.

"Yes," he said before she even spoke. "Him." He pointed to a cameraman finishing up a street shot. "He'll do kids."

She said, "Thank you" to his back as he walked away.

Satisfied, she took her students down North 3rd Street to rehearse. Elated at the prospect of their own "movie," they decided their two songs would be "Purple People Eater" and "Monster Mash." Miss Campbell, Beatrice, and Angela joined in as they coached them through a rehearsal where they emulated the TV show *American Bandstand*, with two lines of dancers and two people at a time dancing through the center of the lines.

Summer harnessed the cameraman, an affable fellow, and he came to the side street to film the kids. He laughed at their performance and told them they did great. He promised to get the film to the school as soon as they finished with the "big movie." The amateur movie stars were thrilled.

"At least one person on that movie crew is nice," Summer told Angela.

Stella pulled at her sleeve. "Miss Summer, I wanna see in there." The girl pointed to the B&B.

"Oh, well." Summer looked at the other women and no one objected. "I guess we can go in the lobby. They aren't filming inside today."

They filed into the side door by the back stairway, the one with the small speakeasy window, but Summer didn't think it prudent to point that out to children. Betty sat at her desk in the lobby and got up to greet them.

"Well, what have we here? Hello, everybody. Welcome to the W.B. B&B. This is like a hotel, where people come to sleep at night when they're traveling and aren't at home."

She squired them around the lobby, taking time to point out the library shelves and the importance of reading.

"I hope you can come back someday when we aren't so busy. It isn't a good idea for us to go upstairs right now because there's movie equipment all over the place," Betty said.

"What's up there?" Stella wanted to know.

"Bedrooms and a ballroom," the innkeeper told her.

"Come along, children. We have to go now," Summer said, herding them toward the back side door where they'd come in. "Thank Miss Betty for showing you around."

A cacophonous chorus of "Thank you, Miss Betty" rang out.

Taking the side street to go back to school, they hadn't gone far when Summer realized one of their chicks had flown the coop.

"Oh no, I have to go find Stella," she told Angela, who nodded.

Summer jogged back to the B&B and headed straight up the stairs. She knew Stella well enough by now to know that's where she'd gone. Not in the vestibule, not in the ballroom, Summer was shocked to see the apartment door standing wide open. She dashed inside.

There in the center of the room stood the girl, mesmerized by the scene around her. Even though boxes had been packed and stacked by the walls, the apartment still held enough charm to hint at its former glory.

"Stella, what are you doing here?" Summer didn't intend to be so harsh, but that's how it came out. Controlling her voice, she added, "How did you get in here?"

The child shook her head, held up her palms, and threw a look at Summer indicating the teacher was a moron. "I walked."

"But the door was locked."

"No it weren't. It were open."

43

"Who wants more coffee?"

Everyone at the café table looked up at Joey.

"I'll take another hit," Sheriff Kowalczyk said.

"Here you go, Aleks," Joey said as he filled the coffee cup.

"Thanks. Me, too," the Detroit police detective said.

Joey poured, took the pot back into the kitchen, and rejoined the group.

"As I was saying," Detective Womack said, "having a name to work with helped us immensely in figuring out what might have gone on here. We still don't know the identity of the dead man or how he came to have the combination to the safe or who killed him. But we're getting closer."

The detective was a large, strong, spit-and-polish man. His tailor-made black suit was immaculate. He wore a white shirt, white pocket handkerchief, and blue and purple patterned tie. His black patent leather shoes let off a bright sheen. His rumbling voice emanated confidence. It struck Summer that he could have been a member of the Purple Gang, according to Hazel's description. Summer liked this man. Maybe he would help them finally figure out the mystery of murder and mayhem in West Branch.

"Detective Womack asked me to invite anyone who spends time in this building and might have insight into what happened," the sheriff added. "That's why you are all here."

Linda Hughes

"Yes," the detective dovetailed, "sometimes with cases like this different people have different pieces to the puzzle, and once we all get together the pieces start to fall into place."

Summer, Betty, Hazel, and Joey sat on one side of the round table. The law circled the other half of the table, Deputies Fitz and Bush, the sheriff, and the detective. Summer's heart raced when Bogey walked into the room, but she forced herself to focus on their reason for being there, which definitely was not her love life. The fact that she and Bogey hadn't had time to talk would never help solve this case.

Detective Womack continued. "I handle cold cases in Detroit, although we have so many active ones I don't get to spend nearly as much time on the cold ones as I'd like. The Purple Gang, however, although now disbanded as a gang, has never really gone away. We're learning that they had connections in small towns all over Michigan. Here, because they liked retreating to this remote area, that connection seems obvious with your speakeasy." He pointed upward to the ballroom directly above. "In other small towns there were businesses like stores and gas stations that laundered money for them, for a cut. We recently uncovered one that had been in Clare, for example. A small farming community."

He took a long sip of his coffee. "We still have unsolved murders we feel certain they masterminded, but we can't prove it. But there is one murder we recently learned about from an old gang member who's in jail.

"He was there, Mrs. Hazen, on the night the woman was killed in the apartment."

So far Hazel hadn't so much as winced, but now she gasped. "Who was the poor woman? His wife?"

"No. According to our informant, his wife had recently di-

240

vorced him because she discovered he had a girlfriend in Detroit. I hope that doesn't hurt your feelings, but that's the way it was."

"I couldn't care less. Not now."

"His ex-wife had moved away with another man and was totally out of the picture. It seems Mr. Aaronson's girlfriend—his Detroit girlfriend—decided to take advantage of the situation. She bought a wedding dress, and when Mr. Aaronson visited she showed him the dress and announced that they needed to get married.

"Our informant, one of Mr. Aaronson's bodyguards, was there to witness what happened next. Mr. Aaronson informed the 'broad,' as the bodyguard called her, that she was 'dumb as a stump' if she thought she could force him into marriage. He said he'd marry whoever-in-hell he wanted. He grabbed the wedding dress, and he and his two bodyguards took off. They came to West Branch. They dropped him off, with the dress, at the apartment, and went to the Ogemaw Hills Hotel. That's where they often stayed while he was at the apartment. Next thing they knew they got a call and the girlfriend was dead."

He stopped, letting that sink in while he drank his coffee. Without being asked, Joey filled cups once again.

"So," Hazel said, "he only asked me to marry him to spite another woman." Her face went pale. "I'm so lucky that marriage never came off."

"Yes," Aleks agreed. "You escaped a real brute."

"We think the girlfriend must have already known about this place or she followed them here," Detective Womack continued his run-down. "Our informant refused to give up the location of her burial. He said she's 'next to all the others' and we'll never find them."

"Her death really was an accident," Hazel explained. "She had the gun pointed right at us. Izzy grabbed the gun so she wouldn't shoot us. I guess I should be grateful to him for saving my life. But, then, he got us into that situation to begin with."

"I hope you all are ready for what comes next, because it's pretty unbelievable. We've known this for a long time. But, of course, we didn't know there might be a connection to West Branch." Detective Womack looked around the table. All eyes and ears were with him.

"Many of the gang members were caught breaking the law and went to jail. Some were killed in gang-related activities, especially when the organization started to implode and infighting took over. One even came up to Lupton, not far from here, and built the Graceland Ballroom after Prohibition ended. But Mr. Aaronson and some of the leaders moved to California. They changed their names; he became Frank Jones."

"Frank Jones?" Hazel quipped. "That's a horrible alias. I'd never use it in a book."

That got a titter out of the group.

"They started legitimate businesses and did very well for themselves. A couple of them, including Aaronson, became extremely wealthy, upstanding citizens in their communities. Supposedly. They've always been suspected of keeping a hand in underworld activities. But there's no proof of that."

"Couldn't they ever be connected to crimes back here in Michigan?" Bogey asked the question most likely on everyone's mind.

"No, try as they might, law enforcement—not Detroit police or the FBI—could ever nail them. We know their legitimacy started in Michigan when they invested tons of money in the oil and gas industry that sprung up in the state. They were in bed especially with one such company in Mt. Pleasant. We know they got that initial investment money illegally, but could never prove it. They took those gains and started their legitimate businesses out West."

"Are they still alive?" Summer asked.

"Some are. Mr. Aaronson is not. Frank Jones, nee Issur Aaronson, was shot to death in his bed two years ago."

"Oh my," Hazel said, "was it an old gangland enemy with a grudge?"

"No, it was his wife. His fifth. She found him in bed with another woman."

"That's a good reason for a grudge if ever there was one," Betty noted.

Hazel nodded agreement. Summer would have sworn her friend suppressed a grin.

"So, where does that leave us in terms of what happened here?" Bogey asked.

"Good question. We speculate that someone inherited something—papers, files, a notebook, a lockbox—we don't know what, that contained information about the money left here, including the combination to the safe. We're still working on who that might have been.

"Hazel, giving us a name was a big help. Now we're running the sketch of the dead man by business associates of Mr. Jones' in California, and by the police out there and the law firm that handled his estate. That's the most promising thing that's happened in a long time, so thank you for that."

"Sure."

"However," Aleks said, "none of this tells us who is gaining access to that apartment right now. Summer, tell them what happened with your student this afternoon."

Summer cleared her throat. "My class was in town to work as extras on the movie. One of the kids got away from us and ran upstairs. I went after her and found her in the apartment. As you know, we always lock that door. But it was wide open. I grabbed the girl and got her out of there, but on the way out I told Betty to go look around."

"I did," Betty said, "and as soon as I walked in I knew I needed to check out the safe in the closet. Sure enough, it was open with another note in it." She unfolded a piece of paper and placed it in the center of the table. All eyes gravitated to it as she read aloud: "Still idiots."

After a thoughtful pause, Hazel said, "The writer isn't very verbal. He needs an education on how to write."

"Hazel, you've hit the nail on the head. That's why we suspect movie producer Monty Miles," Aleks said. "He talks like this. It sounds like him."

"Or," Detective Womack interjected, "it could be someone who wants us to think it's Miles. It could be someone else on that movie crew. Or it could be someone else altogether. We still need all of you who are most often in the building to stay on alert. See if you can catch this Miles or somebody else doing anything nefarious."

Aleks said, "We'll keep Fitz on standby outside every night until this gets solved."

"But what would his purpose be in leaving these stupid notes?" Fitz asked.

"We don't know," Aleks admitted. "But somebody who'd steal old money in a burlap bag and kill a guy on a bike might not be too bright."

Summer couldn't reconcile that with the producer's organized direction of a movie. But she had no better explanation. In fact, she had no explanation for anything at all.

44

"We need to talk."

"I know."

Summer readily acquiesced to Bogey's entreaty.

Lingering in the café after everyone else left following the meeting with the sheriff and the detective, they stood in the center of the room, facing each other uneasily. As always at night, the window shades were drawn. The lights remained on, so the place looked cheerful with its black-and-white and red decor. The mood, however, was anything but cheery.

Betty and Joey could be heard chatting as they washed coffee cups and saucers in the kitchen, but the young couple ignored the sounds of other humans being alive at this moment.

"You need to know," Bogey began, "that Chastity was taken to the psychiatric ward of the hospital in Bay City. She's an alcoholic who needs help. She's not in her right mind."

Summer gnawed at her lower lip. "That doesn't change anything, Bogey. If she's pregnant with your child you can't shirk that responsibility. The fact that she's unstable will make it hard on you, but you will still need to take care of your baby."

"Summer, that's what I'm trying to tell you. She's done this before with different men. There probably is no baby."

"How can they possibly know that for sure? Doesn't it take weeks before the rabbit dies from a pregnancy test?"

"I have no idea. I know they've taken a test and it'll be a while before they have results. But, Summer, you don't know Chastity like people around here know her. Any one of half a dozen guys could be the father of her child if she is pregnant. And she probably isn't."

"But if she is, you could be the father. You would still need to be responsible. A baby shouldn't be abandoned by its father."

"Of course not...Wait a minute. Are you saying you don't believe me? Are you saying you would believe a crazy drunk woman before you would believe me?"

Although they'd kept their voices low up to this point, Bogey struggled to keep control and his volume rose enough to silence the chatter in the kitchen. Both he and Summer looked in that direction. Neither Betty nor Joey appeared.

"Keep your voice down," Summer ordered.

"Fine. I'll keep my voice down," Bogey whispered, "if you'll listen to what I'm saying to you. I am not the father of Chastity's baby, if there even is a baby."

"You don't know that for sure." Frustration strained Summer's voice.

Bogey ran his fingers through his hair and backed away from her. "I swear, you are the most frustrating female I've ever known."

"More frustrating than Chastity?" She knew that was a horrible thing to say, petty and immature. But in her anger, it spilled out anyway.

"What? What are you talking about?"

"I don't know. I... I thought falling in love would be so much easier than this." Summer felt like she should cry but tears would not come. Her fury over this situation wouldn't allow it.

"Wait. Did you say, 'falling in love?'"

Oh crap. She realized she'd totally blown it. If ever there had been any hope for something with Bogey she'd ruined it by professing her love for him. Everyone knew that was like burning a relationship at the stake, or driving a stake through its heart. A woman should always wait for the man to say it first. Men were terrified of being in love. A woman saying it first scared them off. Helen Gurley Brown, editor of the new *Cosmopolitan* magazine, insisted on it, and Carla the jailbird and knower of all things male had mentioned it, too, along with so many other deplorable "caveman" attributes.

"Oh, I don't know. I don't know anything except I need to get some sleep for school tomorrow. I have to go."

She stormed out of the room and through the B&B lobby. Taking the stairs two at a time, she barreled up to her room and slammed the door behind her. Hurling herself onto the bed, she pummeled her fists into the pillow.

A knock came at the door.

"Go away."

"No. We need to talk. I have more to tell you." Bogey tried to keep his voice down, but Summer figured he could be heard all over the place.

"Hey, you. What's all this racket? I need some sleep." The intrusion of Jillian's voice surprised Summer.

"I'm sorry," Bogey could be heard saying. "I need to talk to Summer."

"Well, the way she slammed that door I don't think she wants to talk to you. Go away."

"I will. When she opens this door and we can talk."

"Listen, deputy, I see your uniform and all, but if you don't get out of here I'm calling the police."

"I am the police."

"I'll call more police. Get the hell out of here and let me sleep."

Summer had moved up to her door, her ear pressed to it to hear the contentious conversation on the other side. A tap on the wood, like fingers drumming, made her snap back. Dejection filled her as she heard Bogey's footsteps fading away.

Jillian's door clapped shut, concluding the encounter.

And thus the door to Summer's love life closed, as well.

45

Betty swung her Winston around while telling her story. "And then Mr. Movie Monster demanded that I go to the drug store to get him a Clark Bar. I said, 'Are you kidding? Go get it yourself.'" She took a puff, the little circle of burning tobacco at the end of the stick hypnotizing Summer.

"Betty," Summer interrupted. "Oh, my word, Betty, I know what it is."

"What what is?"

The two women had just finished their Saturday morning breakfast in the café. Summer jumped out of her seat. "Remember I told you about Stella's scars?"

Betty nodded.

"That's it." She pointed to the cigarette.

Betty held out her smoke and twisted her wrist to examine its cindering tip.

"Oh damn. You think her mother burns her with cigarettes?"

Summer nodded. "I have to go help Stella."

"I'm going with you." Betty stubbed out the butt, got up, and rushed to the kitchen. "Joey, I've gotta leave for a while. If I open the door to the lobby, will you listen for the phone?"

"Sure. You okay?"

"Yeah. Thanks, Joey."

Betty yanked her car keys out of her pocket and off they went.

Driving around the streets on the north side of town, not far from the school, they couldn't come up with a house that looked like it would be where anybody lived in abject poverty.

"I'm sure it's out here somewhere," Summer said, "because she always walks this way after school."

They covered all the streets that had houses, then turned onto the dirt road that meandered into the woods. Driving past the path that led to Injun Joe's, the run-down cabin Betty had shown Summer when she first arrived in town, they scoured the area.

"There. Could that be it?" Betty slowed down to let the Beetle crawl past a place that was no more than a shrunken shack. The crunch of gravel under the wheels of the car seemed to say "beware."

"Maybe." Summer stuck her head out her open window and studied the place that sat off the road, tucked into the trees. Dirt and weeds for a front yard. Cracked cement steps leading to the door. A water well a few feet from there. The screen door off one hinge. Two filthy windows. A catawampus roof promising to collapse at any moment. A bramble of wild bushes and vines crawling up the backyard, ready to pounce on the invading domicile and reclaim the space as its own.

A bathtub Mary, rusted and unloved, stood in the center of the dirt yard. Such structures, an old-fashioned porcelain bathtub half buried standing up on end to shelter a statue of the Virgin Mary, were common amongst Catholics in Michigan, especially Catholic farmers. This one, however, showed no sign of anyone caring about religious beliefs. It had obviously been left by former owners long, long ago.

The slum of a house and its surroundings stood alone, remote, in shadow. No wonder no one noticed what might be going on inside.

"Yes," Summer decided. "I bet this is it."

Betty stopped the VW. The gravel's warning ceased.

Bravely, Summer got out, quietly closing the door. "You stay here while I check."

"Okay. Be careful."

Focused on the shack, Summer barely heard the words of caution. She went to the door and before she could raise a hand to knock, Stella appeared behind the screen.

"Miss Summer, how come you're here?"

"Hi, Stella. I like to… visit my students sometimes. Is your mom home?"

"Nah uh."

"May I come in?"

The knowing look on the girl's face told Summer she didn't buy the "visit" ruse for one second. Without answering, she opened the door.

Squalor; the smell of it, the breach of it, the feel of it; assaulted Summer's senses as soon as she stepped into the place.

Stella read the horror on her teacher's face. "I try to clean it up, but Wilma gets mad. She likes it this way."

"I see."

The place had no electricity or running water. A sagging couch sat in the main room, along with a side table holding a kerosene lamp. A beat-up Franklin stove sat on the wall, allowing Summer to feel relief that they had heat in the winter. A door to the side revealed a small bedroom with a messy bed. There was no sign of a bathroom and Summer hadn't seen an outhouse outside.

A counter of sorts lining the back wall had a big bowl and a couple of pans sitting on it, so apparently that served as the kitchen. An empty bread bag and two empty jelly jar glasses used for drinking sat on a rickety kitchen table. There were no chairs.

"Stella, have you had breakfast?"

"Yeah. Well, we only had one piece of bread left so Gloria had toast. 'cept we ain't got no toaster. But we pretend we got us some toast."

"I've noticed you always save some of your snack and lunch to bring home. Is that for Gloria?"

Stella nodded.

Gloria toddled out of a dark space on the side wall and took her sister's hand.

"Hi, Gloria. Remember me from school?" The child stared up at her with big, disbelieving eyes. No one, Summer ventured a guess, ever came to visit this house. Summer slowly stepped behind the girls and looked into the dark room, which was no more than a storage closet. With no windows it was hard to see, but a mat on the floor with a shredded blanket said it all. "Is that where you sleep?"

Stella nodded again.

"Stella, I'm going to go outside and talk to my friend for a minute. But I'll be right back. Is that okay?"

"Uh huh."

Summer sprinted out to tell Betty what she wanted her to do. Betty eyed the shack, nodded, and took off. Summer sat with the girls, struggling to think of a story to tell them to bide the time. She came up with repeats of stories she and Angela had read to the kids at school. Thankfully, it only took Betty half an hour to return with food supplied by Joey. He'd wrapped up scrambled egg and bacon sandwiches. There were glasses of orange juice and milk.

The two little ones dug in.

Minutes later Sheriff Kowalczyk arrived with a woman from Social Services. The woman looked around for less than five minutes and nodded at the sheriff. She invited the adults outside while the children finished their breakfast.

"I've warned Wilma before," she said to the sheriff. "She had to send Stella to school, and she had to provide a decent place for them to sleep and meals. The last time I visited she had things set up quite nicely, but I see she let it all go to hell in a handbasket. That and the cigarette burns on Stella—Wilma gets no more warnings. She's done."

The sheriff nodded. He looked at Summer. "Betty says you know someone who will adopt these girls?"

"Yes."

The social worker said, "A private adoption is allowable, as long as it happens soon. Otherwise, I'm taking the girls as wards of the county."

Right on cue, a Cadillac sedan drove up and Mr. Genks, the lawyer, got out. He held a folder full of papers at the ready.

The grownups greeted him, and Summer said she needed to go inside to talk to Stella.

Inside, the girls had finished eating. Gloria's mouth was joyfully covered in scraps of food and drink, and Stella wiped at it with paper napkins provided by Joey.

"Stella, I have a very important question to ask you." Summer squatted down to Stella's height. "You don't have to answer me right now if you don't want to.

"You see all those people out there?"

The child nodded.

"They are here to take you and Gloria away to live with somebody who will take better care of you than Wilma does. Do you understand?"

Another nod.

"I know some people who would like very much to have two daughters. They would like to adopt you."

Stella looked at her in confusion.

"Do you know what 'adopted' means?"

A shake of the head said no.

"It means these other people would become your new mom and dad, and you would go live with them in another town. I know them very well and they're very kind, nice people. In fact, you met them that day at school: Mr. Harry and Mrs. Ellie. If you agree, they would adopt you and Gloria and you would be their daughters."

A furrow formed between Stella's thin eyebrows as she stared at Summer.

"I know that's a big, big question for you to have to decide right away. If you want to take time to think about it, the sheriff and that nice lady with him will take you to live with somebody here in West Branch. You can wait to have somebody adopt you here. Or take your time to decide if you want those other people to adopt you. Take as much time as you want. You can think about it for a week or a month or… as long as it takes before you get adopted. Okay?"

This time the girl nodded.

"Do you have any questions?"

Stella shook her head. "I already 'cided. We wanna go live with those other people in that other town."

46

Harry and Ellie stood aside, watching while Stella and Gloria looked around the bedroom. Since their marriage twenty years earlier, the couple had lived in the Victorian-era guest cottage, which was actually a large house, behind the family cottage, an enormous house, on Mackinac Island. Harry's one-hundred-and-three-year-old grandfather still lived in the big house, with round-the-clock care. In their house, they had given their two newly adopted daughters a guestroom decked out for girls.

Stella so lightly ran a hand across the pink-and-white quilt on one of the twin beds it seemed she was afraid to touch it. She looked back at her mysterious new "parents." Taking Gloria's hand, she went over to the window seat with its fluffy pillows. She craned her neck to look outside at the pretty view of green lawn and blue lake.

Ellie went over and pulled back the ruffled curtain. "We'll have these tied back so you can see outside better. It's such a pretty view."

Stella looked up at her without speaking, and turned her attention to the spectacular scene outdoors, with twilight rays of sun splaying across the water to make it shimmer.

Harry picked up Gloria and stood her on the window seat so she could see, too. But instead of looking out, the little one turned and hugged his neck, laying her head on his shoulder. It had been a long, momentous, and exhausting day for one so young. He patted her back, a wave of protectiveness overtaking him. The child smelled bad; she was too thin to be healthy; her dirty, matted hair hung in strings around her fragile face. He didn't ever want to let go of her.

"Stella," Ellie said, "we can have the room redecorated if you don't like it."

Stella stared up at her. "We like it," she said, barely audible.

"Oh, I'm so glad. I hope you'll be happy here."

"We're happy." Stella's voice gained strength.

"We don't have any girls' nightgowns, but we can go clothes shopping tomorrow. For tonight, would a couple of my tee shirts be okay?"

The question seemed to befuddle the girl. "Sure."

"This one is ready for bed," Harry said, smiling at the sleeping child in his arms.

"Come," Ellie said, addressing Stella. "Let me show you the bathroom down the hall." She held out her hand. Stella studied the offering, cautiously deciding to take it. They walked hand-in-hand down the hallway with Harry and Gloria in tow.

"Our bedroom is right down there, in case you need anything in the night," Harry said, pointing to the bedroom door at the end of the hall.

Stella gazed up at him quizzically. "We won't need anything."

"Well, in case you do, you can knock on our door right there," he insisted.

Harry walked up and down the hall with Gloria in his arms, not wanting to frighten Stella by going into the bathroom with her and Ellie. Ellie called out for him to get two of her tee shirts, and he did so without Gloria so much as stirring.

It had been a miraculous day, the phone call from Betty coming out of the blue. Within fifteen minutes they caught a ferry from the island to the mainland, jumped in the car they had garaged there, and arrived in West Branch within three hours.

Harry had been stunned at Summer's acumen. She had all the necessary people assembled at a shack on the edge of town. She and Betty had visited the hovel that morning, then Betty went back to the B&B and made the phone calls Summer asked her to make. First Betty called Sheriff Kowalczyk, who called Social Services, the county agency that took care of abused children. By the time Betty called Harry and Ellie, she was able to explain that the retrieval of these two children was already in motion. Then she called the lawyer, Mr. Genks, who they met through the adoption of another one of Summer's students.

By the time Harry and Stella arrived, the girls' mother, Wilma, had returned from an apparent night out. The sheriff had already informed her that she had two options: let the county take her children away or let the girls be privately adopted. Keeping her daughters was not an option.

Harry and Ellie walked up to the shack at the moment the woman said, "Hell, what do I care? You can have the little brats." She'd stood there nonchalantly running her thumb back and forth under the front of the belt on her skirt, as if she had not a care in the world.

It had been as simple as that. Mr. Genks had the paperwork. Everyone signed. Harry wrote a check for two thousand dollars, which the fickle mother clearly had not expected, and they were off.

As Harry and Ellie walked the girls to their car, Ellie turned as if to say something to the girls' mother. Whether it be rage or pity that welled within his wife, Harry couldn't tell, but he put his hand on her shoulder. They locked eyes and she read his unspoken message. As far as Harry was concerned, no conversation of any kind would help with a woman who would mistreat her children. It wasn't a lack of money; it was a lack of love.

Ellie relented and they left West Branch without so much as stopping at the B&B to give the girls much needed baths. They wanted their new daughters to spend their first night away from their old home at their new home.

In the car, Stella sat in-between Harry and Ellie in the front seat, while Gloria stayed on Ellie's lap. The adults had taken turns explaining to the girls about adoption, and how they had always wanted two daughters. They were blessed, they said, to have found them. They didn't know how much of that got through—no doubt none for three-year-old Gloria—but seven-year-old Stella stoically took it in.

When Ellie asked if she had any questions, Stella said, "No."

They rode the ferry in silence and once on the island took a carriage taxi home. Stella had been fascinated with the fact that no cars were allowed on the island, so she would need to learn to ride a bike and a horse in order to get around. They had a quick supper in the kitchen, then came right upstairs to the bedroom. Both girls seemed so tired that without having to say it the new parents determined that a bath and hair washing needed to wait until morning. They had a housekeeper who would gladly wash the sheets to rid the bed linens of the smell of neglect.

Ellie and Stella came out of the bathroom with the child smelling somewhat better and with her hair a tad untangled. A dollop of Vaseline had been put on the scab above her lip. She wore a clean pink tee shirt that hung to her ankles.

While Harry held Gloria upright on her bed, Ellie took off her rag of a dress and covered her with a tee shirt, too. The child didn't even awaken. Gently placing her under the covers, Ellie tucked Gloria in for the night.

When Ellie pulled the covers down on the other bed for Stella, the girl stood in the middle of the room staring at it. "It's... it's awful far away." She pointed at Gloria in her bed.

"Oh. Oh, of course," Ellie said.

"Let me fix that," Harry offered. He took away the lamp on the small table between the beds, then moved the table out of the way. He shoved Stella's bed next to Gloria's. "How's that?"

Stella looked at him in surprise. It seemed she wasn't accustomed to making requests that were granted. "Thank you," she said.

Slowly, still not sure of this strange situation, she crawled into bed. As stiffly as if she had a board strapped to her back, she laid down.

"We have a nightlight here," Ellie said, turning off the overhead light and turning on a small, shell-shaped light. "Will this be enough?"

"Yes."

"Would you like the door open or closed?" Harry asked.

Silence answered until the girl said, "Part-way open."

"Okay. Now, remember, we're right down the hall," Harry said, taking a chance on annoying her by being redundant.

They turned to leave the room.

"Why did you want to 'dopt us?"

The question caught them both off guard. They turned back and went to the side of Stella's bed. Ellie sat down and put a hand on her shoulder. "We told you, sweetheart, we always wanted two daughters. You and Gloria are perfect for us. We hope we'll be perfect for you, too."

Even in the dim light they couldn't miss the expression of skepticism on Stella's face. Her eyes narrowed. Her jaw stiffened.

"But we're ugly."

"What? Oh, no, sweetheart, you are not ugly at all." Ellie was aghast. Harry remained speechless.

"Wilma says we're skinny as a door and ugly as a doormat."

Harry found his voice. "Wilma is wrong, Stella. You and Gloria are both beautiful girls."

"Would you believe," Ellie said, nearly choking on her words, "that I used to be skinny as could be when I was a little girl." She gestured to indicate her ample body. "And look at me. I bet you'll be like me and won't be skinny at all when you grow up. And you know what's best?" Stella shook her head. "You are beautiful inside, in your heart." She gently tapped Stella's chest. "I know it. That's the best kind of beautiful of all."

The girl gazed up into Ellie's face, hanging onto every word, and, without warning, reached up and grabbed her new mother around the neck. Ellie clung to her daughter with all her might.

When the two females parted, Harry collected his courage and said, "Hey, can your new dad have a hug, too?"

"'kay."

He was granted an unsure embrace, not nearly as endearing as what his wife had received, but he was willing to take whatever he could get.

"Good night, sweetheart." Ellie said as they turned to leave the room.

When they reached the door, they heard, "Nobody ever called me 'sweetheart' before."

"Well, get used to it, sweetheart," Harry said.

They were gifted with a grin as they left the room.

47

The next morning, after a night of getting up and down many times to check on the girls, Ellie and Harry were dog-tired after only one day of parenting. But they forced themselves to get up early so they could go tell their ancient grandfather he now had two new great-grandchildren right next door.

"I'll go talk to Popo," Harry said, throwing on some clothes. "You know how early he gets up to read the paper on the porch. I'd better get over there before one of the house workers breaks the news."

"Okay, I'll clean up and get the girls up. We'll have breakfast, give them a good bath, and then take them over to meet him."

Harry hurried downstairs and out of their house, walked down the gravel driveway toward the front of what they called "the big house," and started to turn to the front porch when he heard a familiar little girl's hearty voice. He ducked behind a lilac bush to stay out of sight and eavesdrop.

"I'm Stella. I live here now. My sister and me got 'dopted by those people who live in that other house."

"Well, hello, Stella." Harry's grandfather's words still rung clear, even though his centenarian voice had turned to gravel. "Oh my goodness, that's wonderful that you got adopted. That means I'm your great-grandpa. I saw you come in the carriage last night, so I figured you were going to live here now."

Wouldn't you know, Harry thought, *the old codger is still sharp as a tack, and didn't miss our arrival.*

"Do you like it here so far?" the old man asked.

"Uh huh," the child said. "We have beds with warm blankets and soft pillows."

"Oh, my. There's nothing better than a bed with warm blankets and soft pillows. Believe you me, at my age, that's one thing I know for sure."

Ellie came running out of their house with Gloria in her arms, obviously having discovered Stella wasn't in her room. Harry signaled for his wife to proceed quietly. She silently came to his side and listened as they huddled behind the lilac bush at the side of the porch.

"Yeah." Stella agreed.

"It seems we have something in common. We both love our beds and blankets and pillows."

"Uh huh."

"You know what would make this old man happy?"

"Nah uh. What?"

"Would you call me Popo? All of my other grandchildren and great-grandchildren do."

"Okay. Popo."

He cackled. "That's wonderful."

"So, how old are you?"

"I'm a hundred and three."

"Wow. That's purdy old."

"Yes, I'd say it's very, very old."

"Your back looks all crunchy. Does it hurt?"

"No, not much. It doesn't like to stay up straight anymore, so I'm kind of hunched over, is all."

"Can you see okay?"

"Ah, you spied my magnifying glass here. Yes, I can read the newspaper okay as long as I have this to help me. And my glasses help me see everything else."

"That's good."

"Yes, it's very good. I'm very lucky."

A pause in the conversation indicated that the young girl and old man were comfortable with each other.

Then Stella softly said, "Do you think maybe you might die pretty soon? Hector at school says ever'body dies."

Herbert Sullivan let loose with a hearty guffaw. "Yes. Probably pretty soon."

"Will you go to Heaven?

"I sure hope so. In fact, I believe I will because I've lived a good life. I've loved my family and been nice to people. That's how you get into Heaven."

"I don't know much 'bout Heaven. Hector says when you die you go to Heaven or Hell."

"My oh my, this Hector fellow is quite the authority, isn't he? Well, let me see if I can explain it. When we die we go to Heaven, a very nice place, if we've lived a good life here on Earth. If we haven't been good here on Earth, we go to Hell. It's not a nice place. Up in Heaven, there are all the people we love who died before us. I'm so old, I've got a lot of those, I'll tell you. That's why I was good, so I could go to Heaven and see them again. And our Lord Jesus Christ is there. Do you know about him?"

"Nah uh."

"Oh, he was a wonderful man. He helped a lot of people. Even though he died a long time ago people called Christians still love him and worship him. Your new mom and dad will take you to church so you learn all about him."

"So, he's your friend and you'll get to see him in Heaven?"

"Yes."

"That's nice."

"Yes, very nice. And I'll get to see God, too. So, when I die, I hope nobody here is sad, because I've had my turn on Earth and I'll be with people I love in Heaven."

Another moment of comfortable silence hung in the air.

"I like you," Stella said. The statement was so unexpected and so innocent that Harry and Ellie stood as still as church statues to hear what would come next.

"I like you, too, sweetie. When somebody gets to be as old as me, they can tell when somebody deserves to be liked. In fact, when they deserve to be loved. And you do."

"You do, too… Popo."

"Why thank you, Stella. You've made an old man very happy."

"I'm glad," Stella said. "I'm happy, too."

Harry and Ellie stepped out from behind the lilac bush in time to see Stella throw her skinny arms around her new great-grandpa's spindly turkey neck for a heart-whole hug. His gnarly hands embraced her, and they both laughed.

The warmth of love and caring infused the scene.

48

Summer shivered at the sight. The *Playboy* magazines lay hidden beneath a pile of unfolded Fruit of the Loom whitey-tighty underwear in the dresser in Monty's room. During her regular cleaning time, Summer had taken to snooping more than cleaning to see if she could find any clues to help solve the mystery of the murder.

Trying to find clues about the murder took her mind off her love life. Well, her lack of a love life. This was the first time, however, she'd garnered enough courage to handle a man's underwear.

So, with only a little digging she couldn't miss the stowed pornography.

Sheepishly, she looked at the door. No one was coming. They never did this time of day in the late afternoon. She pulled the magazines out of their hidey hole and bravely dared to flip open the pages. She had never seen a *Playboy* magazine, or any other kind of dirty pictures, for that matter.

"Oh, my word…." As soon as she said it, she realized the irony of her statement. Men didn't look at these for the words, no matter what anybody said. The most recent one, June, 1965, featured the stunning actress Ursula Andress. Summer nervously opened the foldout and proceeded to drop the magazine onto the floor as if it was too hot to handle.

"Oh my."

Snatching it back up, she shoved over a heap of Monty's clothes he'd left in a pile on the bed and sat down to take another look. She turned the magazine sideways, then turned it right-side up again.

"How on earth does she get into that position? Doesn't that hurt?" she marveled.

She shuffled through more pages. The nude women's bodies were so perfect the photographs almost looked like paintings. Casting that issue aside and moving on to another one, she found a similarly contorted playmate in that foldout.

"Okay. I know that must hurt." A dishy dame with her back twisted like a sponge and inconceivably arched backwards like a snake over the side of a bed, and her head thrown back to reveal a long neck and to allow her long hair to touch the floor, smiled at the camera in a come-hither look.

"Ouch. I'll never be able to do that. Is that what men expect?"

"I wonder if that's what that Chastity does." It was a forlorn thought.

She flipped through until running into a joke page. Some of them were funny, although she didn't get them all. She was chuckling when the unmistakable sound of footsteps approached on the wooden floor.

"Oh, crap." Frantic, she gathered the magazines and thrust them back under the underwear. She closed the dresser drawer and grabbed her dust rag at the moment Monty opened the door.

"Oh, hi, Monty," she said as nonchalantly as possible. "I'm finishing up in here." She feared she might be dusting the top of the dresser a bit too fervently, but he didn't seem to notice. "Is there anything I can get you? More towels?"

Distracted, Monty tossed a script onto his bed. "No. Need a nap."

"Oh, yeah, I saw you started really early this morning. Doing the courthouse scenes now, huh? How's it going?"

"Good. Great place. Decent actors. Well-behaved extras. Good as it gets."

"That's nice. Okay then, I'll be going. See you later." Summer took her dust rag and can of Pledge spray, and inched her way out the door, almost making her escape.

"Summer."

She turned back to him. "Yes?"

"You'd be a good extra. Come over. If you can."

"Oh. Um, thanks. I'll see if I can work that out. 'Bye."

She closed the door behind her having no idea what to make of that exchange. He'd been almost civil. No, he'd been decidedly civil. It made her wonder if he made an effort to be nice to confuse her about his involvement in a murder.

Realizing she'd be a terrible spy in the time of war, being too easily distracted and veering off course. Hopefully, world peace would never have to depend on her.

Maybe she'd do better in Jillian's room, she decided, and went up the stairs. She knocked in case the assistant, too, had returned, but got no answer. She opened the door a foot and peeked in. No Jillian.

With her trusty Pledge can and rag she went inside. Unlike Monty's room, this one was neat as a pin. Was it too neat? Summer pondered. Nothing looked any different from other times she'd been in here. The bed was made, square corners and all. Scripts, notebooks, and other papers sat neatly stacked on the dresser. A collection of books, newspaper articles, and reports about the

Purple Gang was piled in a large box. Summer had gone through those before and figured Jillian must be one heck of a researcher. She must know more about the Purple Gang than anybody.

A suitcase on the stand held folded clothes. She'd fingered it before, but hadn't gone through it. She felt around under the garments. Nothing. She already knew the dresser drawers remained empty. Jillian hadn't moved things out of her suitcase.

A hard-sided briefcase sat on the floor. She reached down to pick it up when she heard that sound again. By the time Jillian opened the door, Summer diligently dusted the side table.

"Hi, Jillian. I'm done. The room is all yours." She made an effort to sound as innocently cheerful as possible.

Jillian looked at her without saying anything, her hand still on the knob of the door.

"I'll see you later." Summer had to scooch past the woman to get out. It took all her effort to walk down the stairs instead of run.

She couldn't find one helpful clue in those rooms. If Monty was the killer, and if Jillian had been his assistant in murder as well as in making movies, they were good at it. The problem with that theory was that Jillian openly hated her boss, so it seemed unlikely they were in cahoots together. Besides, Monty hadn't acted like a murderer today, but that could have been acting. And Jillian seemed too milquetoast to have the gumption to kill anybody.

Maybe he was too friendly. Maybe she was too milquetoast.

Summer sure did hope nobody else was going to die.

49

A chill struck Summer. Like frost creeping its way up a window pane, the cold encased her body.

She looked up.

Jillian stood at the door of the apartment, a gun pointed straight at her.

Summer stood still as an ice sculpture, berating herself for getting up late at night and wandering around the apartment for no good reason. Look at what that wrought.

"I want the rest of the money." Jillian's shrill voice bounced off the walls.

"There isn't any more. You read the news. A bag of money was taken by the man who ended up dead, and we don't know who got it. There is no more." Summer struggled to thaw her voice enough to speak.

"That's a lie. You must know where it is. There was supposed to be bags-full all over the place."

"What makes you think that?" *Keep her talking*, Summer frantically decided. *Talking and not shooting.* She stepped sideways, only daring an inch or two.

"Oh, don't act all innocent with me," Jillian growled. "I know it was here. The instructions I found in Frank Jones' lockbox said so. It also told me he was really a gangster named Aaronson."

Irrational, proud, she seemed pleased with herself for being able to brag about having such highly guarded secret information.

"You have his lockbox?" *Keep her talking...* Summer took another indiscernible step sideways.

Jillian smirked and cocked her head, belying arrogance yet nervousness. Beads of sweat sprouted on her forehead. "Yes, I do. And you don't. So that money is mine. Where is it?"

Play to her arrogance, Summer thought. *That's most likely to keep her bragging.*

"Wow, how impressive that you have his lockbox."

"Yes, it is." She swung the gun around menacingly.

"Are you a relative?" Another step sideways.

"Hell, no. Nobody's ever given me a damned thing." Jillian's voice quaked with anger. "I am, however, one ace of a researcher. I used to work for the law firm in California that handled his estate." She filled her lungs, stretching her backbone to full height on her chunky body. Proud. Jillian was very proud of herself. "I was so trusted by the firm they gave me free range to go through the documents and belongings left by rich dead assholes. I found the bank key to the lockbox, and went and got it myself. The firm never even knew about this stash. Now, where's my money?"

Taking a terrifying gamble, lest she be shot, Summer asked, "Who was the man on the bike? The one who took the bag and got killed in the cemetery?"

"Don't you try to pin that on me." Jillian became furious, the gun quaking in her hand. "That idiot killed himself. He tied that stupid bag in such a tight knot he couldn't get it open to show me there was money inside. He took out his jackknife to open it and then slipped into that stupid grave. Fell right on top of his own knife. I had to crawl down there and turn him over to get the money bag out from under him. Idiot." Her eyes averted in morbid memory long enough for Summer to take another step sideways so that she stood squarely in front of the window.

"So he was your partner in this. Not Monty?"

"Are you kidding? That stupid man couldn't find his way out of a stupid paper bag."

"Well, why the bike? Why not drive a car over here?"

"Because I didn't want to get caught, you stupid bitch. Now where's my money?"

Jillian's frustration mounted, the repeated use of the word "stupid" telling Summer her intended murderer came closer and closer to completely losing her cool.

"If there had been more money here, you would have had to drive over to get it anyway. Right?"

"Oh my, aren't you a smarty-pants? What an idiot. Yes, of course. But by then we would have cased the joint and I'd be here for the movie. When I heard about the movie being made I knew that was my chance to have a legitimate reason to stay in this stinking town. Whose idea do you think it was to stay right here at your pathetic little B&B? Monty was so impressed with my knowledge about the Purple Gang he hired me without even checking my references.

"Now, bitch, you have one last chance before I shoot you dead. Where's the money?"

"Jillian, put the gun down," a man's voice boomed.

"Oh, shit! Don't shoot me. Don't shoot me." Jillian burst into tears. "It's a prop gun. Not real. See?" She held the weapon up over her head, turning it from side to side.

Summer finally dared look behind her nemesis to see Deputy

Fitz standing inside the back door, his pistol held in both hands and aimed at Jillian. Amazingly, Betty stood at the side door, her pistol aimed at the same target. If Jillian hadn't scared the life out of her, Summer would feel sorry for the fool, the ineptest extortionist-robber-murderer imaginable.

"Slowly lower the gun to the floor," the deputy commanded as he took long strides into the room, his aim never wavering.

Jillian did as told and sobbed into her hands.

Fitz kicked her gun aside. With his weapon remaining in one hand and trained on the offender, he used his other hand to pull a set of handcuffs off his belt and cuff the woman, who now bawled like a baby, hiccupping spastically.

Betty, her gun set aside, mercifully appeared with a handful of tissues and, with her hands cuffed in front, Jillian was able to wipe her face.

"I heard enough to get the gist of what went down," Fitz said to Summer. "I'm taking her in. Don't touch her gun. I'll send the sheriff to retrieve it and to talk to you to get an official report. Betty, will you look after Summer until he gets here?"

"Sure," Betty said, going to her friend's side.

The big deputy and his culprit clanked down the stairs, another round of wailing trailing along with them.

Summer opened the window, waved, and hollered loudly enough to be heard across the street. "Thanks, Tommy. I knew you'd take care of me."

The teen had perched himself into a tense crouch, but stood and waved happily when Summer opened the window. It was midnight on a Friday night, his usual time for a cigarette break on the roof of the Midstate Theatre by the marquee.

"Sure, Miss Summer. Wow. I'm so glad I was here. Once you

stepped in front of the window I could see everything. You and her behind you with that gun. Scared me to death."

"Me, too. But she didn't know we'd waved at each other just before she came in. Knowing you were there pulled me through. I knew you'd flag down Deputy Fitz for me. You're the best."

"Is she the one who killed the man in the cemetery?"

"We don't know, at least not for sure. Listen, how about you and your mom come over to the café tomorrow and have lunch on me. I'll tell you what I know. Okay?"

"Yeah. Sure. My mom would love that. Me, too. I'm so glad you're okay. Whew. Well, I'd better get home before my mom starts to worry. She'll be shocked to hear about this. See ya tomorrow." He waved again and crawled into his window.

Summer turned to Betty, who smiled. "Only in a small town," Betty said. "Only in a small town."

50

Summer strolled the aisles of Shoemaker's dime store. The wood floorboards creaked, like in the B&B, a comforting sound. Who knew how many feet had passed over these very floors and what troubles those people had survived? Maybe she could survive hers, too.

This store was old, like all of them, in the middle of the same block as the B&B, but on the other side of Houghton Avenue. In the two blocks that made up the main part of town, stores had tall ceilings, many with tin tile, and wood floors. The timber had no doubt come from this very area, seeing that it had been lumbering country. She loved it that most of the stores hadn't "modernized" and had retained their original ambiance from the old days.

The town had been built in the late 1800s and early 1900s. She vaguely remembered Uncle Harry trying to tell her about that when she first came here, but she hadn't been listening. Now everything about West Branch intrigued her.

She fingered the treasure trove of goodies as she walked around the charming, old-time dime store. Toys, marbles, fabrics, yarn, kitchen utensils, dishes, aprons, bandannas, doo-dads, candles, candy, and... ah... records. She didn't have a record player in West Branch and didn't need one for the couple of weeks she had left here. Her transistor radio worked well enough for now. But, flipping through popular records would help pass the time until lunch with Tommy and his mom. She might even find a new pop song to take home with her.

She'd already spent two hours doing her Saturday morning chores around the B&B. After the harrowing incident with Jillian the night before, she couldn't shake her somber mood. Her life hadn't really been in danger, but she hadn't known that. Little Hector's words rang out in her ears: "Ever'body dies." This store provided a quiet space that diverted her attention away from the morbid thought of her own demise.

Rifling through a rack of 45s, she saw many that she already had at home in her huge record collection. But there were some she didn't have yet, hit songs she heard on the radio. "I Can't Get No Satisfaction," by the Rolling Stones. "Ain't that the truth," Summer whispered. "Down in the Boondocks," by Billy Joe Royal. She chuckled at how she'd thought of West Branch as the "boonies" when she first came here. "My Girl," by the Temptations. She wondered if she'd ever be anyone's girl.

"I wish I could have been your knight in shining armor."

Bogey's voice coming from behind her so startled Summer she dropped the handful of records she held.

"Oh, crap," she said, bending down to pick them up off the floor.

Bogey bent over at the same time and they bumped heads.

"Oh, sorry," she said.

"Sorry," he said at the same time.

They gathered the scattered records and stood up. He placed records neatly back in the rack and she nervously held onto hers.

"I wish I could have been there," he said, "but I'm glad Fitz was. Even though it turned out not to be a real gun, you must have been terrified."

Summer's resolve to put Deputy Bogey Bush out of her mind

shattered. Sticking by her guns wasn't her forte, not when the tall man with the black hair and brown eyes, in jeans and a plaid shirt, smelling like Old Spice no less, planted his masculine body right in front of her.

How in blazes could she talk her mind into rock-hard resolve when her body turned to Jell-O every time she saw him?

"Yeah, thank God for Fitz. It was a crazy time." She ran out of words. Pure and simple. What more could she say? *Can we have that Chastity committed to get her out of our lives forever? Will you marry me and let me have your children? Kiss me, please, now.*

"Um," she came up with, "how are you?"

"How am I? How *am* I?" He thrust balled fists onto his hips. "How do you think I am?"

She shrugged. "I dunno." It hit her that she sounded like her kids. But, she couldn't for the life of her formulate a more coherent sentence.

"I'm confused about why you won't talk to me. Has Betty told you I've been calling?"

"Um, uh huh."

"Why won't you talk to me?"

"You know why. Chastity."

"I told you: I never slept with her."

"What?" Stunned, she dropped the records again, but ignored the mess on the floor. "You never said that."

"Yes, I did."

"You did not. You said you weren't the father of her child."

"Same thing."

"Is not."

"Is so. I never slept with her, not that that's anybody's business."

"Why not?'

"Why not what?"

"You know: why didn't you, uh, sleep with her?"

"What are you talking about?" Confusion coated his words.

"Well—you know—she's a... a... floozy."

"So, you think that if a woman is available I'll sleep with her no matter what?"

"No. Well, yeah, I guess."

"Well, damn it all to hell. Are you saying I'm going to have to explain to you why I didn't sleep with every woman I ever met that I didn't sleep with?"

"No. That's not what I'm saying and you know it." Now rising ire rankled Summer.

He ran a hand through his hair. "This is without a doubt the weirdest conversation I've ever had in my life."

Another customer, a young woman with rollers in her hair, came within earshot and they both clammed up. Summer always wondered where a woman was going later that she needed to wear rollers out in public. The woman wandered away.

Gesturing wildly, Bogey continued. "What you're saying is you thought I slept with her and then turned my back on the consequences, on a baby?"

"Well, that's how it sounded."

"That's what you think of me?"

"I didn't know what to think." Summer's anger melted into tears that threatened to spill over.

Bogey shook his head, threw up his hands, backed up a few steps, and turned and walked away.

A pretty, dark-haired, middle-aged store worker appeared at Summer's side. Kindly, she said, "Are you okay?" She bent to pick up the spilt records.

Summer stooped to help. "Oh, yes. I'm so sorry. I, well, I... I don't know what got into me."

They stood up. The woman took the records out of Summer's hands and put them in the rack.

"How about this one?" she said, plucking one out and handing it to Summer. "It's very popular."

Summer looked down to see "Back in My Arms Again" by the Supremes.

"Sure. It's perfect. Thanks."

She paid fifty cents up front for her new record and left the store figuring she'd so totally screwed up her chance with Bogey she'd never be back in his arms again.

51

"Thanks for coming here today. I thought you all would want to hear the update on our murder mystery. It's no longer a mystery." Aleks addressed the group sitting at the café table late on Saturday afternoon. "Detective Womack here agreed to come up from Detroit again to join us to let us know what he's learned, too. Detective, why don't you begin?"

The same crew as before circled the table: Sheriff Aleks Kowalczyk, Deputy Bogey Bush, Deputy Gerald Fitzgerald, Detective Womack, Betty, Hazel, Summer, and Joey. Amongst the sheriff, the detective, the innkeeper, and the cook, cigarette smoke streamed toward the ceiling in fat rivulets. Everyone had a bottle of pop of one brand or another in front of them, with Coca-Cola and Faygo Redpop being favorites.

The detective perched his cigarette on the side of the ashtray and began his report. "When Sheriff Kowalczyk contacted us about the arrest of Jillian Chalmers, we called the police in California, who talked to the law firm that handled Issur Aaronson's estate. They recognized her name immediately. Surprisingly, she hadn't changed her name before coming out here to commit crimes. We're guessing she assumed Michigan was so far away no one would ever figure out her connection to Aaronson."

He paused, took a sip of his Coke, and continued. "She

worked for the law firm for five years and, as she said while holding Summer at gunpoint, she was a trusted employee who was given the task of going through the files and belongings of clients who died. They even gave her a set of lock picks to pry open lockboxes and other locked items, like jewelry boxes, diaries, luggage, even the gloveboxes of cars. She helped them get into houses when needed."

"That, of course," Aleks interjected, "is how she kept getting into the locked apartment."

"So," the detective went on, "someone at the law firm has now gone through the documents of Aaronson's that she'd been trusted with. They didn't find any references to anything here."

Aleks picked up the baton. "But, after we arrested her and went through her room, we found a letter by Aaronson about all the money that was stored in the apartment here. Jewelry, too. It said his 'moll,' Hazel, might have taken some of it, but not all of it, because she didn't have the gumption to do that."

"Hmph. Bastard," Hazel groaned.

Aleks nodded agreement. "He said he knew she couldn't take the money in the safe because she didn't know the combination. It gave the combination."

Detective Womack ran with the story. "We figure Miss Chalmers panicked upon learning that her law firm had sold the apartment. She quit her job and drove out here to Michigan with her boyfriend, one Frederick Dobbin, known in the criminal world as Dobby. They hatched a half-assed plan, pardon my French, to rob this place and find the moll to get more."

"Holy mackerel," Hazel said. "I had no idea I was so popular and in such demand."

"That was forty years ago, though," Bogey said. "How on earth did they think the 'moll,' sorry Hazel, would still be around? Or that anybody here today would know who she was? Maybe that's how it panned out, but that's all been an amazing coincidence. It was illogical for them to think that."

Aleks answered. "They thought that because they weren't very bright. The man at the law firm said Miss Chalmers was a brilliant researcher and recorder, but doesn't have an ounce of common sense."

"That, by the way," Detective Womack said, "is why most criminals get caught."

"So the dead guy is this Dobby?" Betty asked.

"Yes," Aleks said. "She's confessed that he was to come here, case the place out, take what he could, and join her at the cemetery. Then they'd come back with the movie crew, where she'd found a job. He would lay low while she stayed right in the middle of their target."

"Wait." Summer couldn't follow this "half-assed" plot. "The whole bike idea was stupid enough. She told me they did that so she could stay clear that night and not risk getting caught. But why on earth did they decide to meet at the cemetery?"

"Well, first of all, since his last stint in prison this Dobby has been a bicycle courier in L.A.," the detective said. "So, apparently, 'escaping' by bike seemed plausible to those two nitwits."

"Now, this second part is hard to believe, but here goes," Aleks said. "When I asked that very same question about the cemetery she told me that according to Aaronson's records, that's where exchanges took place back in the day. Payoffs. Orders from the boss. Things like that. Always at night. The gang got a kick out of doing that at the cemetery because the police in West Branch weren't on the take. Not the state police or the sheriff's office.

They were all too straight. Doing business right in the backyard of the state police post, in the cemetery, was like thumbing their noses at the law.

"Our felon and her partner in crime wanted to do it the authentic way. They thought it would put them in the same league as the 'real wiseguys.' They fancied themselves the reincarnation of the Purple Gang. Jillian and this Dobby fellow were both Jewish. Both were criminals. Jillian honestly seemed to think they were starting something big, the glory of the good old days. She became fixated on the gang when she had to go through Aaronson's things. She became totally infatuated with them when she did more research. They were real fanatics."

"Well," Hazel said, "I see what you say about Jillian not being too bright. Who in blazes would put that together?"

"Especially after how it ended up." Aleks took a hit off his cigarette, blew a smoke ring, and continued. "It turns out that she waited much longer than expected in the cemetery for her boyfriend to arrive. When he finally got there, he was furious because of the storm. They got into a shouting match. He yelled at her for not coming to pick him up when it started to rain. She yelled at him for being such a 'retard.' This part she told Summer, then repeated to me: He tried to open the money bag to show her the loot, but he'd tied it shut so tight he couldn't get it open. He took out his jackknife to open it. Neither of them noticed an open grave right there. He slashed at the bag and slipped.

"Next thing she knew he and the money were gone. She called out to him but got no response. She saw him in the grave with the money bag underneath him, so she jumped in. It was so dark she couldn't figure out at first what happened. But then she realized he was dead. Horrified, but not so horrified she didn't want the money, she rolled him over and saw that he'd fallen on his own knife. She says she couldn't see well enough to get all the dough because some had fallen out, but she got as much as possible and clawed her way out.

"She was very disturbed that her 'idiot' boyfriend caused her so much trouble. She's much more upset about losing the money now that she's in jail than she was about his death."

The sheriff's audience sat there mesmerized by his sordid tale.

"I'd never write all of that into a book," Hazel noted. "It's too bizarre."

"Yeah, the things criminals do are often too bizarre to be believed. But they do them anyway, especially when fantastical fantasies about getting rich are involved."

"Do you think that's true? That he fell on the knife? Or do you think she killed him to take all the loot herself?" Joey asked.

"We think she's telling the truth because our coroner says the angle of the stab wound was lopsided, sideways instead of straight on. She would have had to stab him from behind, and the truth is he was too fat for that to work, or she would have needed to be left-handed to get the angle if she stood in front of him, and she'd not. We'll never know for sure, but she's probably not lying.

"I've arrested her for theft, assault with a deadly weapon for what she did to Summer, extortion, and everything else we could think of. She'll be in jail a long, long time."

"What about those notes in the safe?" Hazel asked.

"Yeah, what in hell was that all about?" Betty added.

"Oh, well, she hoped to upset the apple cart and get somebody talking, maybe even to the press," Aleks said. "If somebody would've spilled the beans about who had the rest of the money and the jewelry, she planned to go find them."

"What an idiot," Hazel said, and everyone laughed at her reference to what Jillian had called them.

The door to the B&B burst open, giving everyone a jolt.

"Oh my God! Jillian in jail. I'm so sorry. I brought her. I didn't know." Monty was beside himself as he approached the table.

"Oops," Betty said. "I forgot to lock that door. Everybody, this is the movie producer, Monty Miles."

"I promise. I had no idea."

"We know, Monty. Jillian confessed and we know you had nothing to do with the break-in or the robbery or the murder."

"She wanted the movie. She knew everything. About the Purples. I thought... I thought... she was brilliant. She found this town."

"It's okay, Monty. It's all over."

"Oh my. Please. Don't hate me."

Betty paused before responding. "We don't hate you. It's okay."

"Mr. Miles," the sheriff said, "this is Detective Womack." He pointed to the man beside him. "You aren't in any trouble, but we'd like to talk to you to get some background information about Jillian Chalmers. We think we know everything we need to know, but you might be able to fill in a few recent details. Do you have a few minutes right now?"

Monty clapped his chest with an open palm in a flamboyant gesture of distress. "Yes. Of course. Always obey the law." Summer thought the back of his hand might go to his forehead as he fainted to conclude the drama.

Everyone else vacated the café to allow the two lawmen to talk to the movie man.

Bogey went out the front door with Fitz but looked back at Summer as he left. The expression on his face gave her no clue at all about his feelings for her. Did he hate her? Did he love her? Did he have no feelings for her whatsoever? If he didn't want one woman because she was a floozy, did he not want her because she was the real idiot around here?

She had no idea.

52

At the beginning of the summer of 1965, Summer had no idea how her life would be transformed. A freak incident brought her to small-town West Branch. She'd abhorred what had happened to her at the party in Traverse City, at the stranger's house where she apparently accidentally got high on laced brownies and landed in jail.

She'd railed against her Uncle Harry for forcing her to do her community service in this strange place out in the boonies. But these final weeks in West Branch had flown by. Now that her time here was almost over, she knew she would miss this quaint little town with its interesting people, fascinating history, and auspicious connections to big-city crime.

These thoughts meandered through her mind as she walked the path along the west branch of the Rifle River, the creek that trailed behind the main part of town. A couple of her students showed her the path, which they took to school each day. To take advantage of the longest part of the walk, she had to go west from the B&B, away from the school, and hook back behind the town's buildings. Going down a small hill by the bridge, the path wandered through residential backyards with mature trees on one side and the creek on the other, all the way to a block from the school.

She usually rode her bike to school but on some days preferred the path with its burbling clear creek. Every now and then she'd see a fish swim by. Wild Lily of the Valley grew amongst the grass. Purple ground cover that she didn't know the name of tumbled down the rocky bank to almost touch the water. Maple, oak, white birch, cedar, and pine trees lined the way. Some hung over the creek, considering falling all the way over to make foot bridges. The lusty smell of cedar and pine dominated the air. One circle of cedars had a "secret doorway," according to her students, a place to step into the center of the stand of trees, to make a "fort," an open space big enough to hold half a dozen people.

Summer loved ducking into the fort. She'd come to think of it as her most private of time, a time to feel like part of nature.

She'd never have done this if she'd had her car. Smiling at her recollection of originally thinking she'd get someone to bring her treasured Cabriolet convertible, she'd ended up not missing it at all. Well, hardly at all.

The last couple of weeks had flown by at school and at the B&B. She remembered those first days of Head Start when she'd counted down the minutes to the end of each school day. Now it seemed she hardly had time to do everything she wanted to do with her students. Her kids, scurrilous as they were, entertained her every day.

These final weeks of movie-making had been hectic at the B&B, but Summer had come to adjust to Monty and his unusual way of speaking. In fact, the more relaxed he was around her and Betty, the more normally he talked. He planned two premieres for his finished film, one in Detroit and one right here in West Branch. Summer knew she'd come back for that.

In fact, she knew she'd be back again and again to visit her new best friends, Betty and Hazel. She'd also invited them to visit her in Traverse City.

It was ironic that she'd started the summer craving friends her age, which was how she ended up at that unfortunate party in the first place. Now her new friends, Betty and Hazel, were old enough to be her mother and her grandmother. Age didn't seem to matter amongst them. They thoroughly enjoyed each other's company. Summer had learned a lot about life from each of them.

One thing they'd been encouraging her to do was open up about what went wrong with Bogey. As of yet, she hadn't been ready to discuss it. The bottom line was, she figured, she and Bogey must not have been meant for each other. She had no idea why, but what did she know about love? Obviously, nothing.

She'd seen him many times in the past weeks. He'd drive down Houghton Avenue in his cruiser about the time of day she cleaned rooms. She'd take a break and look out the window, yearning for him to stop by like he used to. He never did.

Before going to bed at night she'd look out her window, sometimes waiting for a long time, to see him drive by again on his way to the sheriff's office at the end of his shift at eleven. His head would turn in her direction, and then he'd drive on by.

Her heart ached. Her mind didn't understand. Her body shut down.

Maybe she'd become a nun.

What a summer it had been. She came to appreciate this small town and she made wonderful new friends. She learned she could survive jail, being mired in a murder mystery, cleaning toilets, having her life threatened, being sequestered in a room full of children all day long, and a broken heart. As far as she could tell, that meant she could survive anything.

Her walk down the creek path came to a street to cross in order to continue. She went up a slight hill to cross over and back down to follow the water. Through the trees she could see some pretty backyards. She wondered if she'd ever have a backyard of her own someday. Or would she still be living with her parents into old age? As much as she loved her parents, the thought appalled her.

Moving to an artists' commune in San Francisco or Hawaii would never work, either. She hated sharing her bathroom with others.

As she came to the end of the path, Summer pondered her life and came to not one conclusion. She had no idea where she was going or where she might end up.

All she knew for certain was that she had to finish this final week of Head Start, wrap up her work at the B&B, and say goodbye to her new girlfriends. Then she'd go home to Traverse City, go back to work at her dad's winery, paint pretty pictures, and spend the rest of her life wondering what went wrong.

No, she insisted. *That can't be all. There must be more.*

Isn't there?

53

The Head Start graduation ceremony in the kindergarten room of West Branch School turned out to be adorable. Summer couldn't help but beam with pride for "her" kids. Most wore their Sunday best, and at least one parent, grandparent, aunt, uncle, or sibling attended for each student. This was extremely difficult, Summer knew, for many of these adults who needed to tend nonstop to their farms or who worked in hourly jobs where it was hard to get permission to take time off. A few, like Angela and Deputy "Fitz" Fitzgerald, had so many children that finding time to spend with one or two was a challenge because there were always more needing their attention.

Still, the importance of the event had propelled these grownups to do whatever it took to show up to support their children. Summer felt grateful to them for their sacrifices. It had become obvious to her that most of the parents and extended family members of her Head Start students were good people who loved their children and did the best they could for them. Kenny's and Stella's parents were the exceptions.

Stella and Gloria were there, too, with Ellie and Harry. Stella had jumped at the idea of returning to West Branch for graduation, but insisted on "plain" dresses because she didn't want to "hurt the other girls' feelings." She and Gloria wore plain pastel dresses with no frills. Their matching blond hair shone with cleanliness and had been cut. The cigarette burn scar above Stella's lip had, thankfully, healed to invisibility.

Ellie and Harry stood in the back of the room. The new adoptive parents appeared so proud it seemed they thought their daughter was graduating with an engineering degree from MIT.

Miss Campbell began with a short preamble and then began calling names.

"Mr. Hector James," she announced, waiting for the boy to come to the front of the room and pick up his "diploma." Hector, who'd slimmed down a bit during the summer and looked healthier for it, bellowed, "Hunky-dory." He waved at his mom as he accepted his sheepskin, in this case a rolled-up paper certificate bound with ribbon, and went back to his seat.

"Mr. Jerry Fitzgerald." The first of Angela's sons, one of Fitz's look-a-likes, pranced up front and accepting his diploma.

"Miss Stella O'Neill." Some of the adults oohed approvingly over the girl's new last name. Stella marched with serious pomp to accept her honor.

"Miss Annie Bellows," the principal said, and so it went.

Family members stood around the edge of the classroom, so the place was crowded. Nobody seemed to mind.

Each child finally had a rolled-up diploma in hand and sat excitedly at their desk. Miss Campbell, Summer, and Angela had determined that two of the children were not ready to move on to their next grades in the fall. They had improved over the summer but not enough to pass. They would be held behind in the same grade. Still, all the children received diplomas for attending the program and doing the best they could.

Miss Campbell said, "Students, you all did a fantastic job

this summer with your schoolwork. Thank you for working so hard, and especially for helping each other out so much. I have no doubt you will succeed in school this coming year, and in the years to come. Be proud of your accomplishments. You did good.

"Now, I think we need to give Mrs. Angela a round of applause for being such a wonderful assistant teacher."

The room exploded with clapping.

Angela, looking pretty in a flowered dress and bouncing her squiggly baby in her arms, smiled and mouthed "thank you." Fitz grinned at her side.

"And, of course, we need a round of applause for Miss Summer for being such a wonderful teacher."

Clapping thundered throughout the small space.

"Now, I'll turn it over to Miss Summer, who has something she wants to tell you children."

All eyes became glued to Summer as she went to the front and faced her students. "I had such a good time with all of you. I hope you remember me as much as I'll remember you. I learned more from you than you did from me, and I thank you for that. The sketches I made of you are wrapped up with your diplomas, my humble gift to you. I so enjoyed making them. This has been the most meaningful experience of my life." She figured Stella might be the only child in the room savvy enough to eek out what that meant, but she had to say it. The adults, at least, would appreciate the fact that she'd struggled through this experience. "I wish you the very best in the future.

"As for my future, I'm going home to live in Traverse City. But I want you to know that I'll come back to visit West Branch from time to time, and I hope I'll see you again."

A short pause followed while they absorbed that information, then the same verbal students who always liked to speak up had their say.

"Yeah, come see us," Hector asserted.

"How come you wanna go away?"

"Will you be a teacher in Tra… that other town?"

"Will you come take us on more field trips?"

"What about you and that deputy who were all lovey-dovey?"

"That's okay. My uncle got off our couch and got a new girlfriend. Her name is Chastity."

Summer withheld a response to that.

"I'll tell you what, how about we cut this beautiful cake the bakery made for us," Summer said, pointing to a three-layer chocolate cake sitting on the desk, "and I can answer some of your questions while we eat."

Cake lassoed the children's attention.

Everyone gathered and dug into the delicious confection. With a good mood permeating the crowd, the conversations were fun and the celebration left Summer pleased with herself for sticking in there and finishing this job, even though she'd wanted to quit many times. Of course, the threat of jail always loomed over her head if she bailed out.

Once the room started to clear out, Miss Campbell came up to her. "I can't thank you enough for what you accomplished here, Summer. You're a natural. Would you like to be a certified teacher?"

"Not on your life. Thank you for your faith in me, but this has to be one of the hardest jobs on the face of the earth. I have a new appreciation for real teachers. God bless them. I'll do everything I can to support them and our schools, but I hope I'm never left responsible for a roomful of kids again. I'm done. Thank you for being so patient with me. And for what you do all the time for these kids."

Miss Campbell hugged her. "I can't imagine doing anything else."

"I've been thinking a lot about what you do. The sheriff talked about how kids join gangs for a sense of belonging. Hazel told us about getting stuck in a bad relationship with a gangster because she craved excitement. I can see now how school can provide those things for kids so they don't fall prey to bad situations like that. School can provide a sense of belonging. Learning can be so interesting it provides excitement. Young people don't need to look elsewhere when they have an excellent school.

"I see now why programs like Head Start are so important. It gets young kids going in the right direction before they can get into trouble.

"You and the good teachers here and great volunteers like Angela provide that for these students all the time. I applaud you, Miss Campbell, for being the leader who pulls all of that together and keeps it going."

The principal beamed. "That's the best compliment I could ever receive. Thank you, Summer."

Angela and Fitz came over to them, and Angela said, "Well, another summer down. We taught kids to read and do arithmetic and wash their hands and zip up after going potty. It was a success."

Everyone smiled. "Yes, it was," Summer said. "Thank you so much for all your help. I would have lost my mind without you." She and Angela hugged like sisters.

Ellie and Harry said goodbye to the last of the others to leave, and joined the group with Stella and Gloria.

They all walked out of the room, but Summer turned back to take one last look. The classroom looked cold and stark without her kids. She had learned so much from them in this room: resilience, patience, honesty, self-preservation, humor, community, caring, and more. She'd learned that children were not only a bunch of noisy nuisances. They were real people with hopes and fears and quirks and opinions and dreams. They had introduced her to some of what she might expect from motherhood someday. For that, she would be eternally grateful. She'd fallen in love with each and every child in this room, and would miss them beyond measure. She wished them nothing but goodness for the rest of their lives.

Be that as it may, she knew she'd never work in a classroom again.

54

"He hates me."

"He doesn't hate you."

"At least not much."

They'd been performing this routine for five minutes. Summer would bemoan her love life, Hazel would insist it couldn't be all that bad, and Betty would take up the rear with a shot of reality.

"Hey," Hazel said, pointing at Betty. "We could take our good cop bad cop schtick on the road."

They laughed. Summer didn't.

They sat on Hazel's porch late in the afternoon on a glorious Sunday. Joey had cooked up fried chicken, mashed potatoes and gravy, and Golden Bantam sweet corn on the cob for their dinner, which they enjoyed in the café when Summer and Betty returned from their respective churches. Hazel was Jewish but hadn't practiced her religion since leaving her aunt's home so many years ago.

Over dinner Hazel said she had some personal news that she hoped wouldn't upset her friends. "I know you think Monty is a schmuck," she said, "but he and I have been talking. He found out I'm the former 'moll' and he wants to do a movie about my life."

"Wow. Are you going to do it?" Betty asked in-between bites of succulent chicken.

"Yes, I think so. He's not as bad as you think. In fact, I rather like him." Hazel nonchalantly bit into her corn on the cob, as if having a movie made of her life was no big deal.

Summer fessed up. "I'm sort of warming to him, too. Hazel, I think that's great. It'll be a great movie."

Betty chuckled. "Yeah. I don't know if you want to tell all the details of your love life, though."

Hazel smiled over the side of her corn cob. "Oh, no one will ever know all of that. Not even you, my best friends."

"Aw, come on," Betty chided. "That's the good stuff."

"I tell you what: I'm so much older than you two I'll be a doddering, senile old fool and in a home long before you. If you promise to come visit, I'll tell you then."

"Deal."

Summer couldn't help but laugh. "I can't wait," she said.

"As for working with Monty," Summer added, "he's not so bad. Different, but not bad."

"That's exactly what I think," Hazel said. "And he is a brilliant filmmaker. I called my literary agent in New York. He made some calls and said Monty is considered to be an up-and-coming moviemaker. He's well thought of in the industry."

"Who would've guessed it?"

After dinner, the three of them sauntered across the street from the café to take in the matinee at the Midstate. It was the first time Summer had been inside the theatre and she marveled at the stunning enormous paintings of mountain scenes. The decor seemed a combination of art deco and Western. Unusual for this part of the country, but beautiful in its misplaced uniqueness. The maroon velvet stage curtains opened and, after a Looney Tunes Road Runner cartoon, they saw a new movie, *Cat Ballou* with Jane Fonda and Lee Marvin. They ate popcorn and drank

Coke and laughed and hummed along with the western musical comedy about a young woman who hires an aging gunslinger and a handsome outlaw to help her avenge the murder of her father. At the end of the movie the audience applauded, something they didn't do back home in Traverse City.

The actor who played the outlaw generated quite a conversation once the trio hit Hazel's porch.

"That actor who played Clay…" Hazel said.

"Michael Callen," Betty said.

"Doesn't matter. He's handsome."

"Yeah, I wouldn't kick him out of bed for eating crackers."

"I'd say that, too, if I was forty years younger."

Summer hadn't commented because she didn't want to ruin the fun by saying she thought Bogey was more handsome than any actor and that she'd decimated any chance of being with him. But now, after holding her tongue for a couple of weeks, she couldn't contain her misery any longer.

She'd started the conversation with, "I'm ready to talk about Bogey. It was my own stupidity. I ruined any hope of getting together with him." She knew she sounded pathetic, exactly how she felt.

"Oh, oh. Tell us all about it," Hazel said.

She told them about their "big misunderstanding" and how he now hated her guts. That generated the good cop bad cop routine.

They fell silent. What more could be said?

"You need to go see him and apologize." Hazel pointed in the direction of his farm.

"Yeah, you insulted him," Betty said, pulling her red glasses down her nose and peering over the top of them. "He thinks you think he would abandon his own baby."

"I didn't mean to. It was a misunderstanding. I'm such a dufus."

"Then go talk to him," Hazel insisted. "You don't think all that schmaltzy riding off into the sunset to live happily ever after stuff happens all by itself, do you? Even in my books I make people work for it."

"You do?" Betty seemed surprised. "Maybe I should read one of your books."

"I finished *Once You Have Found Him*. It's really good. You did make them work through their troubles, didn't you?" Summer suddenly felt a tad hopeful. "I want that. I want to end up riding off into the sunset and living happily ever after."

"One thing I've learned in my life," Hazel said, "is that we make our own life stories. How they end is up to us."

A bird chirped boisterously while no one spoke, it's song a merry jig.

"Here, take my car." Betty finally said, tossing over her keys.

Summer hesitated for the moment it took her to make a decision. She stood up, thanked her friends, and jogged the short distance to the garage behind the B&B. She had to do this before she lost her nerve.

She arrived at Bogey's farm twelve minutes later.

55

Pulling into the driveway of Bogey's farm, Summer could hear music blaring from the barn. Elvis Presley sang "It's Now or Never."

How appropriate, Summer thought as she got out of the car.

Bogey's truck sat in the driveway and the horses were in the meadow, so the man himself must be in that barn, she reckoned. She walked up to the wide-open door.

Oh, Lord have mercy, he's half naked. Her knees buckled. She had to force them to behave.

Bogey's shirtless back greeted her as he used a pitchfork to toss hay into the horses' stalls. His muscles shone like rippling gold with the rhythmic movement of his work.

That swooning thing overtook Summer again. She didn't move. She couldn't move.

Still, he turned, slowly, as if sensing her presence. He stopped and stared at her.

She stared at his chest. Then at his shoulders, and then his arms, one of which sported an eagle tattoo. She'd never known a man with a tattoo. It struck her as rugged and exotic. Then her eyes fell to his jeans. She gulped.

Bogey dropped his pitchfork, reached over to retrieve something off the side of a stall, and pulled on a tee shirt.

Summer had never been so disappointed and so relieved in all her life. She loathed the disappearance of his skin but rejoiced in being able to breathe again.

He went over to the radio, turned it off, and stared at her in silence. The intensity of those bedroom eyes of his almost did her in right then and there, her knees threatening to melt away again and render her unable to stand. She breathed deeply to give herself strength. Finally, as if he'd made some kind of decision, he walked up to her in long, deliberate strides.

"I've been hoping you'd come to see me," he said, offering his hand. Delighted, stunned, and nervous, she took it. "I needed to know you don't hate me. That you trust me. If you didn't come, I was going to have to kidnap you. I wasn't going to let you leave town without seeing something. I wanted to show you this on our first date, but we never got the chance."

They walked to the house and went in a back door that led to the kitchen. Amazed at his ability to act as if nothing untoward had happened between them, Summer followed with nary a word, too curious to see what would happen next.

He said, "My dad took down some things from the house, things he and my mom wanted to incorporate into their new one. Like a built-in hutch that used to be over there."

Summer tore her gaze away from his face to see a torn-up spot on the wall where he pointed. She looked around and found that otherwise the room was a typical farmhouse kitchen. Decorations and accessories were sparse, probably taken by his parents, but the room's former charm still showed through.

"Here's what I've been doing." Bogey led her through a hall-way into the living room. "I've pretty much moved into my bed-room while I take this apart. Dad took down the mantle and the ceiling lights, and they have those up in their new house, but the rest is mine to salvage. So, as you can see, I've been taking down that crown molding and the wainscoting. I'll do these wide oak floorboards next." He ran the toe of his work boot through the dust to clear a spot on the floor to make the rich wood visible. "It's a lot of work, but I want to save as much as possible before the state tears the place down. I want to incorporate it in my own home someday."

They stood in the middle of the room, plaster dust and building debris surrounding them. The furniture was long gone. The salvaged materials, stacked along the walls, were indeed magnificently crafted. She marveled at Bogey's desire and ability to save it.

"Next weekend a bunch of the guys are coming out to help me with the barn. I'll reuse as much of that wood as possible to build a stable for my horses, wherever I end up."

She faced him. "How wonderful, Bogey. You'll have a beautiful home someday, one with fond memories as well as new life."

He pulled her to him and gently kissed her. Then he kissed her again, deeply this time.

When they parted, she said, "So, does this mean you aren't mad at me anymore?" She threw him a coquettish grin.

He looked at her quizzically. "Mad? I thought you were mad at me. I thought you thought I was a real jerk."

"Nah uh."

"Well, I'm not mad, either. Not anymore. I guess I let my 'manly pride' get in the way. At first I was angry that you thought I'd abandon a baby, then I was hurt."

"I came to apologize but forgot as soon as I saw you half naked."

"I didn't care about an apology as soon as I saw you. And here you are fully clothed. Can you imagine what would have happened if you'd been half naked, too?"

She blushed.

"Well, I'll be. I've embarrassed you." He led her back into the kitchen and motioned for her to sit at the small table. After pouring them each a glass of water, he sat down beside her. "Here, drink up."

"You see, Bogey... Well, I've never been half naked with a man, let alone completely naked. The only time I was half naked where anybody could see me was in that fountain when I got arrested."

"Ah, I see. So...."

"I've never had sex and want to wait until I'm married."

"Oh. Hmm. Wow. You are without a doubt the first virgin jailbird I've ever known."

She waggled her head from side to side and rolled her eyes. "Yup, that's me."

"I mean," he said, becoming teasingly animated, "you could probably be in *Ripley's Believe It or Not.*"

She swatted his arm. "That's what my cellmate said."

He grinned a cockeyed grin while running a finger down her cheek. "Oh, Summer Rose Krause, you are an enigma. A fascinating woman. I understand now why you didn't understand what I was trying to tell you. I had no idea you had no experience with, well, you know, with sex."

"Hey, you remember my middle name?"

"Sure. I'm the one who has to fill out the reports that go to the judge in Traverse City every week. I want you to know I've always given you good marks."

"You? That's so embarrassing. I figured the sheriff would do it."

"No, he handed it off to me."

"Yikes. I'm so sorry you have to do that. No wonder you hated me at first. That night we had milk in the kitchen you were so brusk."

"Of course. I was on the job. No way would I let my personal feelings become part of my work. Besides, I confess, in the very, very beginning I thought you were nothing more than a pain-in-the-ass spoiled rich girl who liked causing havoc. I didn't know you yet. I didn't know havoc follows you around all by itself."

She threw him a sideways glance. "That's okay. I didn't like you at first, either. So there."

"Really? Whew. I'm glad we got over that." He pulled her onto his lap and kissed her again, this time for a very, very long time.

Summer slipped into another plane of consciousness where she re-evaluated her determination to remain chaste until marriage. Maybe she wanted to be a slut instead. Bogey pulled back in the nick of time. She took a deep breath and struggled to return to her former self.

But Summer Rose Krause knew she would never be the same again. Bogey Bush had changed her forever. He'd taught her that not only could she get romantic love, she could give it as well.

Then it hit her. If this man ever asked her to marry him, she would become Summer Rose Bush. It sounded like a smarmy moniker from a romance novel. Could she live with that?

Bogey kissed her again.

Oh, yeah, I can live with that.

56

The death of Popo, her great-grandfather, weighed down on Summer, the heavy hand of depression crushing her heart. Yet she knew that Herbert Ambrose Sullivan, at age one hundred and three, wanted above all else for his family to celebrate joy in his living rather than sorrow over his demise.

An Irish wake, not entirely traditional, at his sumptuous cottage on Mackinac Island had been planned, according to his nurses, fifteen years earlier. He'd known for a long time how he wanted it to be. Although he was one of the wealthiest men in the state, perhaps in the country, he ordered a plain pine box. It would be a closed casket. There would be no keening, no wailing, as usual with a Celtic wake. He declared he was too old for anyone to cry over his death.

"It isn't as though we don't all see it coming," he'd told his grandson Harry.

Inside the house next to the casket, which sat in what had once been the library but in recent years had been turned into his bedroom so he wouldn't have to navigate the stairs, there were Cuban cigars for the men and plenty of Johnnie Walker Red scotch whiskey for anyone who wanted it. According to Irish lore, tobacco smoke kept away evil spirits and scotch whiskey, well, scotch whiskey made everybody happy.

Family and friends gathered inside and spilled out into the lush yard. The Sullivan clan had grown to be enormous. With entirely Irish beginnings, with Herbert's parents both immigrating from Ireland, and Herbert's one surviving offspring, Meg, marrying an O'Neill, the family had since become an example of the diaspora of America. Some of Meg's eleven surviving children — her third child, Teddy, had tragically died in the Pacific at the very end of World War II — had married a Polanski, a Smith, a LaBlanc, a Järvinen, a Chen, and, of course, a Krause. And Meg had two best friends who had become like family. One, Peggy, was an Irish immigrant but the other, Abby, was a Chippewa Indian. They all came to say their final farewells to the patriarch of this family.

As well as family, it seemed as if every resident of the island knew and loved Herbert. He'd been born on Mackinac Island and his wish to die there had been granted.

Summer stood in the yard by a camellia bush with Bogey, and with Charlotte and her fiancé. Everyone wore black in keeping with Irish tradition, Summer in a sleeveless black dress with a long, flowing skirt. In a week the whole family would gather again for Charlotte's wedding, which Summer knew would be colorful and merry, a good step toward relieving this communal sense of mourning.

Her great-grandfather might have been "old as dirt," as he liked to say, but he was still the solid ground upon which this family stood. Summer couldn't remember a moment of her life when she didn't know he was there, somewhere out there, even though she couldn't always be with him or see him, the rock any Sullivan descendant could rely on to be there for them.

Now he was gone.

"I'll miss him for the rest of my life," Charlotte proclaimed gloomily.

"I'm so glad we had that big party for him for his hundred-

and-third birthday," Summer said. "He sat on the porch drinking scotch and watching us all play yard games," she explained to Bogey.

"We think the scotch is what kept him alive for so long." Charlotte insisted.

"That was the weekend before I came to West Branch." Summer looked around and picked out her West Branch friends from the crowd. She'd already visited with Betty and Hazel, who were accompanied by Joey. He looked downright presentable in a black suit. Hazel had attracted a klatch of women when someone recognized her as the famous author. Betty and Joey sat in a couple of Adirondack chairs, deep in conversation. Summer couldn't believe it never occurred to her they were becoming a couple.

Angela had already called with condolences, apologizing that she and Fitz couldn't get away with the baby and the boys. Summer reassured Angela that her great-grandpa would want the parents of nine children to stay home with their family. She was so touched, though, by the call.

Summer's own mom and dad had returned from Hawaii two weeks earlier, and now greeted visitors inside the house, along with her Uncle Harry, Aunt Ellie, and her grandparents. It was the first time Summer had seen her parents since their return. She'd talked to them at length on the phone, especially about the Purple Gang murder mystery in West Branch. But, once they'd been reassured by Harry that the culprit was in jail and there was no danger, her parents declared they had so much work to catch up on they couldn't come see her in West Branch. Summer suspected, however, that Uncle Harry had advised them to stay away and let her live her own life for at least a little while longer.

This was the first time they had so much as heard about one

Bogey Bush. Her father shook his daughter's suiter's hand and stared him down when first introduced. Her mother had been subtler, but Summer caught her surreptitious inspection of him as he talked to others.

"Miss Summer." Stella appeared from behind them and Summer delighted in seeing the girl again looking healthy and happy.

"Hi, Stella. You don't have to call me 'Miss' Summer anymore. We're cousins now."

The girl frowned. "Aren't you too old to be a cousin?"

The grownups laughed.

"Yeah, See-saw, explain that one," Charlotte teased.

"I tell you what, Stella, I'll explain it when you get older. But for now, you can call me Summer. No 'Miss.'"

"'kay. Hey, you're that wedding lady who came to our school." She pointed at Charlotte.

"Yes. And I'm your aunt."

Stella squinted, not buying it.

"And you're Deputy Bush." Stella pointed at Bogey.

"Yes, I am." He grinned down at the child.

"Hmmm." Her little head moved from side to side, studying Summer, then Bogey, then Summer again. "'kay," she decided, apparently giving her approval.

"Popo said not to be sad," Stella said, dismissing the confusing subject of who was who and what was what with these grownups, "'cuz he's gonna be in Heaven with his friends."

Those words lifted the pall on Summer's heart. "Yes, he is, isn't he?"

"Uh huh. See ya." Stella scampered away to join her sister and a pack of other children playing under a big tree.

Harry came out to announce it was time to move the casket

to the church for mass. A plain black horse-drawn hearse pulled up in front of the house and strong young men carried out the long pine box.

Mass at his historic Catholic church, Ste. Anne's, was moving, with Summer's grandmother, the deceased's daughter Meg Sullivan O'Neill, first lady of the state of Michigan, giving a rousing eulogy in honor of the dad she so dearly loved. Always at the height of fashion, she wore a black ensemble much like the one Jackie Kennedy wore to her husband's presidential funeral a couple of years earlier, minus the long black veil hanging over her face. Meg's hat had a wisp of veil, instead. There wasn't a dry eye when she finished with her touching, humorous, loving memorial to her centenarian dad.

Communion was given, and the throng moved to Ste. Anne's cemetery. They traveled in broughams, drays, and buggies; on horseback and bicycles; and on foot. Almost every available form of transportation on the island had been rented or volunteered for this occasion, seeing that they were needed because automobiles weren't allowed on Mackinac Island.

Summer and Bogey rode with her parents and her younger brother Shane in a crowded four-person carriage with a driver. It's wasn't far, up a hill that meandered into the center of the island. No one felt much like chatting, so conversation waned.

When they arrived at the lovely cemetery set in the woods, the stark reality of seeing her Popo's headstone tugged at Summer's heartstrings again. She had often seen the large gray granite slab because it was shared with his deceased wife. When she visited her Popo, Summer always came here with him when he put a rose on his wife's grave after Sunday mass.

Chiseled into the stone on one side it said: Hannah Sullivan, beloved wife of Herbert Ambrose Sullivan. 1877-1941. His bride had been dead for over twenty years, yet he always spoke of her as if she would appear at any moment. He loved her as deeply as if their souls had been joined since birth. They would finally be together again.

Chiseled into his side it said: Herbert Ambrose Sullivan, nee Shane Finbar O'Sullivan, loving husband and father. 1862—. Now his date of death would be filled in. Born Shane Finbar O'Sullivan, as an infant he became Herbert Ambrose Sullivan through no doing of his own or that of his parents. That had long been one of the secrets this family held.

After prayers by the priest, a long line of family members paraded by, each laying a red rose on the pine box until it was covered in red. The scent of the flowers permeated the air. When the last vestige of Herbert Sullivan was lowered into the earth, women cried and men looked forlorn; but, a sudden peace overcame Summer. Stella had been right. The old man was happy.

As people milled around after the service, Bogey put his arm around Summer's waist and said, "I'm sorry I never got to meet him. He must have loved his Hannah very much, to still want to be buried next to her after she's been gone all these years."

"Oh, yes. He adored her. Unfortunately, she wasn't his first wife. Someday, when we have a lot more privacy and a lot more time, I'll tell you that whole sordid tale. His first wife is my biological grandmother. She caused a tragedy that destroyed Popo at the time. She ended up spending most of her adult life in the asylum in Traverse City. He didn't meet Hannah until he was in his fifties. He always said she was his salvation."

"I want to hear all about it. I want to know your family, to know you."

She took his hand. "Well, then, follow me." Leading him deeper into the cemetery, she had something to show him.

57

Summer took Bogey around trees and past rows of tombstones, some of the stones so old they were for Civil War soldiers. She stopped at another shared headstone, this one pink granite inscribed for Finbar O'Sullivan and Fiona Flanagan O'Sullivan.

"These are my great-great-grandparents, Popo's parents. This is another tragic story I'll have to tell you about later. It's the story of Irish immigrant lovers torn apart by fate and brought back together only in death. She is where my name comes from."

They looked down and Bogey read aloud:

Fiona Flanagan O'Sullivan
My Irish Summer Rose
Born June 9, 1842
Waterford, Ireland
Died November 8, 1862 Mackinac Island

"I already adore this Fiona for giving you such a beautiful name."

"It's from an Irish poem she loved."

"1862. Isn't that the year your Popo was born?"

"Yes. She died in childbirth."

"How horrible. That's so sad."

"Yes, it's hard to imagine. They had hard, cursed lives. I'm so blessed, Bogey, to come from these people, from Finbar and Fiona and Herbert. Theirs are stories of love and loss and grit and survival. Stories about the importance of family.

"They went through hell to give me the wonderful life I have. Being here, standing in front of them, reminds me to honor them by appreciating all that I've been given."

Bogey stared into her eyes before tendering a gentle kiss. He looked around and Summer followed his gaze. Most folks had left the cemetery and those remaining, including her parents, stood gathered around Herbert's grave. He pulled her into further seclusion behind a tall, fragrant wild rose bush beside Fiona and Finbar's graves.

"Honey, I was going to do this later, but this seems perfect, being here with the people who made you." Bogey reached into his suitcoat pocket. "This belonged to my grandmother." He opened his palm to reveal a thin gold band with a small diamond. "She left it to me for my bride. I'll buy you a ring with a bigger diamond someday, if you want, but this is all I have to offer you now. I offer it with all my heart. Summer, will you marry me?"

Summer's gaze went from the ring to his face to the ring and back to his face.

"Don't you dare ever get me another one. This is perfect. I'll wear it every day for the rest of my life. Yes. I'll marry you."

He placed the ring on her finger and this time their kiss lasted a long time.

Beaming with joy, Bogey swept his fiancé up in his arms and twirled her around.

When he set her down, he became serious. "I know you want to live in Traverse City, your hometown. I've applied for a job as deputy there. Keep your fingers crossed for me."

She realized he had no idea about the extent of her family's wealth, about her wealth. Her trust fund from her great-grandfather alone would support them nicely forever. Now there was the added bonus of a huge inheritance on top of the trust. If this man was going to be her husband, of course she had to share her financial status with him.

"Bogey, dear Bogey, you know my family is rich, right?"

"Sure. But there are so many of you, I figure at your place in the family, being generations down the ladder, you might not get anything. Don't worry about that, honey. I'll support us. You don't have to work unless you want to. Continue to work at your dad's winery, or not. I don't care. Paint as much as you want. You'll never again have to be a 'chambermaid' or school teacher. I want to give you a life that makes you happy. That's what'll make me happy."

Summer's heart swelled. She knew she had to break the news to him about her fortune, but decided to save it for another day. In fact, she astutely decided to ask her mom and dad to help with that, when the time was right. First, she would need to break the news of her engagement to them.

"Can we keep this between the two of us until tomorrow morning at breakfast with my parents? Let them mourn today and give them something to be happy about tomorrow."

"Of course. That's perfect."

He turned to Fiona and Finbar's headstone. "Do you think they know what's happening here?"

Summer ran her hand across the top of the stone, feeling warmth in its cold surface. "Yes. I think they do."

"Well, then, thank you, Fiona and Finbar," he said, "for witnessing our betrothal. I promise to love your girl until the day I die. I'm so sorry for your misfortune, but you can rest knowing that you brought great happiness into this world: our happiness. I'll be grateful to you forever."

Holding hands, they walked back to Popo's grave and found that everyone had gone except for a man on a horse, who held the reins to another horse. Summer recognized the farrier who cared for the family's stable of horses on the island.

"Hope you don't mind," he said, "but your parents had to leave in the carriage. They asked that I bring up a horse for the two of you."

"Thank you," the young couple said in unison.

The man tipped his hat and rode off.

Bogey hoisted himself into the saddle and pulled Summer up behind him. Wrapping her arms around his waist and pressing her cheek to his back, she felt life soar through her body. As they rode down the hill toward their future, her hair blew wild and free, her skirt fluttered in the breeze, and her bare legs tingled from the caress of the summer air. Surely, the lives of her ancestors lived on through her.

They turned the corner toward town and Summer could see the afternoon sun casting prismed glows of golden light onto the lake, causing the water to shimmer like a halo sending blessings her way. Her happily ever after loomed out there on the horizon. She intended to snatch it up and hold it dear for the rest of her life, going to her grave someday like her great-grandfather, steadfast and fearless, happy to have lived.

Author's Note

I was born and raised in West Branch, Michigan, population 2,000 seventy years ago when I came into the world and 2,000 today. For years I walked through downtown on my way to school and wondered what went on in the upstairs of the stores that line the main street. I always knew about the Prohibition-era Purple Gang from Detroit that hung out in the area when my parents were growing up there.

A couple of years ago when I learned that the upstairs of one of the buildings had been a speakeasy during the Roaring '20s, my wild imagination put the bits together to conjure up this story. Who knows? Maybe a gangster moll really did live in one of those apartments. Maybe millions of dollars are stashed away up there. And maybe the day will come when we'll find all that loot.

But we probably shouldn't bank on that. Instead, the treasure is in the town itself, a lovely Victorian-era setting where we can picture the lives of people long ago. There are towns like West Branch all over this country, small burghs where buildings and traditions have been kept intact as much as possible by contemporary residents. Those folks need to be appreciated for preserving the history of our communities, because that history made us who we are today.

My heartfelt "thank you" goes out to them all.

Acknowledgements

TCM, Turner Classic Movies, provides endless images and ideas for writing stories about the 1920s, '30s, and '40s. My imagination can't help but blossom under the influence of their "shows," as we called them back in the day. TCM Backlot even made me Fan of the Week a while back. *Midnight Mary*, 1933, starring a drop-dead gorgeous young Loretta Young playing a "gangster moll" to Ricardo Cortez's chilling portrayal of a gangster, especially brought my characters in this book to life. I will be forever grateful to TCM.

Thanks also to my West Branch, Michigan, Class of '66 friend Ron Kimball, who provided a map of the town stores as they were in 1965. Alan Cascadden, Class of '65, wrote a wonderful short story, which gave me the idea for the character Tommy smoking on the roof by the marquee of the theater. That's what Alan used to do! Nancy Rabidue McCauley, Class of '68, also wrote a charming story about growing up there, with some details I'd long since forgotten.

My former neighbors, Sally Rea and Nancy Rea Griffin; along with the Ogemaw County Genealogical and Heritage Society, and others; have given the town a wonderful house of history, the Ogemaw County Museum. Sally was kind enough to take me on a tour that brought back fond memories and served as a reminder of how it used to be.

Then there is my sister Karene, known to locals as Corky, who I've talked to and laughed with all my life about our hometown. Our brothers Barry and Tom have tales to tell, too. I need to thank our cousins, also, for being so helpful. Michele Tetu Ahrent and her husband Rick provide room and board when we go back to visit, and Tammy Finnerty Montague and her husband Richard recently drove us way out into the boonies to see family burial grounds. Our dear friends Barb and Gary Hughey are like family, and never hesitate to keep us out-of-towners up on the place.

As always, thank you to the Deeds Publishing crew: Bob, Jan, and Mark Babcock; and Matt King. Deeds not words, indeed.

And, here's love and adoration to my husband Joe and our three fur babies. They understand me like no one else. For that, I am eternally grateful.

Finally, my heartfelt appreciation goes out to my readers. Your support brings me unbridled joy.

About the Author

Award-winning author Linda Hughes has a dozen books in publication. *Secrets of the Summer* is the third book in her historical romantic suspense trilogy set in her home state of Michigan, with this story in her small hometown. She has spent most of her adult life living in Georgia, so she considers herself to be a Yankee and a Southerner.

Her writing honors—including awards and being a finalist for awards—come from the National Writers Association, Writer's Digest, the American Screenwriters Association, eLit, Indie Book of the Day, Silver Falchion, and the Baltic Writing Residency. You'll find her on Amazon and on social media. Visit her website at: www.lindahughes.com

MAIN STREET WEST BRANCH MICH.